And Death Shall Have No Dominion

A Tribute to Michael Shea

Michael Shea

And Death Shall Have No Dominion

A Tribute to Michael Shea

Edited by Linda Shea and S. T. Joshi

Hippocampus Press

New York

Published by Hippocampus Press
P.O. Box 641, New York, NY 10156
http://www.hippocampuspress.com

Cover design by Barbara Briggs Silbert.
Hippocampus Press logo designed by Anastasia Damianakos.

Thanks to David Kurzman for the cover image by Michael Whelan; Della Shea for the photograph of Michael Shea; the Stewart family for the use of John Stewart's illustrations; and Lori Pearce for the use of the images by Alan Clark commissioned by her husband, Michael.

First Edition

1 3 5 7 9 8 6 4 2

ISBN: 978-1-61498-179-4

Contents

Editor's Note

Linda Shea

To wonder whether Michael was an artist would be akin to wondering if a heron was made to fly. He wrote because he had to, because words were what he loved most and were his way to create beauty in this world. As an adolescent, sitting in his father's converted stable-office across the street from MGM Studios in Culver City, his first literary efforts were poems, so it is fitting that this volume contains his Epic Verse.

Also presented are three new stories: "King Gil Gomez and Monkey Do," written in the early 1980s in San Francisco; "In Memory Drive Slow" (1990), inspired by a handwritten sign on a Sonoma County back road; and "Credit Card" (2008), in which the main character is an older, country-living Ricky Deuce, from Michael's Mythos story "Copping Squid." "The Growlimb" (winner of the 2009 World Fantasy Award for best novella) is the only previously published story.

Michael felt that all the genres were really the same. High and contemporary fantasy, horror, and science fiction were all linked to realism archetypically and to our modern life. He wrote to please himself, believing that his task was to write well and provide some entertainment. I think that for him language was the closest humans could get to truth, and that to produce art was to become whole.

I first met him in San Francisco in the late 1970s. He was a large, handsome man who could pick up a spade or dig a ditch at a moment's notice, but who also spent days at a time at his desk. He was working at house-painting and construction gigs, as that let him stay in the world of his thoughts and balance out all the hours at the desk; but in previous years and for many years after he also taught at universities and junior colleges.

On our first evening together he read Chaucer to me in Middle English, "When in Aprille . . ." His copy of Edward Gibbon's *Decline and Fall of the Roman Empire* had pages that were carefully taped together over and over. Tacitus, Caesar, Marcus Aurelius, Harold Bloom, Shakespeare as well as works of science, philosophy, history and fiction were his constant companions. He was modest and unpretentious and always supportive of others' efforts at art, telling people when asked that all they had to do was to write it down, to "start," and it would happen.

Knowledgeable and enthusiastic about all things in the natural world, he would often carefully bring us creatures he'd found on our little country property. Speaking of an insect or reptile, he would say, "See it's exquisitely shaped," and then proceed to explain its particular adaptations and physiology. The kids would get paid for special bugs they found up on the hill, usually a quarter. Our daughter Della once netted a buck for a miniature scorpion on a leaf.

He was an ebullient, expressive, and intense man. Once, when he took me for a pre-dawn cruise down LA's freeway arteries, we ended up in Watts. There was a scaffold erected around the Towers as they were being repaired, and we climbed it to the top, spending the sunrise up there. At a coastal beach we once found a mother gray whale and her calf. As the kids and I looked on, he went into the water near them. They seemed to know a kindred spirit and were not alarmed. When our kids were of grade-school age and Michael was taking a group of them to the ocean, he stopped our van on a country road, told them to wait, and as they watched, amazed, jumped off the bridge about fifty feet into the river. He shook himself off, got in the driver's seat, and off they went to the coast. I believe that in that moment he was shaking off other considerations, maybe even the story left at his desk, in order to be in the moment with the kids; and the river and its beauty helped him do it.

In whatever spot his desk sat during our years together—the night clerk's cage of a San Francisco men's hotel, a garage or attic—the air would be filled with the patter of "rainfall," his fingers on the keys . . . punctuated by occasional bursts of laughter when he was amused by something he had just written. He would sound out the sentences in his wonderful raspy and sonorous voice. Da-daa, da-daa. Heartbeats in the iambs, testing phrases for their music.

Living with the man was to have a stream of beautifully crafted thoughts surrounding one. So unpretentiously, with so much wonderful laughter, these phrases were like sunlight coming through a window. They encircled me so completely that I didn't even realize they were there until they were gone.

We can still have him talk to us through his verse and prose. The epic verse in this book was originally embedded in stories and novels, serving as a way for him to be true to his first love, rhyming verse. The sound of the beat of the heart.

Thanks for Derrick Hussey of Hippocampus Press, Dr. Danny Temianka, and S. T. Joshi for all their help with this volume. Thanks also to the wonderful writers and artists who have given freely of their time and talent with their contributions, and to our children, Della and Jake.

The day Michael died he was working on a novel until an hour before he passed. I think if there is a way for one to be still writing in the star wheels of the universe after this life, he must be. He once dedicated a book to us, myself and the kids, *with love from the cave.* We dedicate this volume to him in the stars.

—LINDA SHEA

Note: The title of this book is taken from Dylan Thomas's "And Death Shall Have No Dominion," a favorite of Michael's.

This book's Afterword, written by Michael, came like a gift into my hands as I was sorting through some non-writing-related paperwork. Of course, he never knew it would be used in this collection.

Salutation to the World as Beheld at Dawn from Atop Mount Eburon

Long have your continents drifted and merged,
Jostled like whales on the seas,
Then cloven, and sundered, and slowly diverged,
While your mountains arose, and sank to their knees.

Long and long were your eons of ice,
Long were your ages of fire.
Long has there been
The bleeding of men,
And the darkness that cancels desire.

What hosts of hosts—born, grown, and gone—
Have swarmed your million Babylons!
How many pits has mankind dug?
How many peaks has he stood upon?

Many and long were your empires of blood,
Fewer your empires of light.
Now their wisdoms and wars

Lie remote as the stars,
Stone-cold in the blanketing night.

Now even your wisest could never restore

One tithe of the truths Man's lost,
Nor even one book of the radiant lore
That so many treasured so long, at such cost.

For it's many the pages the wind has torn
And their hoarded secrets blown—
Tumbled and chased
Through the eyeless wastes
Where the wreckage of history's thrown.

—Michael Shea, *Nifft the Lean*

Foreword: Michael Shea Remembered

Dan Temianka

I met Michael in high school, in L.A., in the early 1960s. He was a year or two older, an eon at that stage of our lives, and haunted the back of his parents' 1920s clapboard house in Culver City, across from the old MGM Studios on Washington Boulevard. His dad, on whose ancient Remington typewriter Michael wrote his first fiction, worked for the Department of Water and Power and scrawled poetry on the walls of their garage.

I escaped to Michael's company; we smoked and debated. He was astounded that I could whistle Bach. I was amazed at the power of his intellect, which he displayed at salons held by our wonderful American Lit teacher, a heavy, hyper-intellectual chain smoker with a sharp wit and short hair that she curled.

They discussed Proust and *The Waste Land*, and Michael's fiction. He argued with her over his use of the word "progressed" to describe the motion of a bus going down the street. She bought a hot black Chevy 409 convertible, and every boy in our class was horrified at the misplaced good fortune of a middle-aged lesbian English teacher driving such an orgasmic dream car.

We adored our Latin teacher, Mrs. Kelly, whose sternness we accepted for three years. She worshipped the ablative absolute and gripped her desk to explain it, her jaw hardening like a Roman emperor's until the word "denarius" flashed into my mind. She recognized Michael's brilliance and lauded him.

Next thing I recall, we fled to Berkeley and shared a pair of disheveled, poorly heated rooms behind the Darling Flower Shop on Shattuck Avenue. I constructed the word "MUSIC" out of colorful scraps and glued it on the wall of my room. My father, a violinist, visited and was appalled. Hippies wandered in day and night, though we didn't call them that because we were, too. One night four of us sat famously stoned at our kitchen table until dawn, and later swore that we had all shared the same hallucination of beams of blue light connecting our eyes in a parallelogram. We shot pool on Telegraph Avenue, the center of the universe, in a psychedelic haze. I had a series of girlfriends and rode motorcycles. It was the dream time.

For a couple of months we had a job driving for BATSC, the Bay Area Transportation Study Commission, predecessor of BART. The State cars were gray Dodge Darts specially fitted with stopwatches and odometers accurate to a thousandth of a mile. The two others in our crew were Roger, who later became a vice president at Bank of America, and Porky, a pothead pianist from New York who attained local fame when the engine fell out of his Corvair in a Berkeley intersection. Our boss was a short, chubby administrator with bushy eyebrows and the unlikely nickname Spike. He was rightly suspicious of the traffic data we gathered. One afternoon we were arrested by the Highway Patrol and sat handcuffed on the side of a dirt road for an hour, until they realized the bad guys were in Nevada, not Novato. Michael absorbed the experience stoically.

He wrote as if his life depended on it, which it did, and read James Joyce and Swinburne. I was reminded of Jack London's Martin Eden. His discipline with the pen was worthy of Procrustes. One night he burned a stack of his writings on the asphalt parking lot behind us, because they weren't good enough, he said. Much later I learned that Brahms destroyed countless unpublished manuscripts of his chamber music for the same reason. We'll never know what treasures were lost in those solitary potlatches.

He was a writer to the core. "I . . . want you-ou back again," he would sing quietly to himself over and over at his bare table, beseeching his muse and struggling with his demons, most of them arachnids. He spent an entire hot summer writing in an attic. No one I ever met was more a writer, except maybe Ray Bradbury, who wrote every day of his long life.

He taught me his Irish songs: "The Patriot Game" and "Rye whisky, rye whisky, rye whisky I cry" and "Timmy-way-ay-ay! We all shave under our chin, *bam, bam.*" We bawled them drunk.

Somehow I found my way to San Francisco State College. One evening when I had been wrestling with organic chemistry for hours, Michael glanced into my room and caught my intensity. He fixed me with a beady glare and inquired, "In the clinch, eh, Danny?" Meanwhile he was excelling at UC Berkeley and graduated *magna cum laude,* despite being arrested several times at demonstrations for the peace and civil rights movements.

He knew me better than I knew myself. Then we had a falling out, something to do with a navy surplus pea coat, and I went on to medical school and my career.

Over the ensuing years I became passionate about Jack Vance, obsessively collecting all his books and stories and manuscripts and ephemera. Then I re-read everything Jack had written and wrote *The Jack Vance Lexicon: From Ahulph to Zipangote,* a compendium of his invented words. Only after that did I discover that Michael, by a coincidence of literary empathy that borders on the mystical, had meanwhile written *A Quest for Simbilis,* his first novel and a wondrous sequel to Jack's *The Eyes of the Overworld.* It transpired that he had come across a copy of *Overworld* while staying at a flophouse during a hitchhiking jaunt to Alaska, and had written to Jack for his permission to write the sequel, offering him a share of the proceeds. Vance returned a scrap of newsprint with the quizzical typed comment that he was "a bit flummoxed by your offer," but gave Michael permission to make use of his droll character Cugel the Clever. Michael went on to write four more novels in the Vancian style, the first of which, *Nifft the Lean,* won a World Fantasy Award.

Our friendship re-blossomed, and my files filled with our correspondence. He sometimes signed his letters "The ink-stained wretch" or "Yr. Obt. Svt." I inflicted limericks on him—doggerel, really—and was treated to a heartily deserved dose of his crackling wit: "While I view, with sadness, your willingness to traduce every precept of metrical decency (indeed, the Meter Maid should pull this one over and pummel the driver with batons), I have to concede that this effort is at least redeemed by the ingenuity of its puns, and its tastelessness. Even now I scheme riposte." My

"Limerickal feet," he added in further just rebuke, "tread so wantonly as to be fairly described as 'clubbed.'"

Michael published well. His best known fiction included *The Color out of Time, Fat Face, Polyphemus,* "The Autopsy," "The Angel of Death," and *In Yana, the Touch of Undying.* His stories were collected in *The Best from Fantasy and Science Fiction, A Treasury of American Horror Stories, The Best of Modern Horror,* and others. He was translated into French, German, Italian, Japanese, Swedish, Russian, Norwegian, Spanish, and Finnish, and was repeatedly a finalist for the Hugo, Nebula, and World Fantasy Awards; he received the latter for both "Growlimb" and *Nifft the Lean.*

He loved to teach English and painted houses, advertising himself as an "earth-mover"—the well-muscled Shea with a shovel—but nonetheless compelled himself to write for hours every day. My wife and I picnicked and river-rafted and drove around Napa-Sonoma with him and Linda. I burdened him with tales of my exotic travels, and with an overwritten novel which he vivisected with infinite kindness. I eagerly awaited his occasional letters, sensing the weight of his literary labors in the interim. As he ended one to me in 1989, "I utter this hasty bleat of friendship and salutation on the run, but swear an ampler sending soon." Another was signed: "(. . . this entity is actually a troupe of spotted word-hogs cleverly and busily animating a writer-shaped hulk.)" A sort of cubist eloquence imbued even his sendoffs.

My oldest friend sleeps. I miss him.

Fiction

Credit Card

I

Ricky Deuce, at five-five, had always felt short, but you forgot something like that most of the time. He'd been sheet-rocking for Fast Wall eight years now, and when he had his aluminum stilts strapped to his calves and was taping and mudding the joints of the second and third runs of rock, it never crossed his mind. All the tapers used them, and if some could get a bit higher with them, so what?

Not today. Teetering toward quitting time across vertical acres of wall, he felt short. Because Angie was sick. His faithful, hard-working wife had cancer. And because stubborn, self-indulgent Ricky Deuce had made her life so hard, so short of money, she was at a hospital all the way cross-state, masquerading as her insured sister.

Ricky had been trying to grow up. He'd quit drinking six years ago, while their boy Ronnie was still young enough for it to make a difference. The kid was fourteen now—*had* it made a difference? Sometimes the boy was so touchy, as if you were nagging him to death if you asked him the simplest question.

"I don't care what *anyone* says about you"—Zack's bulldog voice echoed off the vast bare walls—"you're OK! Still workin' at three-thirty-*five!*"

"That's me, a *company* man!" Ricky teetered to a stack of rock, sat on it, and unstrapped his stilts. He hurried and caught up with him out in the lot. "Hey, Zack, you know Angie's . . . sick. She's upstate, and I've gotta take a couple days. I've got to go see her."

DeeAnn had been talking to Zack. His quick nod and embarrassed arm-thwack of sympathy scared Ricky. It kept hitting him: Angie had started *dying*.

He drove home through blocks of construction on the city fringe. Yesterday he'd seen Ronnie skateboarding here with his friends, doing jumps and turns along the fresh asphalt and spanking-new sidewalks.

He coasted his rusty old Chevy pickup past the half-sheeted frames of townhouses. Yesterday, all in their baggy pants and helmet-like cloth hats, their innocent energy had struck him, like wolf pups in a nature film all practicing the same moves in a meadow. . . .

He'd already put money in the kid's pocket for him and Rachel, their friend who'd be putting him up. Had given the boy a quick shoulder-hug too, said, "Don't worry about Mom . . ." Ronnie had shrugged the hug off. He knew Mom might die, and Good Old Dad couldn't do shit to stop it.

Yep—there they were, rolling out of a driveway for momentum to do jumps over a small debris-pile in the street. All in turn snatching the boards up under them when airborne, as if by some adhesive on their shoe soles.

They were in one of those cul-de-sacs with driveways radiating off an asphalt circle. As Ricky eased his truck into it, someone big hustled out of one structure. A bulky dude, waxed baldy, suspenders—not even noticing Ricky's truck behind him, menace in his stride.

Ricky noticed the cell phone and measuring tape clipped to the guy's belt, and the new white pickup with the logo Gibbons Construction parked near. Folds of fat crossed the back of his neck: a pre-ulcer site-boss with no people skills.

"Get your punk asses off this property! Come here!" this contradictory command almost roared. The kids were hesitating, their graceful slouch on their boards stiffening up a little. Ricky coasted to a stop, pulled on the handbrake . . .

"You little fucking vandals think you can just waltz around in here!?"

. . . and plucked from the seat his old worn framing hammer with the handle cut down to two-thirds . . .

"I want you to empty out your goddamn pockets! You're gonna stand right there while I call the cops!"

. . . tucked the haft into his belt behind him and slid out of the truck, hurrying over, calling politely, "Sir? Excuse me!" Wearing a big smile, hands held high, he hurried between the contractor and the kids.

The guy had a Genghis Khan 'stache, a tough Pacific Islander face. Utter surprise. "Who the fuck are you?"—so far out in rage, he hadn't sensed Ricky's approach.

"A friend is what I am." Big warm smile on runty Ricky Deuce, seven inches shorter and sixty pounds lighter. "See, I'm that boy's dad, and I know for a fact he's no thief."

"Well, if you're that little shit's dad I can just cut to the chase and kick *your* ass." In that trance of voluptuous fury, he probably had teenage boys of his own.

Backstepping, calming hands lifted, Ricky said, "I know where you're coming from, your cup just runneth over—" But here came the guy, bulging with rage, so Ricky pulled the hammer and showed the snap his sinewy little arm could give it.

Said, "See if you lay hands on me, big guy like you, I'll have to smash some of your teeth in, have to kneecap you—have to crack some of your *bones* . . ." The rant of rage entering his voice, a will to *smite* this fucker waking in him.

A gear slipped in his wrath. He *saw* this guy—too clearly to feel rage. "I bet you got teenagers, right? They act like punks? But just think how you raised them, barking at them all the time because they're boys and you gotta toughen them up! I mean, look at you and me! They act like thugs? *We* scared them into it!"

Something was working in the guy's bunched-up face, something coming loose there.

Ricky became aware of his hammer and tucked it back into his belt. "I'm gonna take these kids to a different block. These construction sites are irresistible to them—no traffic, safest places for them really. We're very sorry to have disturbed you."

Signaling to the boys, Ricky trotted to his truck and swung it over to let them jump into the bed. The guy was trudging back to his trailer, looking a little dazed, gazing around at this shiny new ghost town of his. . . .

A couple blocks away he let the kids out. "Gimme a second before I go, Ronnie." He thought the boy approached him less guardedly. Lean-muscled and already taller than his father, he was so beautiful, knew so little, and was so determined on what he knew—it broke Ricky's heart and made him want to laugh at the same time.

"Listen, son. We don't really know anything yet. We just have to hope. I'll always stand by you. Always." He hugged him quick, not to embarrass him. And now the boy hugged him back a little.

* * *

As full dark fell Ricky swung off the freeway down to an island of fast-food neon. Stepping into all that light, all that bright orange and yellow plastic, he felt like a bit of an eyesore. His cleanest jeans still bore a faded concrete stain, his "good" T-shirt a couple of burn-holes from a cheap cigarillo he'd tried. His hair and beard looked weedy no matter how he trimmed.

The families ahead of him in bright clothes fit right in, but at the register two shag-haired women in trail-worn jeans and jackets were taking their turn. The bulkier, older one, standing mute, wore the kind of high-crowned hat Ricky had seen on Peruvians in *National Geographic.* The leaner, darker one, profiled with a strong Mayan nose, wore a battered black fedora and was using pissed-off-sounding Spanish on the register girl—herself Hispanic, but looking confused at what this scary-eyed woman was saying.

It seemed they wanted refills on their coffee cups. They made the girl explain the refill policy several times. Ricky watched them work her, saw their detachment and their masked amusement. Thought: *Two dykes with 'tude from the Andes.* At last without refills they retired to a table they had already littered with napkins, creamer cuplets, and empty sugar packets.

He admired their brass, knowing what it was to milk a cup of coffee for an extra hour in some warm place with a bathroom. When he bought his order he added two large coffees to the tray and a heap of sugars and creams.

He off-loaded these at their table. "Here. I know. *Yo se lo que es, faltar dinero.*" And was already turning away so they'd know he wasn't trying to wedge in on them.

"You don't know *dick!*" grinned the darker one around her great Mayan beak. "But thanks."

Heading to a table in the rear, Ricky had to laugh. He glanced their way while he ate. So not just Andes—urban ghetto too. Still something authentic about them. That younger one had eyes like match-heads—you could see them just searching for something to strike on.

Pros at sponging, the coffees had been a mistake. They were sure to hit him up for something more. The bulkier one seemed full of slower, grimmer thoughts than her skinny, satirical friend.

"Hey, *pendejito!* You gotta help us out." And here she was, the bigger one, standing a little too close as she said this. On one of her blunt cheeks was a neat little knife-scar.

"Whoa." Ricky smiling angrily now. "Pendejo, OK, call me that once or twice. But Pende*jito?* You can *toma*lo por *coo*olo."

"Hey, man." The leaner one was all beaming now. "Forgive this pig my friend here. She got no education. We jus' need some gas, *jefe*."

"Plata no tengo, ni nada."

"No money, man! We jus' need some from you *ride.* We gotta siphon an' a can!"

Ricky found this irksome, but a bit comic too. The older one, still standing too close, was substantially bigger than he was. He'd never before sat this close to a hostile woman who might actually be able to kick his ass. The body language of both was fearless.

They said they had a siphon and a can. A pair like this would, wouldn't they? Was he afraid of getting mugged out in the lot? He had to struggle to hide a grin. "I could give you a gallon, I guess. I'm low myself."

"Hey, that's all our can holds!"

The parking lot, in the orange gloom of the looming burger logo, seemed oddly empty. He'd parked his mo-fugly truck with its one broken taillight and one missing plate in the far, shadowed corner of the lot. As he led them that way he asked, "So where's your car?"

"Downa street," said skinny Maya. "Where's yours? We in kin' of a hurry." And from under her jacket, she produced a rusty little metal gas can and a siphon. Their car was stolen, he thought, so they'd parked out of sight. As they crossed the lot, they fell slightly behind him to either side. He found he could smell them, a faint feral whiff as of the fur of a large animal. Their boots clocked along on the off-beat to his. His sense of time slipped a cog, and for an instant it seemed to him this walk had begun in the distant past, that these women had always walked at his back, his escorts or his guards.

And then the younger one was kneeling by his tank, cursing at the rusty metal cap of her can. As it gave with a squeak, the big one inserted the siphon, knelt beside her, and with a lewd sidelong look at Ricky and a wiggle of her eyebrows began to suck on it with an exaggerated hollowing of her cheeks.

When the younger received the siphon with her can, the downrush of gas sounded improbably forceful, like a hose at full stream, and it seemed to run on and on.

"What the fuck are you doing?" Ricky was unsure what he was asking. Doing with that siphon? Doing to his head? "It's gonna overflow," he protested lamely.

"Naw," said the big one. "We not gonna waste a drop! This shit's precious, *gavache*." And the stream stopped, the siphon was plucked, coiled, and pocketed.

And then they stood there, as if waiting for something else from him. A dozen different harsh dismissals volunteered themselves, but what at last came out was a laugh at his own confusion. "Lemme see that can a minute."

Absurdly, Ricky hefted it, then, openly clowning, studied its bottom as if for a false chamber. "Well," he said, handing it back, "good luck."

They stared back stone-faced. The skinny one snatched the can so sharply from him that a rusty angle on its strap handle tore his palm. His bright blood spattered on the asphalt.

Then they smiled, beaming on him. "You OK, *gavache*," Skinny grinned. And she slanted him her barbaric profile, the directest look he'd had from her. Molten tar her eyes seemed in the orange light.

"Thanks for the juice, Bruce," said Scarface over her shoulder as they clocked away.

Ricky coasted the truck to a stop in the breakdown lane. His gas gauge was no help—it had been stuck at the half mark for the last few months—but he *knew* he should have at least a quarter-tank left. What the Christ had those bitches *pulled* on him?

A peaceful scene. Dark farmland sprawled to both sides of the empty highway, down which headlights roared past him only at longish intervals, and he could hear the crickety silence in between. He gathered himself for the coming drudgery. He had his own gas can at least. He would trudge along the embankment and up to that overpass a quarter-mile ahead. Since it merited an overpass, that empty-looking street had to lead somewhere.

Headlights flared . . . slowed . . . and tucked into the breakdown lane behind him. He caught the yellow and red from the cherry-rack behind the headlights. Here came the added wattage of the sweep-light flooding his cab with ice-white.

Getting out his wallet, he sat waiting, without looking behind. How many times had he lived this moment? More than the national white-male average surely.

"Good evening. May I see your license and registration and proof of insurance?"

A kid, this one, big and sleek with youth. Bad luck draw. The ones new to the uniform, the uniform wore *them,* they had an engorged sense of the sternness their authority called for. Ricky handed over the documents.

"I ran out of gas, officer. My gauge is broken. I misjudged what I had in the tank."

"Your gauge is broken. Your right taillight appears to be broken too. Would you turn on your headlights?"

"It *is* broken. I've honestly been so short lately that I've been waiting for the extra couple bucks to fix it."

The officer was silent for a beat. "Would you turn on your headlights, please?"

Stone-faced, Ricky turned them on. Downhill from here—his favorite kind of cop, the perfect Type. He sat clamping down on his anger. Say as little as possible. The cop checked his taillights, came around and checked his headlights, and solemnly came back to his window.

"You're missing your front license plate, and your proof of insurance has expired."

He sat there, and they looked at each other through a short silence. The cop's face was smooth and shiny as armor, the uniform on him like some kind of radiation suit in which no vibes from fallible beings could reach him.

Ricky felt trapped in a joke. He sets off cross-state with sixty bucks and a maxed-out credit card. Stops for a bite. Two beaner sharpies steal his gas and strand him here where this robot pops up and condemns the very truck he sits in. And here he sat, perfectly fucked.

"Officer," Ricky said, "I know I'm at fault here, and these . . . automotive violations are only part of it. I ran out of gas because my gas gauge is broken—another thing I haven't fixed yet. I'm on my way right now, I'm trying to *hurry* on my way to commit a crime: fraud. They think my wife has cancer. We don't have insurance, and we don't have the money for this kind of thing—I'm a sheet-rocker. So we've sent her to the hospital for tests over in Conejo Grande because her sister lives there and her sister does have medical insurance and we're all pretending that my wife is her sister so she can have these tests . . ." Surprising that the cop hadn't interrupted him yet. Why was he *saying* these things? ". . . and so I'll be a part of that fraud. I'm telling you this because . . . I'm just trying to do the exact opposite of what you expect, because you probably expect me to make something up and conceal the truth."

Another short silence. Was the cop as amazed as he was at his speech?

"Stay here please," the cop said and went back to his car. Ricky almost laughed aloud. Stay here. No problem! The dykes from the Andes had seen to it. What, oh *what* had he just *said?* While the cop was calling for backup, here he sat, living proof that yes, a sufficiently stupid man, sufficiently frustrated, would actually chew his own legs off to facilitate his escape from a dilemma.

He heard a metallic noise close behind. The cop was unscrewing his gas cap. Downloading a five-gallon gas can into his tank. He nodded at a second can by his foot. "Splash some of that in your carb and put the rest in your tank."

As Ricky did this, the cop was writing in his ticket-book. When Ricky was back behind the wheel, the cop handed him the yellow flimsy. "This is a fix-it ticket for all your violations. I'm just writing *your* copy, in case you get pulled over for the taillight. I'm not logging in the citation. Just fix those things as soon as you can."

Now Ricky really surprised himself: *tears* jumped into his eyes. He just sat there gaping. The cop reached in and—a little awkward at this gesture with an older man—gave him a thwack on the shoulder. "Good luck, sir."

* * *

When the Greyhound rolled out of the station near midnight, Ronnie had a window seat on it near the back. Mom had called from the hospital in Conejo Grande, and Rachel had gotten him to the station just in time.

Ronnie didn't like busses usually, but this kind of cross-country night ride wasn't so bad. He felt private, a view of dark, flowing farmlands all his own, like a TV. Most of all, though, he felt relieved that Mom had called and told him to come, that she wanted him with her however sick she was.

He felt sorry for Dad. It was true he was a fuckup, always colliding with life, but he was a unique kind of fuckup. It was *him*. That stuff he was saying to that goon—who else but Dad would come out and say things like that to a stranger? Ronnie had asked friends over the years, cautiously and indirectly, about their fathers. His researches had persuaded him that no other fathers would ever say that kind of shit.

But sometimes Dad's outbursts were . . . excruciating. Ronnie hated it when Dad enthused, "You're such a fine-looking lad, son! You've got the class genes, thank God for Mom!"—trying to make Ronnie comfortable with being already taller than he was. Hated it especially now that things were so screwed up, with Mom sick and all. . . .

A bulky woman in a kind of Stetson hat loomed out of the aisle and settled into the empty seat beside him—gave off a leathery, earthy smell. "This seat taken, *jefe*?"

Ronnie got that sinking feeling. Loony adults—they sensed when you were too polite to fend them off. Plenty of other seats were empty—why'd she choose the one next to him?

"Who you goin' to see, *'manito*?"

"My mom."

"You don' live witchoo mom?"

"She's sick." It popped out, feeling like betrayal to give it to this big tramp lady. She had a scar on her cheek.

"You know 'bout sickness, *flaco*? Kind that kill you? It's in the *air*."

Another woman took the empty seat across the aisle, looked Mexican too but skinny, with a curved blade of a nose and a hungry smile. She sat sidesaddle, feet in the aisle. "Thass right, *hijo*. They floatin' up there, waitin' for you to weaken, to tell 'em, 'Yeah, you got *poder*.' Entiendes *poder*?"

"Power."

The two women looked at each other, exchanging big smiles like doting aunts. Bladenose told him, "You smart! An' so *guapo* too!"

"His momma mus' be *muy guapa*." The big one, so close, almost growled it. "You lucky. 'Cause you sure don' take after your daddy."

"How do *you* know?" An anger half fear rising in Ronnie's voice now.

Bladenose: "We met him. He give us some gas! Then our piece-a-shit ride crash an' burn, can you feature that?"

"What's his name?"

Scarface: "We don' know, nor your name neither. We know your daddy, though."

"Describe him."

Another shared look, and both laughed. Ronnie's anger was rising. Bladenose said, "He a gnarly little dude, gray beard, shaggy. Got a bunched-up little face, look like he been beat on here an' there."

"Good talker too," purred Scarface. "Cuss you up in Mex like a *campesino*."

No two ways about it—they knew Dad. They still looked pretty intense, but somehow less threatening now.

"So how did you find me?"

"We didn' *find* you!" Scarface hoisted her broad brows. In that hat she looked like some kind of gangster protesting his innocence, like a button in a Mexican Mafia, but a sociable one whose business wasn't with him. "We cop this bus when our *ride* crap out."

"But how did you know who I was?"

"We knew. Thass all." They grinned at him, as if they'd made a dare and were waiting to see if he had the right answer.

This lay wholly outside the spectrum of adult behavior that Ronnie had experienced. It felt like a scam, but what did he possess to be scammed for?

And what they'd said about sickness kept tugging at him. Sickness was his destination because that was where Mom was: it *had* her, and it could take her right off the earth while he stood empty-handed to help her.

"So you just knew who I was." His voice felt like someone else's, trying this out. He paused, felt them waiting to judge his next words. "Why are you talking to me?"

Again they gave each other their scary smiles. The Mafiosa slanted her shadowy hat-brim at Ronnie. "We're talkin' to you about *la Enfermeza, 'manito.* About *la Muerte,* you understand?"

Speaking his next words was like stepping out onto a creaky plank above an abyss. "What do you know about . . . sickness and death?"

Again they looked at each other, a steely look now like a mutual accusation in their bright black eyes. Bladenose turned him a gentler, more affable face. "We can take you where they keep 'em. It's right on the way. We can take you to the Warehouse of Woe, *'manito.*"

"Thass right," growled Mafiosa. "You wanna help you *mamacita,* onlies' way be you look 'em inna face *youself,* la enfermeza y la muerte." Her own big dark face, so blunt and scarred, leaned closer to his as if in illustration. A bitter smell came off her, like . . . ashes.

"Thassit!" said Bladenose, leaning across the aisle. "You face 'em *youself,* that mean you *mamacita* got a *ally,* gotta strong soul to stan' her *back!* If you game, we get down this nex' *town,* an' we take you where they *hang.* Face 'em *for* her. Sittin' by her bed don' do shit for her, 'less you do that *first!*"

Ronnie had been feeling exactly that—how helpless and useless he'd feel, sitting by Mom's hospital bed. He didn't know who the hell these two were, but they spoke his own heart to him. How could he say anything but yes?

The highway that led to Conejo Grande could only be reached by branching through the town of Skelton, which filled a midsized valley. Here Ricky began looking for a gas station.

One more full tank would take him all the rest of the way to Angie from here, but he was pretty sure his card was maxed out. He wished he'd asked Zack for a cash advance. He'd be in a real bind if he couldn't somehow get a break on a tankful here. He hoped to strike up a friendly enough relation that maybe they'd take a check. Maybe if he offered to leave his license with them for collateral . . .

There, set a block back from the central highway through town, was a little independent Supreme Service station.

He went hopefully inside, where a large elderly lady with big hair and a pale, blandly smiling face accepted his card . . . pulled out a card-swiper and made a regretful face at him.

"Oh. I'm afraid you're card's declined."

"I was afraid of that. Ma'am, my wife's in a hospital at Conejo Grande. I've got to get there. If you would be so kind as to accept a check, I can *swear* to you it is absolutely good. If you want, I'll leave my license with you for—"

She'd held up a polite palm, requesting silence, her calm gaze seeming to say they both had all the time in the world. "I don't doubt your check is good. I'll fill your tank, and a container as well, but for a service, not for money."

Amazed relief filled Ricky, followed by unease. Something in her manner made him feel that her business here had less to do with the sale of petroleum products than he'd assumed. "Uh . . . what's the service, ma'am?"

"I believe you're northbound." She didn't pause to confirm this. "On that end of town are two hitchhikers, both young. I want you to drive them as far on their way as you're going."

"Are they friends of yours?"

"No. I'm sure they don't know me at all."

"You want me to bring them back here first?"

"No. I'll trust you just to take them along with you."

He couldn't believe his luck. First the cop, then this! "I can't thank you enough."

She shook her head, smiling. . . .

With a full tank, and a full ten-gallon can in his bed, Ricky drove slowly to the north end of town, and a bit beyond it, before he saw his promised passengers: a last, sole streetlamp lit the pair of them on the highway's shoulder.

One of them, a lanky, pea-coated shape, sat on the pavement hugging his knees, in a slump that seemed to express complete exhaustion; a shorter, slighter figure in a pork-pie cap and a dark sweater much too big for it was standing by the seated one and waving at Ricky to stop. He'd been slightly uneasy about whom he'd agreed to pick up. But hey! It was a couple of youngsters!

He pulled over and threw open the passenger door. The seated one started to get to his feet—had to struggle to do it, while the smaller one helped him up. The smaller one was much smaller, and the larger one seemed very weak and dizzy indeed. They limped, arms interlocked, to the open door, which spilled out enough light to show Ricky a very skinny black boy, hair growing nappy, his arm draped over the much smaller shoulders of a much littler black person—whose cap partly swallowed equally weedy hair, and whose more delicate face was almost surely a girl's, save for what looked like a pencil-moustache on the upper lip.

The girl, grunting and gasping her larger companion up into the center of the seat, was speechless, till she had clambered in and pulled the door to after them. Then she pulled something from her pocket and, reaching across her companion, thrust a small pistol in Ricky's face.

"Aaah-*ite* bitch!!!" squeaked this miniature gunsel. "You gon' drive us to *Coneeeho,* or I'ma *cap* you ass!" Now Ricky could see that the pencil moustache was in fact exactly that—drawn, a bit crookedly, with a grease pencil. He figured her to be twelve or thirteen at the outside.

He shot his hand out and plucked the pistol from hers: found it to be a little twenty-two, and loaded indeed. He slipped it into the front pouch of his sweater.

"Jesus Christ! You drew on a moustache with a makeup pencil, right?"

Her wrath confirmed it. "That piece *mine!* Gimme it back!"

Ricky nodded. "When I get you to Conejo and get you to somebody who can take care of you, I'll give it to *them,* and it'll be up to *them* whether you get it back or not. Now: you two hungry? We'll get you some food the next town down the road."

He had them rolling now, taking it easy till he could see if the boy could sit upright, and finding he was almost too dizzy for it. "You switch with him. I'll go slow. You help him scoot over there where he can lean against the door—and make *sure* that door's *locked.*"

He pitched his voice low, repeating it all in a soothing tone. The girl got the young man moved over and settled, sat herself between them, and leaned against her exhausted companion's side.

"Here," Ricky said. "Bunch up my jacket and get it between his head and the door." He now saw the boy's face was beaded with sweat. Ricky leaned toward him as he drove and spoke louder. "You look pretty sick, son. Do you know what's wrong with you? Have you been feeling this sick for long?" He kept urging his questions, trying to see if the boy could focus at all. The boy's eyes found him, and very faintly he nodded.

"He got the AIDS," the girl said. She didn't look even twelve, her voice much smaller now. AIDS. Right.

He touched her shoulder. "Sweetie—"

"Kameesha," she piped.

"Kameesha, sweetie, you're a brave girl. Really brave for standing by your brother . . ."

"Rap my cousin."

"—real brave for standing by Rap, but if I ever see you with a gun in your hands again, I'll whip your skinny little ass clear across the state. You got that?"

"Umm."

"Do you have someplace to go where they can take care of Rap?"

"He stepmomma live in Conee-ho. She look after him."

"What about you? Who's taking care of you? You got your mom and dad?" The kid made a movement of her shoulder, a turning aside from the question. Since they were going his way, he decided he would drop them at a hospital, maybe get the girl to the stepmother. "What about Rap's stepmom? Do you have her phone number? Can you find her house?"

"Don' know her phone. Rap find her house."

"Rap? You gonna be able to help me find her house?" But the kid was out. "He's exhausted. We're gonna get to Conejo before too long, an' there's a hospital we'll take him to, get him straight to Emergency. Then I'll try to get you to his stepmomma's house if that doesn't take too long. Otherwise I'll leave you at the hospital with him, because my *wife's* in another hospital on the other side of the state, and I've got to get to her."

"You goin' to a hospital too?"

"Yes, I am, 'Meesha. You can call me Ricky."

"Ricky," she said, trying it out, as if it might explain why he was helping them. Then she added, in an apparent non sequitur, "My daddy he name Tye."

"Well, I bet he just loves you, 'cause you're a fine brave girl the way you're helping Rap. That moustache . . . was a sharp idea. You wanna wipe it off, though?"

"He do love me." Dragging her sleeve across the moustache. "He take me to Magic Mountain."

"Whoa! Those are some good rides."

"Yeah, they *fast*, an' my daddy hold onto me so I be *safe*."

"Which ride you like best?"

"All of 'em. I don't remember 'em ecksackly."

Ricky hesitated. "How old were you?"

"Six. It was my six birthday."

"Man, that's just the kind of birthday party I always wanted, but my dad never had the money for it."

"My daddy didn' have no money either. Thass why he lef' to look for work."

"When did he leave?"

"Right then, on my six birthday. My momma tol' me we drive home from Magic Mountain, an' he take a bus goin' the other way."

"Well . . . he still loves you, 'Meesh. Fathers never stop loving their kids."

Central Skelton was mean streets, Ronnie thought. Big shabby buildings with street-level shops all padlocked behind gratings, wet alleys packed with overflowing dumpsters and their spill, little square cinderblock bars with hard-driven trucks nosed around them. Litter tumbled the pavements in the bus's after-draft. The bus station was the only lit structure on its block. The two she-thugs were leading Ronnie to the front of the bus to be the first to debark.

Ronnie was amazed at this wild decision of his, now that he was actually executing it. Getting off the bus at mid-journey to Mom just because these crazy . . . *witches* suggested it?

Maybe they had met Dad, but still, how would they know Ronnie was on this bus? *Dad* didn't know, had said he wasn't going to wake Rachel or Mom up by calling them on route. But maybe the women did break down, found him by accident and Dad's description—because he was going the same direction as Dad—and decided to con him.

But for what? Just the fun of it? Make like you've got mystic powers of knowing him, and then say you've got knowledge of disease and death.

Hint you've got *power* over disease and death. That was the hook, the precise pitch that the sucker *wants* to be true.

But he *did* want it to be true. Didn't any chance of help for Mom, however insane, have to be taken? Wasn't that his responsibility? He thought of Mom's level look when she talked to him about decisions. "Always think it through before you do it. Use your imagination, picture the different ways it might go."

Should he follow these two? Mom's level eyes said *no way*. But he was going to do it.

The bus spun into the station ramp and surged majestically toward its berth. The two Latinas stepped down into the stair well.

Mom's eyes said no way, but disease *had* Mom. Ronnie now stood outside that wall around her. He was alone, and she needed any help at all that he could find for her.

Mafiosa descended with a jaunty little jump—surprisingly supple for her mass. Hawkface took the door-pole two-handed and swung out with a parting grin for the driver. As soon as Ronnie's soles touched the pavement, they were hustling him double-time back along the bus and out down the ramp, Hawkface asking him, "You got your ticket, *hijo*?" He pulled the ticket from his coat pocket. "Good, now you tuck it safe away."

Out on the sidewalk, the women stopped and traded a look. The long blocks of signals were set on blink, but a sparse traffic growled by here and there, miscellaneous vehicles that shared an air of being on the prowl. What were this spooky pair's eyes saying to each other? Hawkface led off to the left.

They walked a casual pace, as if they had no set goal. The sky, scorched by the sodium vapor lamps, was like lead. The city's ugliness was the only dimension. The women's worn boots seemed to make too much noise in its silence, having a drummer's conversation, converging, then dissenting. . . .

They turned at the first cross-street. This one was narrower and darker, the next streetlamp far ahead. Its litter seemed menacing—a torn, foul shirt . . . a bottle smashed amidst a starburst stain of red . . . a car by the curb sitting low on its bolt-studded wheel mounts, its rear doors gone and the front one graffitied: *don't tow have gone to call help*. Their boot heels woke echoes in alley mouths.

And then, as if they'd conjured it by walking just far enough down this grim lane, a pair of headlights swung into view a long block ahead. One light was dimmer, browner, like a cataracted eye. Its motor had that lurching, hesitant growl of being headed nowhere but straight to them.

The big old black boat of a car drew up alongside, its unevenly idling engine like an endless, angry argument . . . and Ronnie's guides stopped and turned sociably to meet it!

The passenger was a big guy with a long Scandinavian face starting to collapse. His eyelids were piled folds; seams and sags bracketed a mouth wide and dangerously thin. His pouched eyes blankly worked them, looking for something . . . usable, but his face told them it wasn't going to speak, that it was waiting for the driver, who now leaned forward.

The driver had a full, flushed face, round and chubby-chinned like a cartoon bear's, with gray stubble and a sociable potato-nose. "How you ladies doin' tonight?" He looked at all three of them saying this. When his eyes met Ronnie's, Ronnie felt his gaze a fraction off-center, as if he were looking at eyes just to one side of Ronnie's. The guy made a cheery grin. "You wanna know somethin' about the cops on this beat? I know 'em. Right now they're up at the Triple-X jerkin' off. There's nobody around here but us. You wanna take a ride with us?"

Mafiosa smiled ingratiatingly. "Oh, hey, we don' do the deed wit' *men, pendejo!*" She gave a little placating chuckle . . . and the two women just stood there, frighteningly inert. The guy pulled aside one flap of his jacket. A bright, bulky revolver was tucked in his belt.

"Hey," he smiled, "we like *all* kinds of pussy!" Again he looked at Ronnie, or just beside him.

Ronnie's hands went into his pockets, a blind reflexive search for resources. Disliking luggage, he'd done his packing in his pea-coat's pockets for this trip—was carrying two pairs of socks, his toothbrush . . . and in the right side pocket his hand met something unexpected. A solid little lock-back Buck that Dad had given him. It was already in his coat, from a camping trip, when he'd packed for this journey. His hand closed around it. The heft of this knife was like a touch from Dad now, and Ronnie felt less alone. And the moment he gripped the knife, both women turned and looked at him, then looked at each other, and smiled.

Mafiosa approached the car and rested her forearm on its roof, slanted her hat-brim down through the open window. "That really true about the pigs on this beat?"

"Oh, yeah. One of 'em's my cousin."

"Is that a Smith three five seven you got there?" She asked this almost girlishly, with envy and awe.

"That's right, lady."

"Whoa! How'd a piece-a-shit like you get a class roscoe like that?"

The smile on the guy's stubbly happy-bear face gave just one brief flicker. "I got it from the guy that owned it. He was dead."

The passenger reached for his door handle.

"Thass not what I want you to do," smiled Mafiosa. "Jus' sit right there's what I want you to *do*."

Something strange happened to Ronnie's eyes. There she was leaning in her shabby black coat on the car, her size unchanged with respect to the car, but all at once she was *bigger* than the hulking, thin-mouthed man. Looking between them you saw her mass engorged, dwarfing him. The passenger blinked. He seemed to see it too.

"What you want us to do—" said Stubbly-Bear, his hate bunching his face like glee, looking not quite into her eyes, "—what a fat, dyke, taco-burner wants us to *do* don't mean *dick* to us." He drew the Smith and showed her its short brute muzzle.

"What I want you to *do, payaso,*" smiled Mafiosa, "is stick that thing in you *mouth*."

As if he'd suddenly become aware of something strange, Stubbly-Bear looked at his partner. Razor-Lips sat there, not looking back at him. Then Stubbly-Bear looked at his Smith, as if a voice in his head were telling him something he'd never before realized about the revolver. With amazed eyes, he tucked the two-inch barrel in his mouth.

Her hat-brim gave him a nod of approval. "Now put you 'bout two poun's, naw, *three* poun's of pressure on that trigger . . . a little bit more now . . . thass good. Now you keep that trigger squeezed jus' that tight. We gon' give you a chance for a lucky break here. Look there now." Pointing through his windshield. "See that power pole on the main drag there? I wanchoo to *collide* widdit, hit it *muy rapido, maricon*. Wanchoo to put the pedal to the metal an hit it right square between you headlights. Go, *pendejo! Andale!*"

With a screech the car launched, Stubbly-Bear lipping the muzzle tight as a limpet, and rocketed off leaving a haze of burnt rubber, accelerating desperately. Hawkface plucked Ronnie's coat. "This way now, *guapo.* We leave 'em to their biz." They continued on their way, boots clocking, like a countdown accompanying the engine-roar receding behind them.

A ringing, banging, clashing, clattering impact—a *symphonic* impact—billowed out through the citywide silence, littering miles of empty pavement with its echoes, and at the core of that huge racket came a sharp thin *crack* like a driven spike.

"Whaddya think, *'manito*?" Hawkface nudged him. "You hear that roscoe go off?"

"Who *are* you?" Ronnie wanted to halt right there, but his legs moved like clockwork, obeying the rhythm of their boots.

"We jus' two workin' girls. We make deliveries for the Organization. Le's keep the pace here, *guapito.*" Hawkface laid a hand on his shoulder. Not a heavy hand, but one that felt as sharply outlined as a statue's.

"What organization?"

Mafiosa looked back and smiled, and her arm made an all-inclusive sweep.

"But just explain to me . . ." Explain? Ronnie saw it again: a stone killer sticking his gun in his own mouth and looking surprised. "Just please tell me what we're *doing.*"

"We doin' our *thing*. We helpin' our *community*"—her bootheels accenting her words as they walked. "You our guest! But tell you what—le's forget about dat *bus*. We jus' gonna walk the rest of the way to you momma—be jus' as quick in the end!"

"What are you saying? We can't walk all the way cross-state from here! It's hundreds of miles!"

Mafiosa took him by the shoulders and gave him a look of amazement. "Whachoo *mean,* we can't walk it? We got some stops to make on the way, but hell, you can *see it from here!*"

"See *what?*"

"See the hospital you momma's at! Looka there!"

At an indeterminate distance, where the street's darkness shrank to a knife-blade point, and the whole city shaded off into the night, there was *something* . . . a far, far-away pale mass that seemed to hover in the dark, something that had to be pretty big to show at all at such a distance: a tiny pale mass dotted with stacked rows of infinitesimal square flecks of light like . . . lit windows?

Ronnie squinted at it, saying—his voice a faint whine of protest as he repeated—"The hospital's clear across the *state!*"

"Jus' stick widd*us*. We getchoo there *rapidito, hermanito!*"

As their boots clocked on ahead, Ronnie glanced behind him and saw the distant wreck smoldering against the power pole.

And when he looked ahead again . . . the city had vanished from before him. They were on a country road, snaking through hills, the thick ceiling of stars the only light for miles around.

"Hold tight," he told himself, and kept walking after them. For he understood that he had just stepped out of his own world and was entirely in theirs. . . .

II

The emergency room's electric glass doors pulled back, and Ricky stepped through carrying Rap bride-wise in his arms. He'd wrapped the shivering boy in his work jacket. Kameesha walked close, her hands gingerly holding Rap's dangling ankles, less to support him than in fear of losing him in this big swarming place.

The kid felt light as a bundle of sticks, though Ricky knew he looked ridiculous, carrying a body so much larger than his own. But this was tactical: they'd have to take immediate charge of the boy with Ricky holding him right in their faces. He came up to the desk.

"Ma'am, I picked these kids up by the highway. Kameesha there says her cousin here has AIDS. He's in bad shape, sweating and piss—ah, wetting himself."

She leaned forward, a rail-thin woman with a long, gaunt prairie face and an unsettling gaze: the lenses of her glasses were of unequal thickness, and one of her eyes was more powerfully magnified than the other. First her look gimleted Ricky, giving him that sinking feeling. Then she reached out. When she actually touched Rap, Ricky knew it would be all right. She thumbed back his eyelid.

"Gurney!" she shouted. "Front desk!" Voice sharp as an icepick. As an EMT and a guy in greens laid Rap on his white, wheeled bed, the woman told them, "They say he has AIDS. Check him for any kind of bleeding. *This* man *carried* him in."

Ricky added, "And check the girl here too, please. She's been hitch-hiking with him I don't know for how long, and helping him . . ."

"What's your name, dear?"

"Kameesha."

"Come here." The woman plucked some Kleenex, wet them from a bottle of drinking water, steadied the girl's face with her left hand—"You need to wash your hair, Kameesha; you need a bath"—and began to wipe the remaining smudges from her upper lip. "Where's your family?"

"Rap stepmomma live in Skelton."

"Here in town? What address?"

Kameesha shook her head. The woman looked at Ricky. "In there please, sir."

"Mr. Deuce."

"OK, Mr. Deuce. We want you to go in that washroom. There's a shower. Take a thorough scrubdown, please. We'll see to Kameesha." Returning her gaze for a few moments, Ricky discovered that her unequal eyes somehow simultaneously beamed both implacable command and . . . kind intent.

More than half an hour after Ricky had washed up, another nurse brought Kameesha back out, obviously bathed and wearing fresh clothes.

The head nurse at the desk was writing something. "Ma'am? I'm sorry to interrupt . . ."

"Just a moment, Mr. Deuce. . . . Now. As best we can ascertain from the young man—who has responded well to some fluid nourishment—here is a map to his stepmother's house. I am afraid that its neighborhood is not . . . in the best part of town, but in cases like these we always seek family first. The phone number he provided appears to be disconnected. Of course, the county's Protective Services can take over Kameesha's care. But if you are willing to find the stepmother and bring her or send her here, it would, uh, complete your good services to both these young people and provide Kameesha with a place to stay."

Ricky found that the woman's schizoid gaze made a strangely irresistible appeal to his conscience. One of her eyes appeared frostily to expect the worst of him, while the other seemed to see his better nature. "Well, my own wife is in the hospital—in Conejo Grande across the state, and I'm on my way to see her now."

"I'm so sorry. Is her condition critical?" Her tone was not so much one of concern as a sly question about degrees of urgency.

Ricky's heart reached a swift decision. Rather than affirm in his heart that Angie was critical, was in danger, he would make the choice that assumed her deliverance. He would regard Kameesha here as the more imperiled.

"Can I use your phone to call her? My cell's defunct."

"Certainly."

When his call went through to Angie's room, the receiver was plucked up to the sound of female laughter. Angie's laugh and her sister Nicky's. Angie merrily asked, "Is that you, Ronnie?"

"No, hon. It's Ricky."

"Hey, stranger. You coming out to see me?"

"I'm in Skelton. I'm just calling to tell you I'll be a bit late—I'm making a short detour to help out some kids I picked up hitchhiking."

"Well, it's good you're looking out for kids on the road, because your own boy's on his way out here. I called and got him on the bus."

"That's wonderful! I felt so bad leaving him—I drove by where he was skating to say goodbye to him again."

"It's good we're all convening like this, Ricky, because Nicky and I are going into business together. We just decided. We were sitting in this Courtesy Room they gave me, and Nickie was talking about her and Ron's agency, and well, I'm gonna start selling real estate out of her office in Conejo Grande."

That made Ricky lose a beat. He'd always suspected that his sister-in-law Nicky would have talked her out of marrying him if she could. "Well . . . you mind if I move out there with you? I mean, this isn't—"

"Of course! She says there's plenty of construction work out here. I just assumed you'd see the logic of a move."

"I do! I do! Thanks for taking me along!" For right now, for this slender stretch of time, it seemed to him that Angie's refusal of fear, and her excitement for a new career, were her cure itself, were maybe—praytogod—the end of her danger. . . . "Honey, I'm gonna run this one more errand to find these kids' stepmomma so they can hook up. She's right here in town—we're in Skelton. Another hour and bam, I'm back on the road to you."

"Don't speed. Nicky and I have got lots to work out. Drive carefully and get here in one piece."

It put heart back in him, her strength and love. He stood there, feeling its sweetness. . . .

OK. Kameesha first. She was safe now, because the authorities had her—but also *un*safe, because the authorities had her. Child Protective Services could scoop her right up.

"Ma'am, I guess I'll go look for the stepmother now. As I say, I can't spend *too* much time because—"

"I understand perfectly—here's where you are now . . ." She thrust the map before him. And when he'd studied it, she said, "The boy's too exhausted to tell us much about his family, and the girl knows very little. Rap's last name is Peoples. Kameesha says his stepmother raised him after his father left. She's now living with another man. We sense there's something doubtful about him. Will you tell us what you think?"

"Of course."

"Ah, here she is."

Somewhere they'd found a bulky wool sweater for the girl. She'd been bathed, and her freshly washed hair was pulled back into two little five-inch pigtails. She stubbornly clutched her cap, apparently the focus of some objection from the motherly Asian nurse escorting her. The girl walked with her chin tucked down, having none of it, but the rest of her body showed a kind of compliance toward the nurse. Ricky could see that bathing and grooming had called back a younger child in her, one who had been better loved. . . .

This nurse said, "Mr. Deuce? Will you please tell Kameesha that she must *not* put this dirty old hat on her nice clean hair?"

He saw that once she left this bright, safe place, she'd want to hide those pigtails—seemed not at all sure she'd find safety, even if they did find Rap's stepmother. "Thank you, ma'am. While we're in the truck together, she can just hold onto it, OK, 'Meesh?"

A faint nod. Ricky weighed his further questions for the girl, then excused himself from the nurses and drew her a bit aside before asking them. "OK. Now, you know if there's anybody living with Rap's stepmom?"

"Rap say she been livin' with Melvin that was a fren' of my daddy Tye's. He say, maybe Melvin be in jail, but maybe now he be *out*."

"What's his stepmom's name, honey?"

"She name Jasmine."

"OK, hon. You know anything else about what kind of place it is where Melvin and Jasmine live?"

"Well . . . Rap say they a chop-shop cross the street from 'em."

Great. "Do you know what that is, honey? A chop-shop?"

"No . . ."

"Well, OK. Now maybe you're gonna have to stay in the car when we get there, 'Meesh, you understand? You gotta agree to do what I tell you when we get there, OK?"

"Mmmm."

Ricky drove them down streets roofed by big old trees. In their shadows, though it wasn't quite ten P.M., the lit houses in this declining neighborhood were fewer than the dark ones, and a few of the dark ones were dirty-windowed hulks in nests of weeds. . . .

Jasmine's address had a dim porchlight, but a stronger light within the curtained windows. The "chop-shop" was probably four houses down the opposite side of the street, where a nimbus of strong yard-light rose from behind an unusually high plank fence. When Ricky and 'Meesha were out of the truck, faint voices and metallic sounds wafted from the place. He led the girl crunching through the leaf-fall of a huge old sycamore and climbed the steps of Jasmine's porch.

Ricky's knock woke firm, even aggressive-sounding footsteps The front door was pulled wide open. It was a woman, mostly silhouette. A solid woman in a loose sweatshirt.

"Whaddya want?" She sounded young. Ricky made out hair styled in curves around her ears.

"Hi, I'm sorry to intrude—"

He had to jump back as the screen door came smartly open and the woman thrust out of it. She had a couple inches of height on him and surprised him by being white.

"What's your name, darlin'? Aren't you that *Tye's* little girl?"

"Yes'm, I Kameesha."

"Who's this here?"

"I'm—"

"This *Ricky!* When me'n Rap be comin' up here Ricky pick us up an' he drive Rap'n me up to the *hospital!*"

"The *hospital?* Why did you go there?"

"'Cause Rap got the AIDS!"

Ricky saw it hit her, the woman not moving at all for a moment but her whole silhouette shrinking ever so slightly.

"How bad do they think it is?" This she asked Ricky.

"They were hitchhiking—Rap was hungry and exhausted. When they take care of that, I think he'll be OK. They can treat it pretty well nowadays—I really don't know, ma'am. We came looking for you because I didn't want to leave 'Meesha with the county, and I have to get on east, because my wife's in the hospital too."

"Come inside," she said.

The living room furniture was well worn, but everything was dusted and waxed and had a fresh-cleaned smell. Jasmine was the most vivid thing in the room, a large handsome woman. Her mouth didn't show much, looked slightly pissed if anything, but her broad lovely eyelids, shaded violet, had a tired, ironic droop that was not unkind. "Ka-mee-sha," she said, putting her hands on the girl's shoulders, "are you hungry?"

"Yes'm. I hungry."

To Ricky, after looking him over a bit, "Thank you for helping my stepson."

In the kitchen she made baloney and lettuce sandwiches for 'Meesha. Ricky felt too tired to eat but accepted some coffee. They sat around the kitchen table.

"I couldn't live with his father," said Jasmine. "It got down to a him-or-me situation. He took off and left Eugene with me—that's the boy's real name—then he showed up again, and he was all like, 'I've gotta right to be his dad! I've *changed!'* I didn't believe it, but Eugene was thirteen, and he wasn't going to be a 'step-momma's boy.' I work for minimum wage, and I had no way to hold him. Of course he took him away, and then just took *off* couple months later."

"I'm really sorry. He seemed to me like a really nice kid."

"I know she can't stay here. See, this is my boyfriend *Melvin's* house, and he doesn't ever let me forget it . . ."

She broke off and seemed to be listening. "Oh shit," she said. Then Ricky too heard footsteps out front. "He was supposed to be gone all night." Heavy footsteps on the porch now. "You two stay back in here!"

Jasmine rushed out. Ricky eyed the back door behind them. A man's voice burst in through the front door.

"Those bitches are trying to burn me! That's an almost new Bronco engine!"

"Melvin, I got a little niece who just showed up. She needs some help, needs a place to stay."

"We aren't taking any *niece* in here! You aren't bringing anyone in my house! I told you that when you were goin' on about that little bitch Rap!"

"You just wait now! I've been contributing all the utilities and half the rent! We only need a room for her till I get us someplace of our own."

"Whachoo saying? *You* aren't leaving! We gotta contract here! You're supposed to pay your share for our business!"

"What *our* business? I've got nothing to do with what you and that lowlife—"

"Outta my way! She's in the kitchen eatin' my food, I know it."

"Don't you shove me, you son of a bitch! You lay another hand on me an' I'll cut you a new asshole! I'm not your pitiful *wife!*"

Sounds of a struggle followed. "I've gotta help her," Ricky told 'Meesha. "You stay put, and you hear any trouble you get right out that back door, hide behind the house, and wait for me. You understand?"

Melvin had Jasmine by both wrists but stood back amazed when Ricky emerged. Melvin was a big guy, standing there leaning back in an almost comic posture of shock, till he pushed Jasmine back and took a step forward. Then Ricky saw that he *was* slightly canted back. One of his legs was shorter than the other, and he stood with his stronger side slightly outthrust. All of him looked plenty strong, actually. He wore a baldy, and one of his ears was a mere lumpy nub of scar tissue.

"I'm not here to intrude," Ricky piped, hands up placatingly. "I'll take that little girl right outta here"—and realized that here 'Meesha was, right at his side—"and we'll be totally outta your way! We'll give you a ride too, Jasmine, if—"

"You ain't doin' *shit* with her!" Ricky could now see, by the slight wobble he gave screeching *shit,* that Melvin wasn't sober. Great.

"Well, to be honest, Melvin, if she wants a ride, I'm not gonna—"

Melvin slugged him surprisingly fast, laid a nice solid crush on his nose and knocked him sideways, bang onto the floor. Ricky rolled back, scrambling his legs under him, rose and launched a desperate counter-lunge, but his feet snagged in the pleats of the rucked-back rug, and he pitched forward just above floor-level. His head drove into Melvin's stomach, and as they both hit the floor he felt something small and heavy leave the stomach-pouch of his parka and rattle on the floor.

He struggled backward, and got on his feet, still half-clocked by that blow to his nose, from which gushed copious hot gore that poured across his mouth and fell ropily from his chin.

Wheezing Melvin was getting up too, like a golem with stiff inhuman joints. As he rose, his right hand snatched something up from the floor. He extended this toward Ricky . . .

CRACK!—the wall to Ricky's right spat plaster. "Geddout the back, geddout the back door!" he shouted, his articulation blunted by his crushed nose. 'Meesha, perhaps a veteran of domestic violence, was already vanishing down the short hall to the kitchen. Ricky swept his arm around to thrust the still immobile Jasmine ahead of him in the same direction. Just as his hand came up before her face, CRACK!

It felt like the edge of his hand had been crushed by a sledgehammer. Amazing, **AMAZING** pain! He shoved Jasmine back toward the kitchen with his shoulder, and she stumbled. There was a moment, as she started scrambling low for the kitchen, when Ricky didn't dare move from between her and Melvin, when all he could do—after looking and discovering that his destroyed hand was missing its little finger and bleeding appallingly from a splintered stump—was to stare at that furious, lopsided giant.

Melvin had the pistol out straight-arm ('Meesha's pistol, of course!), and he was going to do it right this time. Aiming *carefully* at Ricky's face, he took one brisk step closer to be doubly sure, caught his foot sharply in the rucked-up rug, and pitched straight off his feet.

As he toppled, he caught his head on the edge of the coffee table. A very serious snapping sound came from his neck as he struck it. He tremored slightly and lay still.

Ricky stood swaying like a teetering bucket, brimful of pain and nausea. He could not remember *ever* experiencing so much discomfort at one time as this excruciating duet of his little finger's stump and his crushed nose. Jasmine reappeared cautiously in the kitchen doorway.

"He docked hibself out," Ricky reported in a voice he seemed to have rented from a very old and disoriented man. He cleared his throat. "I deed a baddage. You godda flashlight? I dick we should turd off the lights."

When the lights were off the three of them crowded clumsily into the little bathroom. The flashlight beam discovered, in the cabinet under the sink, a bottle of hydrogen peroxide and a box of gauze, but the box was empty. A box of sanitary napkins produced a substitute. 'Meesha used one of these, with peroxide, to clean Ricky's nose, mouth, and chin, while Jasmine rinsed his finger-stump with the peroxide over the sink.

Gazing on that flashlit ruin, Ricky learned that however awful it is to see one of your own bones, it is far more awful to see the *splintered end* of one of your own bones. He realized after long woozy moments that Jasmine and Meesh were propping him up with their shoulders from either side as they worked on him.

They folded a cut-down pad in half over the stump. "We godda tape it tight to slow the bleedig," Ricky rasped. Jasmine took the flashlight into the kitchen, where cupboard doors slammed. She came back with a roll of duct tape. They taped all his fingers together in a silvery mitten with one fatly padded edge. Found scissors and plugged both his nostrils with shaped chunks of sanitary napkin.

"Dere!" Ricky croaked. "Good as dew!"

He saw his helpers, underlit by the flashlight, look at him anxiously, as if he might be delirious.

But their danger here was dawning fast on Ricky. Fear for his continued freedom from prison was beginning to concentrate his thoughts wonderfully. "Do peeble rebort gud shots aroud here?"

"Sometimes."

"Do the cobs cub?"

"Sometimes."

"Kabeesha? You godda cleed ub. Belvids asleeb. Jazzbeed's gudda helb be poodib idda chair."

"What?"

"We gonna put 'im in his chair to sleep it off, hon," Jasmine told her. "You gotta straighten up the rug an' wipe up the floor. Take a couple more pads an' wet 'em."

As Ricky led with the flashlight back down the hall, he froze in front of something spot-lit on the floor. "Jazzbeed? You godda Ziblog bag?"

"A what?"

"A Zib Log Bag. Like for sadwidges."

She too saw it on the floor then: Ricky's little finger. "Oh."

They put it in the bag, poured in a little peroxide, locked the bag, and put it where it wouldn't be crushed: in the pouch of Ricky's sweater.

Faint streetlight sifted in through the thin curtains of the front window. Just enough to gather up Melvin by either end and, with severe agony to Ricky's left hand, haul him up into the big armchair, which moved on its casters as his weight hit it. His head lolled impossibly loose on the backrest, and Ricky saw the flash of Jasmine's eye as she took in his true condition. But she said nothing, and Ricky gained confidence in her steadiness.

"He's still got that pistol in his hand . . ." she muttered.

Ricky moved to retrieve it, and she said, "Wait. Leave it on 'im. Let 'em find him with it. But he can't be *here,* or they'll be looking for me."

They both looked around. 'Meesha had gone into the bathroom with the the other flashlight for more pads. "I doad udderstad."

"We gotta leave him someplace else."

"I cad carry—"

"Naw, in the chair we could roll him. Just down the block a little way—I know just where to put him."

At last, the truth dawned on Ricky. None of this was really happening! He was not really here, was deep in a nightmare or a sustained hallucination. It was obvious! He could not *really* be standing here beside a two hundred-pound murder rap, with his finger in a Ziploc bag in the pouch of his sweater!

"The back steps rotted out," Jasmine whispered. "He just laid a ramp of plywood back there. We can roll this chair down that, and I know how to leave him like he died at this other place."

Ricky, trying to weigh this, found he had been totally stripped of his powers of judgment. He knew there were many intelligent questions that needed to be asked at this juncture but said only, "Led's geddit dud."

Jasmine went to pack a shoulder bag, then emptied a lamp-stand drawer—apparently of mail that had her name on it, into the bag. . . .

Five minutes later Ricky stepped down the echoey plywood ramp into the weedy back yard and braced himself at its foot, arms reaching upward to the doorway where 'Meesha and Jasmine stood behind Melvin's chair. Melvin looked as if he'd fallen asleep while gazing at the stars.

"OK, ease ib dowd," Ricky hissed. As they tried to ease him onto the incline, the slick naugahyde slipped from their grips and here came Melvin. Ricky just barely held against the shock, and as the chair crashed against his shins, he realized that these had been, till that instant, two completely painless portions of his body.

The castors of the chair made a crisp crackling on the dirty driveway going out to the street. Ricky found the best leverage by pushing on the chair's arms, leaning face-to-face over the slouched Melvin. The man lay there with his gun-hand dreaming on his lap. It occurred to Ricky that this was the calmest he'd ever been, this furious man. . . .

On the sidewalk the castors screeched even louder. Jasmine hissed, "Cross the street—darker that side."

Even louder, across the pitted asphalt, screeched the castors.

Up on the opposite sidewalk, in tree-shadow: *screeeek-eeek-eeek—screek-eek!* The direction Jasmine led them did not surprise Ricky: the chop-shop, of course. There were lights on in one or two of the houses they passed—dim, thickly screened by shade and drape—but the main light on the block was where they were headed, that halo above the tall fence, with its growing gnat-swarm of noises rising within it. Were these guys as stupid as this looked? A chop-shop with its own midnight aura like a beacon?

But Jasmine was smart. If the body could be found on or near this property before the choppers inside knew it was there, it might detach his death from Jasmine's residence and suggest his criminal associates as its cause.

Just two houses ahead now. The castors seemed to cut right through those half-guarded mutters, laughs, clatterings and clankings. "Waid," he whispered. He knelt to daub spit on the tiny axles of the castors . . . then, inspired, plucked the blood-drenched plugs from his nostrils. With these he more thickly swabbed the castors. In the dark, Melvin looked young, trustful. Had this broken-necked bastard ever slept like this as a kid?

"OK," he whispered.

Now the screeching was muffled, and Ricky could breathe better too. Another fifty feet, and Jasmine swerved the back of the chair and steered them up onto mute grass. They were on the lawn of the dark, deep-porched old house right next door to the chop-shop—evidently a house Jasmine knew to be vacated.. The men in the yard were perhaps twenty feet away, with just some one-inch-thick plank fencing and air separating them from the three secret corpse-shifters.

". . . *Sho* you is . . ."

rattle-clink

". . . boy's pecker *got* a pecker . . ."

clank-ratchet, ratchet, ratchet

". . . wid *my* bitch, he better . . ."

*tink-tink-tink-**click!***

". . . Haw! She bitch-slap him from here to Houston!"

Ricky sighed, whispered, "Le's geddit dud." He stooped to drape Melvin on his shoulder for the final hard carry up onto the dark porch above them when Jasmine gripped his arm. With come-here gestures, she led him to the low front wall of the porch and indicated two of the bottom planks of siding, both of which had come loose at one end. She tugged at one and, with a rusty whisper of nails, pulled it free. Then she gestured with this plank toward the porch steps.

Prepped for unreality, Ricky saw it instantly. They could leave Melvin *and* the chair, *in* the chair, up on the porch.

The second plank came free as easily—all attached, it seemed, to soft-rotted studs. They laid them, parallel tracks, up the steps. *Eased* the chair into position. In dumb-show he told them they should pull on the chair-back from behind as he pushed on its arms from in front—thinking right now was just the moment for some neighbor's headlights to swing onto the street. . . .

At his nod he thrust, and they heaved. In the intense labor, his finger-stump felt like a tongue of fire. He tried to imagine he was Melvin, the guy at the other end of this track-shoe in his face, riding the elevator up to his repose, to a posthumous revenge on the guys who'd tried to stiff him on that Bronco engine, the guys on the other side of that fence.

As the chair made the porch, it leveraged up one of the planks, which *clapped* softly back into place. A frozen pause before they all moved, and a voice next door said, "Whass that?"

The groan of the yard's metal gate opening.

Jasmine and 'Meesha snatched up the planks and stowed them behind the railing. The three of them sped tiptoe to crouch behind the chair and softly drag it and dreaming Melvin into a shadowed corner.

From next door, considerable weight advanced on heavy boots. A big shape emerged from the fence-corner—dreads, the flash of an ear-stud, mucho shoulders, and scant waist. His shadow face swept the lawn, began scanning the street as, belatedly, the last of the lights in the chop-shop yard went out.

Now the dark was satiny and deep. The big shoulders relaxed slightly, and he turned, his face once more sweeping the front of the house.

Maybe he was looking for some threat as big as he was, maybe expecting to confront a goon in cammies with a Mac-10. The shadow-shape of a chair on one end of the dark porch didn't seem to mean anything to him. Moments after he was back in the yard, the lights came on again, and the tinking and ratcheting resumed.

". . . *para*noid, dawg!"

". . . pay to stay *alert*, Homes!"

*Chink-chink-chink-**sproink**.*

With his sleeves, Ricky wiped down every inch of the armchair. After pressing the nails in the planks back into the chalky lower frame of the porch-front, they tiptoe-sprinted back to Ricky's truck.

They went slow till they hit the corner and, once around it, accelerated steadily. Ricky said, "We gotta call it in right away. The police have to find him before the choppers do. If *they* find him first, they might put him back in his house. I've gotta head north to see my wife. Where can I leave you two that's safe?"

"I'll show you."

"Write down your numbers, where I can find you, where I can call you. As soon as I see Angie and know she's OK, I'm coming back for you both."

They drove in silence a moment. 'Meesha, wedged between them, piped, "Ricky *save* our *lives!*" She sounded exultant, as if somebody had once told her that no one would ever save her life.

"No, I didn't, sweetie. He was just fixing to shoot me, and he tripped and hit his head on the table. Knocked himself out."

"Uh-uh. He *dead*."

"Yes, he is, sweetheart," Jasmine said comfortingly. "Killed himself with his own meanness. Don't you ever feel bad about somebody dyin' that can't feel good unless he's hurtin' someone else. You're right—our friend Ricky here saved us." Ricky thought her expression as she smiled at him held at least as much irony as gratitude. To Kameesha she said, "Here, take this"—handing the girl another sanitary napkin—"and wipe his nose for him."

The witches led Ronnie across the hills. Unendingly the pale path ribboned away before them, its starlit dust like a vast encryption in cursive, and every so often that hospital, a little jeweled cube with tiny golden windows, snaked into view still far, far ahead.

His escorts marched slightly to either side of him, so that it seemed—by a strange gravitation—that they pulled his legs after them, the left, the right, the left. But pulled him, it seemed, to no end, the little jeweled box of the hospital always fixed at sight's very limit.

Until they rounded the next shoulder, and there—astonishingly huge and bright, quite filling a small valley before them—blazed a titan of high white walls and countless amber windows. It was six stories high and a whole city block in bulk. Their path was all concrete now, and it swept down to the luminous entry: big sextuple doors of glass and chrome.

"We're there already!" Ronnie cried, astonished.

"No you ain't!" boomed Mafiosa. "This *a* hospital, but it ain't *the* hospital! You see any town there? You see Conejo Grande anywhere? Don' worry, we get you to you Momma. But *firs'*, we jus' showin' you what *kinda* place she in."

The big doors gasped open on their approach. They passed inside, Ronnie between, their arms across his shoulders now, as if they thought that he might bolt.

His captors—black-clad in this temple of cleanness, big dirty boots booming—didn't seem to disturb in the least the teeming business of the place. The bright floor shone underfoot, and the corridor stretched so far ahead it seemed contracted almost to the vanishing point.

"Ain't it gorgeous?" grinned Hawk, spreading her arms. "A giant meat-an'-bone repair shop! Short a blood? You can *buy* more here! Got extra blood? Hell! S*ell* it here!" And she jabbed her thumb at a door with a buzzer by it off to one side of the reception desk.

Everywhere medical clergy in white or blue were on the move, their chrome trays gliding on silent wheels, glinting with medical magics. A doctor passed them intent on a clipboard, and Mafiosa plucked it from his hand. He looked at them—a shag-browed man with sadly friendly eyes. The witches winked at him. He blinked and turned and walked on past the room he'd seemed about to enter. The witches ushered Ronnie into it.

A legless man lay propped, unconscious, the television bathing him with ads, his lamp on, a radio murmuring out of sync with the almost muted TV. Under the blanket he was just two thigh-length ridges and no more. His face was an unreal garish red, his scalp as well glowing redly beneath his buzz-cut white hair. His bulky upper body tremored faintly as if some inward upheaval convulsed him at the core. The sisters faced each other across him.

"So you down?" Mafiosa asked.

"I stan' by my work," her gaunt sib grinned.

The Thug reached something small from her jacket pocket and flung it at his truncated lap. Dice of tarnished ivory jounced off his blanketed thighs and settled obscenely where the man's balls would lie. The Thug snatched them up at once, but not before Ronnie saw that they seemed to be blank.

The sisters waited, and Ronnie waited with them.

The man's deep tremor seemed to intensify. Mafiosa smiled with half her mouth. "I think the ol' dude's showin' you somethin' here, sis. Looka there!" The man's face was sweating. His eyes snapped open—like a homeowner roused by intruders. His hands pressed on his heart, as if to crush some tumult there. His eyes touched the TV's muted ads, the murmuring radio, the book at his side, his lamp, his walls—his world's continuance. . . .

"Le's go, *hijito,*" Hawk told Ronnie. "I guess I lost that roll for now. C'mon. So many patients, eh? An' so little time!"

"Ho now—you hear that?"—Mafiosa, cocking an ear. "You good witchoo hands, *'mano*?" Ronnie's Spanish was good enough to detect his sudden promotion from "little brother" to "brother."

"I don't know," he said. "Hear what?"—but heard it now in the corridor: doors bursting open, voices and wheels and a ripple of footfalls. . . .

A gurney swung round a corner, masted with IV racks, flanked by folk in greens and blues like islanders rushing a dugout into the surf. As it swept down they were snatched into its rush—were gripping its rails and sprinting, Ronnie looking down on a shuddering young man, his clothes cut away from red traumas in his ribs, midriff, and inner thigh.

This damaged man's lips were gently parted, his eyes shut, his brows lifted in the rapture of one who listens alone to a lofty music, and amidst the flurry of pressure packs and tourniquetting—all at a run—his shudderings were growing slower and losing power.

A hand like living stone took Ronnie's wrist. Thug's eyes glinted close to his. "He bleedin' out—that tourniquet won' close that pipe—but you can save his life."

She shoved his hand into a red rent, a frightful hole in the man's thigh, where Ronnie's knuckles knocked the naked thighbone. "Feel for it, that little sliced *tube,* an' pinch it *shut.*"

Hot leg-meat mouthed Ronnie's hand as his fingertips found it—that delicate elastic lip—felt the blood outwelling and pinched it shut. *Had* it then: the man's life pinched like a gold coin, secure between the pressure of his thumb and forefinger.

It lifted Ronnie's heart. Here he was, saving the man's treasure for him, preventing his very existence from leaking out into the dark as they were all running, the bright floor sweeping under them like a river as they steered the torn life back into the light. . . . They swept the gurney through a turn to the waiting surgery—and with the turn, the man's weight shifted, snagging his leg on Ronnie's intruding hand. The leg convulsed with pain, tearing the artery from Ronnie's grip.

Desperately he rummaged for the slim and slippery pipe, while the broken meat gummed his hand like a toothless maw. Disgorged blood bloomed, an unfolding flower on the gurney's linen.

Thug gripped Ronnie by the neck and dragged him back.

As Ronnie's hand came free, the man's eyes came open, stark amazed, as if they were for the first time discovering the miracle it was to *see*. In the next instant his eyes—still open—had stopped seeing, as the emergency team piloted his corpse into the surgery.

And at that moment of the man's dying, Ronnie felt a catch in the earth's gravity—exactly as if the world were an immense Ferris wheel that reached at that instant a pause at the apex of its turning. With that brief lurch, the little weight of the young man's life left the planet, and the planet plunged back down on its carnival spin, its grand web all gaudy with lights, whirling amid cries and music and laughter through the evening air.

It astonished Ronnie, finding out how *here* everything was. It seemed he saw all the world at once—hills and sky, seas and trees and stones and cities of lights—all of it fixed to the great wheeling moment, all sharing these suns and these moons—how *here* it all was and how sharply you could fall right off of the wheel . . . but he and Mom and Dad all *on* it now, and now, and now—all sharing these moments of its gargantuan dance.

The surgery doors flapped shut behind the gurney. Ronnie felt the red warmth on his hand grow chill and sticky.

He looked to either side of him. The Thug and the Hawk were gone.

What had they brought him here for? Was all this to tell him . . . that Mom was going to die?

When they were absent like this, he found he could almost disbelieve their reality. Either way, *fuck* what they were telling him! He was going to Mom. And once he was with her, he wasn't going to *let* her die.

He rinsed his hand at a drinking fountain in the hall. He reached into his pocket, to touch the reassurance of his bus ticket . . . and then he *knew* the sisters' reality. His wallet was gone. Neither searching all his pockets nor groaning and cursing could change the fact: he didn't have a wallet, he didn't have a ticket, and he didn't have a dime.

And now, back in the Emergency reception area, he gazed with new understanding at the far door with its buzzer and waiting bench. All right then. But was he going to blow this? They would say he was too young. He probably had to be eighteen! Well, that's what he would *tell* them! They'd never swallow it. He did have some hair on his lip and chin, but it was thin and wispy. . . . Screw that! They'd *have* to believe him—of *course* he had ID, but his wallet was stolen and that's why he was selling blood in the first place! He wouldn't take no for an answer. He went to the door and thumbed the buzzer.

The door with its frosted-glass pane was pulled sharply open, startling him. A lean, white-haired nurse stepped out and aimed up into his face a pair of grossly unequal eyes behind lenses of unequal thickness. She looked half-outraged in advance.

"Hello," said Ronnie suavely. "I'd like to sell you some blood." His voice betrayed him with the slightest squeak on *sell,* but sounded good otherwise. "I lost my bus ticket."

Shit! Utterly lame! He struggled to hold his suave smile.

"Are you eighteen years of age?" Did her voice, grainy with age, have a sarcastic edge?

"Yes, ma'am, I am."

"What's your name, sir?" Ronnie now began to feel her smaller eye was dominant. Its littler focus gave her an air of knowing something about him.

"Ronald Deuce."

"Yes. You resemble your father."

"My *dad* was here?"

"He carried a boy with AIDS into Emergency."

Ronnie stood there trying to picture it—*could* picture it: Dad carrying some sick kid into Emergency. But where did he *get* him? What the fuck was Dad *doing?*

"Come in," the nurse concluded. "Take your coat off and lie on that examining table."

Suddenly, things were moving right along. She was tying off his upper arm with a limber rubber tube, sitting beside him with a very substantial looking needle-and-nozzle. "You have good veins, Mr. Deuce. What brings *you* to Skelton?"

She was arranging a clear-plastic tube-and-bloodbag. Ronnie could actually see a little black hole in the tip of that needle. That was one honkin' big-bore needle. . . . Her question—he saw there was no way he could honestly report his trip here thus far. She might refuse to buy his blood if he seemed insane.

"I got off the bus to stretch my legs, and it left without me. I lost my wallet."

Now it was her big eye that seemed dominant. It devoured him fiercely, but with a hint of approval—as if she knew he lied and thought it was the right thing for him to do.

"This will just sting a little at first." Watching the big needle dart at him, Ronnie suppressed the sudden thought that the witches had not left him, that he was in the hands of their accomplice right now, surrendering his blood to her. . . .

But with this cash, he could get to Mom. What did he care what they took from him for it? He watched the needle go into the vein . . . a startling bite it had. And after a moment, surprising too—its neatness, the skillful minimum of pain it gave.

His blood like a red smoke filling the bag . . . like an image of nausea, it began to make him feel the real thing. Until, like an antidote, came a different feeling. That coiling blood of his was power. All this rich, red life in him! Mojo juice! He had it to spare! He was the Magic Man! Need fifty bucks? Just bleed it out and pocket the cash!

"I can see by your veins you get plenty of exercise, Mr. Deuce. That's so important, a young person's *vitality*. There . . . now fold your elbow and clamp this cotton pad in there."

He watched her turn away with the blood-pouch. That red nugget of himself in there. It would be warm to her hand. Just the kind of thing a witch would want. A witches' fee.

Then he thought of Stubbly-Bear with that stubby barrel in his mouth . . . And he felt, obscurely, *relieved* that this blood payment was being accepted from him. Was this like the "vig" on a street-loan in a Mob-movie? Wasn't *everybody* paying off a loan to this Mob?

Look at Mom, whose payments had all of a sudden gone through the roof—shot up past their reach overnight. Was it any wonder, this long nightmare Ronnie had stepped into tonight? His whole family was out in the Wastelands together. Dad was carrying some strange sick kid in his arms . . . Ronnie was trying to pinch the life back into a dying young man . . . And strangers were drawing Mom's blood and reading it and seeing . . . her *death* in it?

What was going to happen to them if Mom died? How could they go on living if they let her die?

The nurse sat down behind her desk. Hefting the bag of his blood, she looked at him. "How is the woman who gave you this?" she asked.

His heart seemed to understand the question before his stunned brain got it—began hammering in him as he tried to read her tight, etched face, looking from the huge eye . . . to the piercing one . . . and back again, searching for her intention.

"You mean . . ." he croaked.

"Your mother, yes. How is she? Your father said she was in the hospital."

"Well . . . she might be sick."

Without withdrawing from his eyes her schismatic stare, she slid the bag into a lower drawer. Could that be right? Did they keep blood in drawers? From the top drawer, she took three bills and fanned them out on the blotter. "We all might be sick, Mr. Deuce, so we should never let that . . . stop us. But move carefully for a while—you may feel slightly dizzy."

He *did* feel slightly dizzy, but it seemed to be her eyes doing it to him. He had an unexplainable urge to blurt out, "Will she be all right?"—and felt a sudden fear, equally unaccountable, of asking it. As if she were daring him to ask it, and if he did it would mean he had weakened, had failed some crucial test.

Two twenties and a ten—he reached down for them and she brought up a Band-Aid and neatly patched his puncture as he did it. "The streets around the bus station are confusing." The smaller eye ruled now, amused, like her grainy old voice. "You'd better go back exactly the way you came."

A few moments later this advice rang strangely in his ears as he stepped out the gasping doors.

There were no dark hills anywhere. He was on the mean empty streets of Skelton, where the two strange women had led him away from the bus. He slanted across the wide, empty street that bordered the hospital, signals on blink as far as he could see in both directions to the dark mouth of that narrow backstreet he'd come by.

Here was that most terrifying cross-street. Ronnie staggered into its dimness, onto its pavements crackly and stained with smashed bottles . . . till he came to the precise place and stood there a moment.

Here he had faced death for the first time and hadn't pissed himself. He could be proud of that, couldn't he?

Here that car had idled, those dim-brained demons sitting in it looking at him like crocodiles scanning meat. In their dull eyes, his death had coiled like silt in a sluggish stream.

Two more who'd fallen off the Ferris Wheel, two who had liked to push others off, before they fell so spectacularly themselves. There was their wreck against that distant power pole. What a mess they'd made. . . .

The witches had killed those killers for him. Would they kill *Mom's* killer? She deserved it. But that man whose blood-pipe Ronnie had let slip—maybe *he'd* deserved to live too.

At the terminal, a young black woman sat watching his approach from behind her bars. She looked a little amused. He thought she looked a little as if she thought he was kind of cute too. He tried to seem older by using careful courtesy. "I'd like a ticket on the very next bus to Conejo Grande, please." Then chided himself, thinking that the "very" was too much, that an older guy wouldn't have said it.

She smiled a little more, and with sweet insolence asked, "Can I help you?"

As he repeated himself word for word, except for "very." A balding, middle-aged man appeared behind her in the booth, his eyes seizing on Ronnie with an intensity that made him uneasy. The man leaned past the young woman and asked,

"Are you Ronnie Deuce?"

"Yes," he replied. Even in his amazement he already knew who had set this man onto him.

"You already have a seat on the next bus to Conejo Grande, Mr. Deuce, no need for a ticket. And if you'll excuse me, I'm going to see you to your seat on it personally. Will you please come with me to the office? I promised your mother we would call her as soon as you showed up."

III

Driving north through miles of dark countryside, Ricky cradled his left hand in his lap. The stump of his little finger ached and ached in its crusted gauze while the weight and mass of the finger itself in his parka's pouch, so slight though it was, poked at his pain and stirred his nausea.

A half-moon was just across the zenith and shedding a goodly light on the low hills and grassy flats that flanked the highway.

A black flaw streaked across it. Ricky blinked.

There it went again crossing it anew: a somewhat larger scrap of darkness, moving faster.

It was a windy night. His truck, trusty but feeling its age, rocked with the wind's punches as it hurtled along at seventy.

Again that blackness—larger still—zagged across the moon.

He experienced a sudden tingle of premonition. More pain was coming.

No! Mere nerves! Stay focused.

But here, by God, came huge black wings! Here were outthrust claws exploding through his windshield!

A blizzard of sharp-edged glass cubes scrubbed his face as if with dozens of tiny teeth. His neck, head, and shoulders were seized by claws, too many of them, as if this impossible vulture had four legs rather than two—until he realized it was a *pair* of the brutes. Ricky's own right foot betrayed him at first, staying frozen on the accelerator, while with his whole upper body he fought the pull of those wings, working so mightily right in his face to drag him out through the empty frame of the windshield.

Nothing to hold onto but the wheel, and the raptors' dire strength dragged the wheel awry. At last his foot found the brake just as the truck was angling off the shoulder, was *launched,* was airborne out over the pasture. Plunging, he watched his headlights spray across a sea of dark, ripply grass below him.

Plunging, cursing the seatbelt that he never wore, locking his elbows, bracing against the wheel as the talons tore at his face and shoulders, hauling his legs up from the pedal-well, planting his heels against the dash, he wedged his shoulders high up in the corner of the cab's frame, the claws still raking him but losing their grip. . . .

WHOOMPH. The truck bellied down to earth—Ricky slamming steel on every side—and launched off shuddering wheels to leap again, and plunge again more briefly, his bumper now bulldozing deep dirt to a halt.

His skull rang like a struck bell. He pried himself out of the cab and staggered out into the grass. Incredibly, the impact hadn't killed the engine. It was knocked into neutral, was growling and grunting away against its dike of torn dirt like a pig after acorns. One of the headlights was still working too. . . .

Buffets of air pummeled Ricky's face, and his chest and claws seized him again, and the great black wings blotted the sky with their demon labor to *lift* him. His fucking *feet* were leaving the ground! He gripped two of those legs—steel sinew in feathered armor—and pulled at them like someone in a cartoon trying to pull jail-bars apart, while his kicking legs grabbed violently for the stolen earth.

Then, in a convulsion of fury, Ricky hoisted his feet and rammed his heels up against the toiling pectoral muscles working the wings. The claws slackened and his heels thrust him free, ramming him shoulders-first down into the grass, where he rolled and bucked, got his legs under him, and sprinted dizzily toward a lone tree islanded in the field.

He sprinted, ducking low at the last as talons raked his back just missing their grip—and then he was under the sheltering boughs.

The winged demons angled after him in under the canopy. Their flight constricted in this closer space, they lit on a branch above him, holding half-spread their huge tar-black pinions. Their plumage *dripped* darkness, seemed to shed droplets that glinted like jet as they fell through the moonshadow.

Ricky searched the sparse grass and found an oaken club near thick as his calf. He brandished it two-handed.

"Come on! I'll snap your fucking legs off! You think I don't *know* you? I can *smell* you! Dirty hair under dirty hats! Both you bitches smell like ashes and axle-grease! You thugs! You've been fucking with me all night!"

"An' you look it, too!" screeched one of the high-shouldered shadows. In the leaf-filtered moonlight their beaks' recurved tips were like great black meat-hooks, and yet somehow seemed to grin, the inhuman yellow eyes gleeful. "Course we fuckin' witchoo! You a *laugh riot!*"

"Leave me ALONE! I gotta get to my wife! She needs me!"

They leapt from their perches, swept down on him in opposing arcs, perfectly faking him out so that—*one-two*—their talons scored his arms left and right, and evaded both his swings of the club.

They glided out from under the boughs. He shook both his fist and his branch at them, his blood drizzling down, as they oared lazily upwards to where the moonlight draped their wings in silver—paused on the wing to unleash two fecal bombs in token of their disrespect, then more powerfully climbed higher, and higher, two dwindling darknesses against the moon.

He had gone insane. Was this what it was like? All his fresh blood was real enough!

He felt he had rendered a payment. That his blood and terror were *buying* something. This, of course, *was* insanity. Angie was in death's hand. How could a little of his blood buy her way out of that?

He stepped out of the tree-shadow, surprised to feel how many new places he was bleeding from. He raised the parka's hood and tenderly bagged his battered head in it. He spoke, singling out the moon—as good a hearer as any. "Look, for God's sake leave me *alone*—or even help me a little! Leave me with a working truck! Don't strand me here!"

Praying inwardly, he got behind the wheel and shifted into reverse. Yes! The truck backed off the dirt-heap.

Now the real test. Ricky swung the truck's single headlight beam upslope, shoved it in first, and began the climb through the grass for the highway's embankment.

By the time he had crawled back onto the pavement, he knew he definitely had a fucking front-end problem. The vital thing was—how bad? He was less than sixty miles from Conejo Grande. Cautiously he shifted up . . . please please let the front end be drivable . . .

In the slow lane of the empty, forest-flanked highway he cautiously assayed third gear. There it was, a whuffle and a chafe, like a metronome that sped up as he did. He found it didn't get too bad at just under thirty miles an hour.

He could do it, if the front end didn't start twisting itself apart. If the wind pouring into his windowless cab didn't freeze him too stiff to drive. He could no longer feel his ears. He dared not think of Angie, not touch with his fear the dangling sword of her fate.

Angie and Nicky sat at the kitchenette table, which was strewn with sheets of paper they'd gotten from the nurse's station. They were playing War again—Angie now kicking some ass with face cards and aces, both of them smoking, the tea-cup jammed with butts, the pair of them crowing and cursing over their cards.

They'd covered many sheets of hospital stationery with the arithmetic involved in setting Angie up with her own phone, computer, and workspace at Nicky's real estate agency in Conejo Grande, and with the surprisingly clear maps Nicky dashed off, of the many neighborhoods in and around Conejo where real estate was moving.

What a godsend Nicky had been! This was the way to think—of plans and projects, and screw this cancer! Every minute she let this scare her was another minute lost, not lived after all. She *had* to say fuck it and let it go. Love Ronnie as he was now. Ricky too. Find out what selling real estate was like and not look beyond.

The door opened, and a doctor neither of them had met leaned in. "Excuse me, Nicole?"

Both of them said, "Yes?" And after a beat Nicky, smiling inanely, said, "He means you, sweetie."

Angie's smile for the doctor had curdled, become a sick thing like the dread in her belly. The man's eyes cringed slightly from hers, and he was holding a folder. She understood his mission. He bore her some final answer, and it was dark and cold. She wanted to tell him to say it—just *say* it—but she couldn't find her voice.

"We don't know how to apologize for this, Nicole." There was a helpless burr in his voice on *apologize,* and though her heart still hung in the absolute cold of space, Angie felt faintly touched by his fumbling compassion. The cancer was hers after all—they didn't give it to her. Her eyes filled with tears.

"You're very kind," she said.

"No." His voice was urgent. "We're very *sorry*. There was no need for you to have a biopsy! Your initial tests didn't call for it! On the contrary, they show you in *perfect health*. We're doing everything we can to find out how they could have been misread."

"They show me in perfect health . . ."

"Yes! The anguish you must have been feeling! I want you to know that we are not billing your insurance for anything, not even your initial tests. We just can't tell you . . ."

But both sisters had him, one by either shoulder.

"She's OK? There's nothing wrong?"

"I'm in perfect health?"

"Yes! Yes! Please let me assure you—"

But he had to let them hug him first, and they weren't gentle about it.

And then the sisters were in each other's arms.

"You're not gonna change your mind about working together?"

"No way!"

"You're still gonna do it with me?"

"Yes way! When Ricky and Ronnie get here, they're gonna have to like it or lump it! I'm in perfect health! It's so hilarious! I mean, I *felt* in perfect health all along, except for the fear when they told me."

"Oh, yes," said the doctor, addressing Angie, "your son's here, Mrs. Deuce."

Both women rounded on him.

"Send him up!"

"Bring him in!"

And then they looked at each other and burst out laughing. The doctor, mildly puzzled, sped graciously on the errand.

Angie gripped Nicky's arms. "We're still going to start tomorrow. They can go back, fix up the place to get our deposit back. Ricky's got friends with trucks. Ronnie's semester ends in five weeks."

"I've got two good agents in mind we might get to come in with us. They're good with the middle market, all those places tucked in corners on unconventional lots. Good houses for people looking for a fifty or a seventy-five K below going rates. You think they'll be OK, five weeks on their own?"

"They'll have to be," Angie said grimly. "But I think it'll be good for them. They were both so scared for me. It'll just make them closer."

"Here we are!" The doctor ushered Ronnie into the room. From the boy's first step inside, both women could see that Ronnie, in one of those freakish outbursts of filial affection in adolescent males, was marching straight toward his mother to embrace her. Almost too late, Nicky darted forward and tackled him with her own hug. "Hi, sweetie! Your aunt Nicole is completely OK! The tests were a mistake! She's in perfect health!"—swinging him over to confront his mother. Now he stood stunned, till Angie opened her arms.

The doctor took his leave. Ronnie, his arms still around her, stood looking his mother wonderingly in the face. It struck Angie that it had been years since her son had studied her so candidly. She remembered that wonderful feeling his unselfconscious gaze could give her when he was a small boy. At last he brought out, in a rusty voice, "You're totally OK, Mom?"

"Totally! They read the charts wrong! I'm perfectly healthy! What's this on your arm?"

"Oh . . . I sold some blood to get my ticket from Skelton. These two—I mean, I lost my wallet with my ticket in it."

"You were on the bus. How did you get separated from it?"

"I . . . don't think I can tell you. I mean, till I can think it over, I don't know if I *should* tell you."

Angie was a little stunned by this unprecedented disclosiveness. She found herself replying as if to someone older, and less known to her. "Do you mean *should* for my sake, or for yours?"

More serious weighing before he answered. "Maybe both . . . or maybe either one."

"Well . . . are you OK?"

"Yeah! *You're* OK? You're a hundred percent healthy?"

"A hundred percent healthy. And after this semester, you're moving up here—"

A knock on the door. It was an orderly, a tall, elegant black woman in blues. "Excuse me. Is one of you ladies Nicole Knight?"

"I am," said Angie.

"A man who says he's your husband is down in Emergency."

"In Emergency!" both women exclaimed simultaneously.

"Well, they were trying to get him to *go* to Emergency. But he might still be down at Admissions, trying to come up here."

"*Trying* to—" Nicky began.

"What does he look like?" asked Angie.

"Short man in his early fifties, got a beard. He's . . . messed up. I mean *banged* up. Very coherent though."

"It's Ricky," said Angie.

Ricky had parked in the darkest corner of the lot. E-e-e-ased himself out. Peered in the side mirror and winced: a vaguely head-shaped mass—all crusts and scars and bulges. Tenderly he tried to groom his hair. All tufts and spiky scabs, it mocked his efforts.

Walking through the entry's shining glass and chrome, his wounded hand snugly parked in his parka's pouch, where its finger also nested. He would plow through all resistance. Angie must see him before her and know he was with her, and he must hear from her own lips how it stood with her.

He wasn't halfway to Admissions when an orderly intercepted him.

"Emergency's over here, sir. Can you tell us what happened?"

Reflecting on the man's question, Ricky had to laugh. "Look, I know I look a fright, but I'm really OK for the moment, and before I do anything else I have to see my wife. Nicole Knight. She's in Oncology." The word felt as if it cut him coming out.

A doctor had joined them and stepped in close, checking Ricky's eyes for signs of concussion. "You're going to be fine, you just have some lacerations, some contusions . . . some punctures. . . . We'll let your wife know immediately once we've—"

"I *am* sorry," said Ricky, stepping back from the pair of them, "I totally appreciate that you want to see that I'm properly treated, but you must understand"—still retreating as he talked, he made it to the Admission's counter and took a firm grip on it—"I've come a very long way, and it's *urgent* that before I do *anything else* I *see* my wife."

Another orderly had joined them, and another tired, gaunt young doctor in greens with a stethoscope necklace. The situation was getting more political. "You're perspiring heavily," the first doctor observed.

And he was. His hidden hand was sending long seismic currents of pain through him, and he realized he had to take a ripping leak. "Doctor, if you looked like me, wouldn't *you* be sweating?" It made the orderlies laugh. "My wife's totally mobile. Can you bring her down to me? She's just resting in one of your courtesy rooms. I know you're obligated to take care of me. I appreciate the . . . beneficence of your motives. I'm just asking for a moment of compassion here, and then I'll go right with you."

"Well," said the first doctor smiling slightly, "you don't *sound* concussed."

The call was made. Ricky, seeing he'd succeeded, said, "I'm deeply grateful to you. Do you have a restroom? I've been on the road for hours."

"One of the orderlies will have to go in with you."

"That's fine. I just need to take a leak."

The chunky orderly closed the door after them and stood just inside it. Standing at the toilet, Ricky could see himself, brightly lit, in a big mirror on the wall to the left of him. He gazed at this urinating ruin with astonishment.

"Holy shit," he said, and the orderly laughed again.

"You got that right, homes. You look like someone's been rubbing you on a cheese grater." Ricky, his piss still clattering, watched the marveling mess watch him back.

"It's amazing," Ricky muttered, shaking the dew from the lily, still staring, "how we keep healing."

"Yeah, it is, isn't it? That's the only reason I can stand working here."

Coming out of the restroom, Ricky stepped right into the midst of Angie and Ronnie and Nicky.

"Good Lord!"

"Jesus Christ, Dad!"

"What *happened* to you?"

"It's just some scratches—the truck rolled over. I'm not hurt and I haven't hurt anyone else! How are you honey? How *are you?*"

"I'm fine! I'm totally healthy! They mixed up the charts! What have you been *doing?*"

For the second time tonight, the second time in more than thirty years, tears welled out of Ricky's eyes. Angie wrapped her arms around his neck and murmured tenderly against his chest, "What have you been *doing*, you moron?"

"Everything's OK? You're completely OK?"

"I'm completely OK."

"I'm fine too! I'm totally wonderful! Everything's totally wonderful!"

"So why are you keeping your hand in your pouch? Let me see it."

"I'm just keeping it warm! I'm gonna go to Emergency and get myself all fixed up."

"Hey, I can't tell if you're awake or not."

He smiled slowly. "But I'm looking right at you."

"You look spaced."

"They gave me some painkillers. They're such wonderful people."

"Listen, Ricky. Are you tracking me?"

"Yes. Speak on."

"Something odd is going on. I know I should let you sleep, but I just have to ask. What was the balance on our credit card?"

"It was maxed out."

"Yes. I was afraid of that, so I just called the credit card company. They say we have a credit of twenty-five thousand dollars. How could that be?"

"Are you sure?"

"I double-checked."

"Well, all I can say is some strange things have been happening lately."

"Are you going to tell me about them?"

"I *have* to tell you about them. You're the only person in the world I *can* tell about them, you and Ronnie. . . . And I think Ronnie has some strange things of his own to tell us both."

"Well . . . OK. Sleep now, dear moron. We'll talk tomorrow. After they put your finger back on."

Ricky smiled contentedly. "That sounds like a good idea."

Two months later, Ronnie and Ricky were graveling their drive. The Deuces now had an acre and a half in one of Conejo Grande's "canyon" neighborhoods and had plunked a big, nearly-new double-wide on it. The neighborhood was full of trees and unconventional houses all variously perched among them. The people seemed friendly, and at night there were coons, and possums, and deer, and coyotes, and foxes, and more coons.

Ricky shoveled down the pea gravel from the bed of his pickup (resplendent with a new blue paint job) and Ronnie raked it over the dirt of the drive. They were halfway down the hundred yards to the street. They had started out talking—as they always did nowadays when they worked together—about their two strange journeys to join Mom, but they had been working in silence for some minutes now. Ricky held quiet, sensing, as he was learning to do, that his son—so wary of disclosure—wanted to say something.

"Dad?"

"Yeah?"

"What keeps bothering me, is what's it *mean?* I mean it, like, makes the world totally different, and so . . . what are we supposed to *do* about it?"

That, he thought, was the hard thing about talking to kids. They always went straight to the essence—straight to what you didn't know. Here was the classic father and son moment. The Big Issues. The father was supposed to have answers for his son on the Big Issues.

"Well, one thing I think it means . . ." He groped. Yes? What *do* you think it means? ". . . is that whenever you meet someone new, you should pay close attention to who it is that you're dealing with."

There was a pause, the kid looking a little surprised and then seeming to find that useful.

There was a bus's gasp and a groan out on the street, and pneumatic doors clapping open. A moment later Kameesha came trudging up the drive. The skinny little thing in her sweatshirt and jeans was definitely taller than when she'd stuck a pistol in his face two months ago. He realized that she too was going to be taller than he was. At present, there was discontent in 'Meesha's gait. She was carrying her cap, not wearing it.

"Hi, Ronnie"—this said glumly, inviting him to ask what was wrong. Ronnie, in 'Meesha's eyes, knew All Things.

The boy seemed to like this older brother thing and took his cue. "You OK, 'Meesh?"

"I wanna get one a those hats you got." And she looked up at Ricky. She meant the skateboarder's knit helmet Ronnie wore.

"That would look sweet on you, 'Meesh," said the kid, backing her pitch to the Buyer of Hats. "We call 'em beanies."

Ricky stroked his beard and weighed this. "Here's the deal, 'Meesh. You bring me your *carefully finished* homework out from your room, and I'll take you down and get you one right then."

"I'll come help you pick it," Ronnie told her. "You need a good fit."

Scorning further palaver, 'Meesha turned and strode with a will toward the double-wide. Some homework was going to fly, let the chips fall where they may.

"Oh, hey, 'Meesh!" Ricky suddenly remembering. "Call Jasmine. She's found a place near the clinic here where she and Rap can move in. Now you'll have two houses." Jasmine, Ricky, and Angela were Kameesha's co-guardians—and the meager checks they drew for her support they put in an account for the girl. Jasmine was burning rubber through the books for her agent's exam—she'd already made an under-the-table commission from Nicole and Angie for a sale she'd set up but couldn't yet sign for. With her understatement and her ironic eyes, Jazz seemed to have a gift for helping people to agree.

Ricky shoveled down more gravel. He kept the little finger splinted and didn't use it yet, but the day was coming. True, it was shorter, but still three joints! Yes, indeed, miracles *could* be worked.

Not that the Prime miracle, life itself, went on forever . . . Inevitably, he was going to meet those sisters from the Andes again someday—was going to *be* this dirt he scuffed now with his boot. Amazing, though, how life picked up its body's pieces and kept on shoveling. He was dirt *now,* and look how this frame of his could move! Look how he could *see* this sky, see these trees, and every leaf of them. . . .

"Hey, Dad?"

Ricky turned, beaming. "Yes, my beloved son?"

"I think we saved Mom's life."

"No. I think *you* did. Me . . . I was just *entertaining* them."

Epilogue

The Thug and the Hawk, those two cruel bitches!
Some call them gods, and some call them witches.
Their eyes show no mercy, the Hawk and the Thug,
While they're racking your flesh, or pulling your plug.

Their sister is Vita, they make quite a trio.
They birth you, and bust you, and bag you with brio.
We give Vita short shrift and jump in the race—
It's only the Hawk and the Thug that we *face.*

Hawk swoops from the sky on your liver and lights,
Or spools up the air so you can't breathe it right,
Or lock-picks your bloodstream and leaks in marauders,
Or clutches your pipes till your heart-muscle shudders.

Thug hangs the tag on you, pushes the gurney
Out the back door of the End of your journey
To the alley outside of Forever's rear wall
Where the dead eons moulder, and fester, and crawl. . . .

The Growlimb

In the offices of Humanity Incorporated, Marjorie, Program Director of Different Path, had her own cubicle. From her desk she could look across the floor directly into the corner nook—not a cubicle really, with only a standing screen to half-partition it off—where Carl Larken had his desk.

Larken was on the phone, his chair tilted back, his outthrust feet toed under his desktop, his body poised almost horizontal to the floor. In cut-offs and worn Nikes, a brambly gray beard and raked-back gray locks ten-drilled on his neck, the man's toughness showed. A lean and sunburned man in his fifties.

Marjorie tried to decide why Larken stood out so. It wasn't his dress. Humanity Inc. was a sizable human services nonprofit, and didn't insist on office drag—most of its program managers had social activist backgrounds and liberal views. What nagged at her was the man's . . . tautness. He was a very personable, articulate guy, sociable on demand, but he had an agenda, an undistracted inwardness. He could be talking to you about your program, deep in the details of a write-up with you, showing perfect grasp and sensitive awareness, and you would suddenly know he wasn't really there, was working his tongue and his face like a puppet, flawlessly managing his half of the exchange, light-years away in his mind. Over the months, she had formed the whimsical but persistent notion that Carl Larken was insane.

She recognized that this secret alienation she saw in him could be from her own lack of real involvement in her work. She was rich. Her parents owned a flourishing winery. After her B.A. in Fine Arts, a sense of aimlessness had overtaken her. This job was her Term of Involvement with Reality, an immersion in the hard and hurting strata of the world. Different Path was a criminal justice diversionary program, counseling and community services for the drug-riddled, the sick, and the desperate. She worked it, pulled her Beemer into the lot at eight sharp, waded into her case files, made her house calls, networked with the D.A.'s office—the whole nine yards. But ultimately, she didn't believe it made any difference. Didn't believe counseling and community service did a thing for the already damaged, the already damned. And her own underlying contempt for her work made her sure of Larken's. It was a felt thing, a sympathetic vibration between them.

Being indifferent, though, was a far cry from being insane. What was there about him, when she studied him from a distance like this, that always ended by sending that cold thrill of suspicion up her spine? This conviction that the man was not really here, was deeply, utterly somewhere else?

She had to go meet with a counseling group. On impulse, she went over and leaned into Larken's nook on her way out.

"Hi, Carl."

"Hey, Marjorie. The *Press Republican* says they'll run a feature for us."

"Super! Just put the copy on my desk."

"It's done. Take it with you. I'm going for a run soon. If you're out on the road, don't run me over."

A little standing joke. Larken worked a loose schedule, often taking long midday runs in the nearby countryside. She'd passed him a number of times, smiling and waving, wondering at what drove the guy—far from young, but every inch of him honed down to sinew and vein and tireless muscle. Heading out, she glanced at the copy of his feature:

For those stricken by chemical addictions, shoplifting and other petty property misdemeanors are more the symptoms of an affliction than the acts of a real criminal. At Different Path, with the generous cooperation of the Superior Court of Sonoma County, we take these afflicted folks out of the criminal justice loop, and into a circle of care, counseling, and rehabilitation—

And so on. The usual. She paused at the exit to the parking lot and glanced back at Larken, balanced on his chair, murmuring into the phone. Those humanitarian homilies that he composed so glibly—they didn't really fit the man at all. He had all the standard smiles, the affable, earnest expressions. But the whole shape and aura of him . . . he looked about as compassionate as a coyote.

* * *

Larken's phone interview with "Dan G." was going well. It was amazing what people would just tell you about themselves. Back when he had taught at the junior college, he'd been delighted by how much personal revelation he could draw from his students with his writing assignments. He was always struck by how *faintly* these kids seemed to feel their own existence. They had to squint to see their own feelings. They had to strain to remember the things they had seen with their own eyes in the course of a single day. But when driven by an instructor, and the need of a grade, they could scrape some of it together, report what life was like for them.

"So, Guy, if I have this straight . . ." Guy Blankenship was "Dan G.'s" real name, which Larken had gotten out of him easily enough, "the meth cost you your wife and kids first, and then your house, and now, because you started spiking it, it's given you AIDS. And you're what? Only twenty-six?"

"It did a major number on me." This was spoken solemnly, almost with a kind of satisfaction.

"Well, I have to tell you that your story is one of the most moving ones I've ever heard, Guy. I want to suggest something to you. I want you to bear with me for a minute here, because I want to suggest an idea to you, and I need to work up to it a little, okay?"

"Sure. I don't mind." And you could hear his comfort with the conversation; Guy was well along in the morphine phase of his AIDS-related cancer.

"Okay. When you look out your window, what do you see? I want to get a feel for your neighborhood."

"Well, Mim's Market is right across the street, like a mom-and-pop. And boy, those kids with their skateboards and earrings, they like live on the sidewalk in front of it, I swear."

"You're on Prince over toward the Fairgrounds, right?"

"Right."

"And if you head down Prince, you hit Crestview. You probably turn on Crestview when you go down to the hospital, right?"

"That's right."

"So Guy, did you ever keep going up Crestview, into the hills behind the Fairgrounds?"

"Yeah. Marjorie took us up there to a picnic like just a few days ago."

"Oh right, she told me that. That's a great view up there, isn't it, Guy? Those big crooked oak trees down on the slope below that turnout there? Four centuries old, minimum, those oaks. You remember them, don't you? Huge big crooked old trees?"

"Big trees, yeah, sure."

"Well, just imagine this, okay, Guy? Imagine a blue jay landing on one of those trees' branches. Just fluttering down, and landing, pecking up a couple little bugs, *peck, peck,* and then flying right off again. Say he's there four seconds. Imagine how brief, how short, his time in that tree was, compared to the whole span of that tree's life. Just a quick blue blip that scarcely touches the tree at all. And that's how short your life on this Earth will have been, Guy, when you check out a year or so from now. Your whole stay on this glorious green globe . . . it'll hardly have happened at all."

"What're you . . . you're sayin' like . . ." The guy's morphine patches definitely had him on glide. You could hear him trying to hook in to this idea, startled by suddenly realizing that his own existence, and his own death, were the focus of this conversation.

"I'm just telling you I feel for you, man. I wanted to share with you the *poignancy* I feel in your situation. My good thoughts go out to you. I'm going to write up what you gave me. We'll talk soon, okay?"

"Okay . . ." Guy was more than morphine vague now. You could hear him struggling to bring these imponderables into focus. His own existence. His own death.

Larken gently hung up the phone. He very much craved a run. A couple hours chugging down the country blacktop would bring him back to a nearly empty building, and he could put the last few touches on the corporate newsletter. He slipped into his sleeveless running jersey, its once-black laundered to a light gray. Out the back, he broke into an easy trot across the parking lot.

For a mile or so it was all body shops and strip malls, gas stations and burger chains—lots of cars and mucho monoxide . . . But after that, the street became a county two-lane that ran past rural lots and sprawling fields, some orchards and dairy farms still surviving here and there, but increasingly, grapevines out to the horizons.

He had an easy lope that ate the miles and never tired. He cruised in the tough vehicle of his bone and muscle, lightly oiled with sweat, and thought of his words to Blankenship. Reckless words if the guy should wake up enough to resent them. Reckless if Larken wanted to keep this job.

His problem was this exaltation, this high and reckless humor in his heart. For days now it had filled him, sneaked into him at odd moments as he worked, and set his heart floating. A foretremor of hope. A limbic tingle of something approaching—at long, long last!

His meditation as he ran was what it always was out here: Behold the visible world! How simply impossibly beautiful it was! The fields, the far-flung quilt of treelines over the hills, giant hermit oaks, swollen and crooked with vegetal muscle! Those towering windbreaks of eucalyptus, cascading with silver applause for the wind! Those hillsides of cattle gorgeously mottled black and white like antique ceramics. Those turkey-vultures hanging on man-sized wingspans above the roadkill feasts that were spread on the two-lane by the hustling Mercedes, Beemers, and SUVs, above all the pizzaed possums and skunks decorating the webbed highways . . .

Life! All its parts mortal, but in their aggregate, immortal and unstoppable. Life the star-conqueror. It spread and spread everywhere, slipping itself like a green glove over the bare, steaming bones of the universe.

All living things were dangerous miracles. Each tree brimmed with majesty as it wore the light, and the wind moved through it, but anything that lived could blow up in your face. And if you *did* win your own immortality, then you must live it in the web of these mortal lives, and you must endure all of their deaths, death after death after death. And if the beauty of it all—fields farms trees skies suns stars—was almost unendurable now, must not immortality itself kill you if you did attain it? Kill you with all that excruciating beauty?

His run had passed the two-hour mark, and he decided to push it to three. First, a piss. In recent years, with San Francisco fortunes being pumped into the wine country, new fence lines and country estates had stripped the roadsides of the margins of old-growth trees and weedy coverts wherein a man might duck to pee concealed. Bleeding your lizard now required thought, and retention skills. He chose a crossroad toward a spot he knew.

There it was. A rank of big old eucalypti stood between the margin of the road and the fence of a vineyard. In a little strip of brush behind the trees stood the roofless ruin of a little cinder block hut.

Several well-trod footpaths crossed the poison oak and foxtail and blackberry vines, threading through the litter of trash in the weeds outside the hut: castoff shirts and shoes, a torn, stained mattress. He stepped through the concrete door frame. In the center of the heavily littered concrete floor was a little grass-choked drain-grate. He stood there, downloading hours of coffee into it, while high over his unroofed head the cascade-shaped eucalypti splashed and glittered in the breeze.

He liked the square solidity of this cinder block hull, which he guessed had been a tool shed. Its simple shape, tucked in this green nook, made him think of a little country temple in ancient Greece.

It was surprising how much of the litter in here was discarded clothing. Many a fieldworker who had tended the adjacent vineyard had surely found free sleep-space here in the warm months, and free drinking space, to judge by the beer cans and flattened cardboard of six-packs. Clothes, thrift-store stuff, were something the poor seemed to have in abundance. He noticed as he was zipping up that there was one little snarl of clothing, isolated slightly from the rest, that possessed the most amazing suggestion of personality.

Here lay a pair of khaki workpants whose legs seemed to leap, and just above the pants' waist a red-and-black checked flannel shirt, its sleeves wide-flung, which seemed to be the top half of the same leap. To provide the clinching touch, one black tennis shoe lay just below one of the pantleg's cuffs. The shoe presented its sole to the cuff, but in every other respect it was oriented perfectly to become the leading foot of this clothes-fossil's leap. Just rotate the tennie one-eighty around its long axis and the effect would be perfect . . .

With a sense of ceremony, of an augmented silence surrounding him, he bent and inverted the shoe.

The result was remarkably expressive. This was a grand, balletic leap, an outburst of eloquence and power, a leap of jubilation . . . or an explosive escape. A surge of will to be shut of it all, to shed the body with one fierce shake, burst free and clear of the shabby garment of bone and skin.

The strangest surge of inspiration welled up in Larken. He'd noted a roadkilled possum a little way back down the road. Suppose he—

Don't weigh it, spontaneity was everything. With a leap of his own, he bolted from the hut, and ran back down the two-lane, retracing his approach.

Here was the possum, flat as a puddle, and baked crispy by several days of summer suns. It was a Cubist possum, where inner and outer possum parts—front, back, left, right—all shared the same plane. Hair, intestine, a ten-key piano-fragment of flattened vertebrae, a spill of teeth surrounding one raisin eye, a parenthesis of sinewy tail as naked as a rat's—all sides of the animal could be possessed at a glance without the trouble of walking around it.

Careful not to pause but to move fluidly at the prompting of his imagination, he took out his Buck knife and sawed through one leathery drumstick, obtaining a hind paw, and then he sawed and peeled free the tail's sharp comma. With his trophies he trotted back to the cinderblock hut, feeling surer with each stride, more convinced he had found something real.

Stepping back inside the hut, Larken felt he was stepping into a pool of waiting silence, a tension of expectation. He knelt, and tucked the bone of the leg into the cuff of the hinder pantleg, so the possum's little clawed foot was providing the thrust for the leap. Then he tucked the root of the tail through the rearmost belt loop of the slacks.

This was a decisive, perfecting touch. The little up-curving tailspike clarified the clothes-fossil's leap. Its emotion was both gleeful and savagely furious. This was a demon's frolicsome, vengeful leap.

And then, as if his enhancements themselves opened his eyes to a further one, he saw something he had not noticed. A little flattened hat lying not far above the shirt's collar. He darted his hands out, half unfolded the hat, tilted it by half an inch—perfect!

It was one of those small-brimmed fedoras that bookies in old movies wore, and it was now cocked at just the exact angle to be perched upon the clothes-fossil's invisible head.

Larken was captivated. For a long moment he could only stand and gaze at what he had made. The original fossil was a ghost, and full of a ghost's haunting questions. And these marsupial parts Larken had given it were an answer, a new touch of evolution.

And then he felt a stirring somewhere near . . . and realized there was someone else in the little roofless room with him.

Though the knowledge crackled through him like lightning, he did not move by the slightest fraction. This Someone Else felt far nearer than anything visible could feel. This Someone's presence was like a chord struck ever so lightly, a fugitive coherence that reached his nerves without identifiable route through any of his senses.

Once long before, bellying cautiously up toward some possibly occupied bump in the jungle, Larken had heard (except he could not possibly have really heard) the faint thrum of a claymore's tripwire, as the guy off to that side of him tripped it—Harry Pogue, that had been—and Larken had slammed his face in mud with only that precious nanosecond of micro-noise for warning, and in consequence Larken had lived, while Pogue's head had been brightly sprayed across an acre of green.

Not a sound he had heard, no. He'd known it even then. A Someone who had warned, had thrown him a fine filament of intimation, a slender bridge across the abyss of Annihilation Everlasting.

A Someone who was with him now.

What must Larken do? What was wanted? And because he had framed these panicky questions, instead of acting with instant instinct, and drawing understanding after, because in his heart, in his awe, he had hesitated—he could not grasp what must be done, could not capture the deep, veiled prompting. The moment passed, and then Larken knew that what this Someone wanted was solitude in this shrine. It wanted his withdrawal.

He backed out of the hut, slowly, ceremoniously, eyes downcast. He should speak something, some acknowledgment, some valediction. Again, his instincts failed him, no inspiration came, and he completed his withdrawal feeling the silence hanging there sullenly behind him, feeling his tongue-tied failure of grace in this first encounter.

Marjorie gave her cell phone number to some of her clients at Different Path. She was wryly aware of a certain insincerity in this "personal touch," because she always left the phone in her Beemer, so she surrendered none of her real privacy with the gesture. It rang as she pulled into the parking structure of the downtown mall. She thought it would be Pat Bonds, her currently significant other. Guy Blankenship's vague, whiny voice disoriented her for a moment. She carried him and her conversation with him out of the parking structure and into the mall.

"It was like . . . it was unreal. It suddenly hit me, he was like saying my life, my whole life. It was like this bluebird landing on a branch and pecking twice. My whole life was that short! He just . . . told me that. He just said that to me . . ."

Marjorie, making tracks toward the fountain, where she and Pat were to decide on their dinner destination, was saying things like, "Well, that's ridiculous, Guy! You've got your whole life still ahead of you!" but meanwhile the image of those massive old oak trees, of the blue jay's quick flutter and flash among their leaves, struck her imagination indelibly as she strode past windows where Technicolor jellybeans gleamed in barrels, and Technicolor lingerie flaunted on headless white mannequins. And just as vividly, she visualized Guy Blankenship then: his plump red underlip, so slack and unprepared; his narrow, tufted eyebrows—minimal, as if the man was drawn in haste, and economy in materials was a priority.

That this poor, simple guy, his past and his memory of it so abbreviated by childhood abuse and hard drugs' erasure, and his future so short . . . that this Guy should also be seeing that same bird dance on that green bough, that he should be looking at his existence for the first time in his life like a wise man—it struck Marjorie as a minor miracle that Carl Larken had planted this vision in Guy Blankenship's mind.

And this made her see Larken again as she had once seen him, loping along in the dusk past orchards where the gloom had begun to gather under the tangled branches. He was a wolf-lean, muscled shape in her headlights who turned at her honk and waved as she passed. His face was a shadow-holed mask, the brambly hair thick on his brow like the undercover he lurked in. She had feared him then, and she feared him now because she realized that something in her applauded the little mental cruelty he had done to Guy, that soft little twit from whose fingers the gift of life was leaking so swiftly away.

"I'm going to talk to Carl tomorrow, Guy, about that upsetting kind of talk."

"Well . . ."

"I'll call you tomorrow, Guy." She clicked off. There was Pat sitting handsomely ankle-on-knee, on one of the ornate benches surrounding the fountain, the picture of understated class. He saluted her with a white-capped latte, and handed her one of her own as she joined him on the bench.

"Fifty more acres of Zin," he told her. "A done deal."

He was just Marjorie's age, a bright, mellow guy, with a clarity of ambition beyond his years, who unlike her had no trouble with his class identity: a WineYuppie and proud of it. Bankrolled by his dad, a corporate attorney in San Francisco, Pat's lack of intellectual pretensions had made him content with the local junior college for the first two years of his B.A. in Business, and he'd had Carl Larken for an English instructor five or six years ago.

When Marjorie had first described her coworker to Pat and they had discovered this funny little piece of common ground, it had struck her that Pat was covertly amused, that he had instantly perceived her hidden interest in the older man. Herself still unsure what that interest was, she told him now how Larken had tweaked Guy's imagination. "On one level it's kind of a raw thing to do," she offered in conclusion.

"Telling some terminal guy how short his life's gonna be? I guess you could call it that," Pat smiled. "He'd get on that note in class, I remember. Mortality, I guess you'd call it."

"I guess you would." Smiling back at him. "Would you say, Pat, that Larken was, well, insane? Like quietly insane?"

There it was, the thing that kept bringing Larken up between them. She thought Pat's eyes confirmed her question, even while he was saying, "I don't know. Everyone's had one or two teachers like that, right? They've got a crazy routine, but they can be really entertaining sometimes."

She let a beat go by. "Would you say, Pat" (batting her eyes as if the question were occurring to her for the first time), "that Larken is, like, quietly insane?"

She wrung a laugh out of him with that. "Well, I remember one thing he told us. He compared a guy being blown apart by a mine to a guy dying of old age. He said the years hit the old guy just like the frags hit the soldier—the years blew the old guy to a fog too, they just took longer to impact him. . . . But hey, the guy acts like he's got a purpose. I see him on the road chuggin' away. Could an insane guy stay in the kind of shape he's in?"

"You still haven't answered me, but screw it. Let's eat. How 'bout sushi?"

The sun was declining when Larken locked the offices' back door behind him, unlocked his ten-speed and mounted it.

He didn't head straight home. He pedaled for hours through town, ricocheting randomly through the city's maze, whirring down long ranks of street lamps, down streets of houses and treed lawns, down streets of neons and flashing signals—trying to wear out the eagerness and fear that struggled in him.

At last it was time to aim his flight out toward the darkness surrounding the city. Along four miles of lampless two-lane, the last two winding through gentle hills, he sped deep into the crickety country night. The waxing moon, well up, said nearly midnight when he steered into the narrow gravel driveway that branched from the road up into his seven acres of wooded slope.

He dismounted and shouldered the bike, carried it up the drive amidst the tree-shadows. He had spread with his own spade this blue-shale gravel. He practiced the skill of silently treading it—liked to come soundless into his property. As he climbed the slope, the leafy gloom chirred with bug life and breathed down on him the dry scents of bay and manzanita and oak and madrone. Something at least coon-sized skittered in dry leaves upslope of him. A pair of owls were trading their tentative syllables.

He branched from his driveway onto a much narrower deer-trail that crooked its way steeply up. Near the crest of his property, on a crescent of levelish ground, a slant-grown oak laid the dome of its branches partly on the grass. Under this crook-ribbed canopy Larken had his sleeping bag. His little aluminum food locker dangled from a branch above his Sierra trailstove: a number-ten can with its ends cut out and a flap cut in its rim for feeding sticks through. It channeled enough heat from a few handfuls of twigs to boil his oatmeal, and the fire was near invisible at any distance.

He unrolled his leather mat and sleeping bag, and lay half-curled around the little stove and its bubbling one-quart pot of porridge studded with nuts and dried fruits. He garnished his meal with black strap molasses and ate it with a spoon, eating faster as it cooled.

Afterward he lay on top of his bag, looking up at the stars that blazed thick through his oak-leaf dome. These hills were a maze of little valleys—in all directions were pocket vineyards, small ranches, country houses. Here and there, faint in distance, dogs sometimes barked, taunted perhaps by fox, coyote, coon, or bobcat.

His body lay slumped in fatigue, but his senses ate up the wide-flung night. Homecoming tires hissed on the road, coming fewer and fewer as the stars blazed more thickly. Four-legged things were afoot in several places on his own acres. The peremptory little tearing sounds of what had to be coon paws were shredding something down in the old overgrown garden where potatoes and tomatoes thinly persisted. A clumsier, more faintly heard scrabbling, from just about down at the compost heap . . . that would be possum.

The thought conjured the clothes-fossil, never far from his thoughts these eight hours past. It dawned on him only then. He had found it a footless, anchored thing, but he had left it clawed and shod. And those claws, whose awkwardness on asphalt made the possum the commonest species of road-pizza, made him a nimble traveler up in the trees, a nomad of the arboreal highway.

The Someone Else who joined him in that but today . . . could he follow Larken now?

He lay there on the little piece of earth he owned, trying to detect something like a footfall, or a faint, faint click of claw on branch. Joy and terror hammered at his heart. Could he be on the threshold at last, the threshold of the thing he had sought all his life? He had exiled himself from so much, left his precious family behind—Jolly, his wife, sweet Maxie, and sweet little Jack, his daughter and son . . .

He could not bear to think of them, of leaving them behind forever. How many years now? More than three. From that moment of departure, he had stepped into this absolute solitude . . .

Perhaps a half mile off, coyote voices began kindling, as if in direct answer to his train of thought. Of course, the settling in of the midnight chill—as now—was often the signal for their song. Larken was wary of seeing omens everywhere, the mark of the lunatic. Still . . . it had been coyotes who had conveyed to Larken his first revelation—had shown him the promise for whose sake he had left his dearly beloved ones behind. The animals' ghostly sound was wholly undoglike. It was a giddy wailing and hooting, a sardonic gibbering—the music of exiled demons begging for readmittance to the underworld.

Larken had long made a practice of extended moonlit treks through the hills. All this land was owned, of course, and so there would be fences even in the deepest hills—fences around the vineyards, around the more sprawling yellow-grass ranches where cattle grazed, around the country estates. He carried a small bolt cutter for the stubborn few fences he could not otherwise penetrate. When he had to pass near houses, he found it amusing to revive his jungle patrol skills, learned so well in Vietnam, modified for this sparser cover.

His goal was the entry of the hills themselves, to move through them as their inhabitant, as linked to the earth as any fox, as roofed by the sky. His night vision, given only a strong moon to work with, was excellent, as were his skills for quiet movement, and he had surprised many a deer on his travels, a silver fox, and twice a wildcat, but never, before that night, a coyote.

It seemed they caught your slightest move a mile away and politely, invariably declined contact. And yet they went everywhere in these hills. They fed from men's very decks and porches, fearlessly devouring unwary cats and small dogs practically from their owners' laps. The coyotes filled their world to the brim without once confronting the simian squatters who claimed every foot of it, and roared up and down their roads killing every other natural denizen—even, rarely, the foxes—but never, to Larken's knowledge, claiming a single coyote as roadkill. Like colliding galaxies, the two nations drifted right through each other—or theirs drifted through ours.

It had been a windy night, that night where his life had taken its turning. The atmosphere, in flood, was trying to wash the trees right off the hills. The big oaks twisted and shuddered like black flames in the moonlight, and the white grass rippled and bannered.

The wind that night made him feel his chronic longing. The wind, trying to stampede the trees, was roaring for a grand, universal departure to another solar system, a better deal, and the grass struggled to join the rootless giant of the air. All that lives strives to fly, to master time. All tribes of beings strain to rise in insurrection, all knowing their time is short, all, when the wind blows, wanting to climb aboard.

He climbed in the wind's teeth, up to the last ridge line before the plain, where the city glowed. He rounded a hill-shoulder toward a vantage point he liked when, completing the curve, he stopped just short of walking into three coyotes who were oppositely bound. All four of them froze, and stood staring at each other.

The gibbous moon, declining at Larken's back, put a glint in the six canine eyes. He looked at each in turn and settled on the eyes, not of the largest, but of the one who stood foremost, a lean bitch with a jaw that was slightly crooked.

Larken was moved by their beauty, not the least uncomfortable. At first he thought they were shocked, embarrassed even at this direct discovery. Animal etiquette would call for a slow side step, a careful withdrawal that avoided any signal of a wish to flee . . . But the bitch, head low, stood planted, fixedly regarding him. Though the wind was contrary, she dabbed her nose toward him. The two males flanking her then did the same, were probably her big-grown pups, still in training for all their size.

The fixity of their stare became fascinating to him. He dabbed his own face at them, snuffed their air, in case this was a necessary greeting. Snuffed, and a whiff of something ice-cold came to him.

It was a scent of . . . terror. Awe. The coyotes reeked of it—it was raising their hackles, was causing them to crouch and tense . . .

He watched enraptured until it dawned on him, finally came to him. He turned—the turning seemed to take forever—turned to look behind him.

Hovering above the wind-whipped grass, revealed against the distant fields of city lights behind it, something towered in the air, a transparent something that twisted the lightfield into a snarled weave, as if the lights were a colored net just barely containing the fight of a huge translucent catch.

Even as he struggled to make out its giant form . . . it was no more. The moonlight dissolved it. The city lights gleamed undisturbed.

The coyotes stirred now, shaking off their holy awe. They gazed at Larken a moment, perhaps with interest. Then they turned, wet muzzles glinting in the moonlight, and melted into the grass.

Larken stood there. All his life—long before 'Nam, which had just clarified it—all his life he had longed to find this doorway, this path that could lead him off the treadmill of time and death.

His legs buckled under, he dropped like lead and sat in the deep grass, staring at the lightfield where that Someone had stood. He found himself slowed to a synchrony with the Earth-clock itself, and sat there unmoving as the starfield inched across the sky. He then knew that when he returned to his wife and children, it would be to take his leave of them forever.

He knew he had been mocked in this revelation. Here he'd been tramping through the night, the earnest searcher, while the power and glory he was dogging followed him unperceived. How long had this Someone mocked him?

How long had this Someone mocked Larken? Back through the decades, had every cloud of crows that burst in flight before him been, in reality, exploding in mirth at oncoming Larken with his giant follower, the derisive god behind him?

Well, it was the gods' prerogative to mock. Larken had been shown at last. He had accrued fifty years of spiritual hunger, poverty, and nonentity and finally, it seemed, had amassed his down payment on eternity.

Oh the price! It was an unending agony to pay, to be denied forever dear Jolly, sweet, sweet Maxie and Jack. But it was a father's place to die before his children, to show them, with his calm as he steps out into the great Dark, that they have nothing to fear, that their own path will be bearable. How could he abide with them while they aged year by year, and he aged no further? Far easier for them to know no more of him beyond tonight than to learn that he was not of their world, and was to live beyond even his own memory of their existence.

So when that morning's sun rose, Carl Larken turned forever onto his present path, and lived in solitude.

He smiled a barbed smile now that tore his heart and felt the scald of bitter tears. He'd put down everything he had that very day—turned aside from his life, and the careless god, having beckoned him, had left him hanging, utterly alone, these three years since.

But what are years to a god? What are a man's tears? And now the god, or perhaps the god's messenger, had touched him between the eyes, and run a finger down his spine. Said *Yes. I am here.*

Larken crushed out his coals, washed out his oatmeal pan from the jug of water in his food locker—locked everything up and rehung it from the branch. Then he carried his mat and sleeping bag out from under the oak to a level spot and lay down, still clothed, on top of the bag, lay scanning the thick strew of stars visible through this gap in the trees.

And heard, or almost heard, that faint, clawed tread—the clothes-ghost he had conjured, coming now, drawing nearer, coming to offer Larken what he had lived for. Coming to tell him the price.

He realized it didn't matter whether he actually heard this or not. Because now, after fifty-five years, he was about to step up to his threshold and confront the god. This had been granted, he knew it in his spine.

Strangely, the most immediate effect on him was not jubilation, but a renewed agony at the price he had paid for this victory. Dear Christ, his precious Jolly! His precious Maxie, and little Jack! Eternal exile from them! How had he mustered the strength, the resolution?

They were his only riches, a fortune he had stumbled blindly into, undeservingly. His and Jolly's first years together, after he had come back, drugged and raging, from the war, had been dissolute years. They drank and drugged and fucked and fought. On the wings of substances, as they took wobbly flight together, he had tried to show her his most private faith—his mad hope that time could be broken like shackles, and a soul, a fiercely desiring soul, could burn forever.

But then priceless, accidental Maxie befell them, and Jolly became wholly Mother overnight. Larken himself took three more years, sullenly sucking booze and powders, before turning to at last and taking on his fatherhood. By then, equally accidental Jack had arrived, and the rusty doors of Larken's heart were forced all the way open.

In that deep, tricky torrent of parental love and nurturing, the next ten years fled away. The immortal fire persisted in Larken's inmost self, but he could not share it with his children. He found it a faith too perilous to speak—a magic he would lose if he tried to bestow it. His children's minds grew strong and agile, but he could not find the words. Before he knew it, Maxie was in middle school, Jack in elementary. Behold, they had friends, passionate interests, lives laid out before them in the world! They had already left him when at last the god vouchsafed to beckon him. Only that made it possible for him to renounce them.

He wiped his tears and listened to the night. The price he had paid was past counting, but his purchase was vast. He had bought nothing less than this whole world, night and day, north and south, now and forever. Was he insane, to feel this reckless certainty? Wasn't this blasphemy? Hubris? Wouldn't it cost him his prize?

He could not think so. This bitter joy refused to leave him. He listened to the night, deep night now, where living things moved quietly about their mortal business. Upslope of him, deer moved very carefully, small-footed through the scarcely rustling oak leaves. Far down on the two-lane he heard the faint, awkward *scritch* of a skunk (awkward as possums, skunks) beginning to cross the asphalt.

Whoops. Far down the two-lane, the beefy growl of a grunt-mobile. Enter Man on the stage of night, roaring high, wide and handsome in a muscle-truck—a tinny sprinkle of radio music above the roar. Closing fast, with a coming-home-from-the-bar aura. It must be just after two . . .

Larken listened to the tires as it roared near, roared past—and yes, there it came, that *whump-crunch-thumpa-thumpa* as the skunk was taken for a high-speed dribble down the court beneath the sixty-mile-an-hour underframe of the truck.

He lay listening. All the dyings! Everywhere, all the time. The coyotes announced themselves, very far off now, but with the gibbering intensity of a group kill. Webbed wings made a tiny, soft commotion—a bat, zigzagging bugs from the air. All the mulch, all the broken, gutted things settling down to decay . . . He felt a shift in his bowels.

He rose and got his little entrenching tool, and a small canteen of water—set out slantwise up the hill, and upwind of his camp.

High on the slope, he crouched on a crescent of deep soil, and a fine, round shit came loose from him. Filling his cupped hand from the canteen, he washed and rinsed himself, and washed his hands. He buried his accomplishments, thinking how coyotes and foxes left their scat right on the trail. When those animals retraced their steps at later times, they nosed the scats and knew themselves, sniffed the ghosts of previous meals. Each time they nosed the fading map of former days, the ever-fainter proofs of their own being, dwindling to rumors. Was this their sense of Time?

Men, more murderous animals, secreted their shit, hiding the lees of their innumerable victims . . . fearing vengeance?

Larken must make an offering to the clothes-ghost. Tomorrow. Must give it . . . something for a heart.

Precisely at the sun's first kindling on the eastern hills, Larken, his bike propped by a tree, stood again before the little cinder block shrine.

He had pedaled for an hour in the dawn's light, scouting the country roads for a fit offering. He had hoped for the rare luck to find something he'd happened on before: a road-struck animal whose life had not yet left it. He remembered once running and coming up eye to eye with a possum that had not yet finished dying. There was still a little bit of him left there in his inky little possum's eyes. The beast was looking back forgetfully at life, looking into Larken's eyes forgetful that he was human, seeming to struggle to remember something they had in common long ago . . .

Had he been given such a find it would have amounted to an omen from the god that his improvised ritual was welcomed. As it was, he found a rare enough thing indeed—a silver fox, whose bush, ruffled by the breeze, had caught his eye. The fox was beautifully intact—back-broken, not mauled—and dead not very many days.

This was much, he reflected as he eased it into his old khaki knapsack. Enough to be a kind of warrant from the god. Foxes, these sharp-muzzled tricksters, were almost never nailed by monkey Man's grunting pig machines. He had to pedal hard to bring this rarity to the shrine before the sun's rising, and made it there just at the instant that the first light struck the gray wall.

He knew, seeing that, that this rite of his was welcomed, and the god was present to receive his offering.

He stepped inside, his knapsack cupped before him in both hands. The clothes-ghost seemed to float on the floor, to glow, so full of feral insolence, of fierce and graceful glee its posture was. Under the hat's slanted bill, the spark of an eye almost glinted. The jauntiness of that up-hooked tail, the sinewy thrust of that clawed foot . . . it knew!

Larken knelt down slowly on one knee. He felt the ghost's seething aura of energy, waiting for Larken to find the awakening magic to give him form and force.

He drew the reeking fox-that-was from the sack. Sun had shrunk its tendons—there was a stiffness that made the little corpse more wieldy. He gripped the gray pelt at the spine just below the neck, and with his other hand lifted one flap of the ghost's shirt. He felt no need for words. He shrouded the fox inside the ghost's shirt, willing spirit into this inhuman gatekeeper. His hidden hand felt in an alien space, felt the heat and menace of a hostile dimension.

Just as he withdrew his hand, it was powerfully, searingly bitten.

Torn to the bone, both the palm and the back of his hand. Blood, its astonishing crimson, welled blazing out of him in the morning light.

He stood staring at his hand full of blood.

Was this a message?

What was the message?

An engine, something big and huffy, was idling not far off. Larken had to stand a moment, struggling to decide if the sound came from that eternal world where his hand had been torn or from this one his feet were planted on.

He seized up a sun-bleached fragment of T-shirt from one corner, bound his hand, and knotted it with his teeth. The bandage went instantly red as he thrust the hand inside the light windbreaker he wore. His bike outside already declared him. He stepped out into the slanting sun, picked up his bike with his left hand, and stepped through the trees to the road with it. A young man stood by a black jeep Cherokee, arm draped on the roof.

Larken smiled easily at him, straddled his bike with his hand still tucked away, stood on one pedal, and slowly coasted over to him.

"The pause that refreshes," he said to the young man who, looking surprised, said:

"Mr. Larken!"

Larken, when teaching junior college, had infallibly Mistered and Mized all his students, and after a beat he said, "Mr. Bonds! This *is* a pleasure! Is this your . . . estate you're viewing?"

Pat was remembering Marjorie's question yesterday. No doubt about it, there was something subtly but deeply not normal about this guy. He steps out of a ruined shed at dawn, steps smiling out of the trees with his hidden hand, making what looked as if it might be a bloodstain in the armpit of his jacket, then cruises over to Pat, totally suave and smiling. And not only does he remember Pat after what, six years? But he even remembers the little standing jokes between them about Pat's pragmatism, his fiscal realism, his good-humored lack of interest in big ideas.

The old man had a real . . . charisma. Complete self-possession. But sitting here with a bloodstain spreading across his jacket, having just stepped out of a flicking abandoned shed at sunrise . . . this self-possession looked more than a little unreal.

"I don't own these grapes themselves. I'm in the development sector of the viticulture industry. We design acquisitions, financing. We're going to get fifty more acres of Zin out of this field."

Larken looked across a sea of grapes from fence to fence. "Where are you going to get it?"

"Here and there along the margins. We'll get a good ten acres here when we tear out that shed and this border strip."

At this Larken just nodded, but he let a beat go by. "Are you leaving any eucalyptus?"

"Just one line at the roadside. We'll take those out later this year. They create a shadowing problem for the new acres." Pat found himself getting a little stiffer as he went on. He still *amused* Larken on a level he didn't get. That was okay when he was the guy's student—a teacher is supposed to run some attitude on you, poke at your perspective. But this man, this wacko old man with his chickenfeed job, found something genuinely funny about the way Pat was, after all, engineering this entire environment here.

And the man seemed to sense his thought. "A world-shaper," he smiled at Pat. "I saw it long ago."

"Well, every generation shapes things, right? Every generation makes what it can, builds what it can make use of."

""You are absolutely right, Mr. Bonds. You can't take a single step on this old globe without changing it. So when are you clearing this section?"

"Tomorrow." And Pat had scored something, he felt it. Where's your contempt for money and power now, he asked the old man in his mind. There's something he values here, and just twenty-four hours from now I'm making it disappear.

Then Larken smiled again. "Time is on the wing, isn't it? On the wing. Which reminds me, I've got to get to work. Good to see you!"

When Larken had pedaled off, right hand still tucked beneath his arm, Pat entered the weedy margin behind the trees. He wondered how he'd failed to ask Larken how he hurt his hand. He stepped into the cinderblock shed.

Nothing. Trash and discarded clothing everywhere. Just a useless eyesore. A perfect place to be scraped clean. Developed.

As he climbed back in his jeep, he thought of Larken's eyes, gray eyes under shaggy brows. There was an intention behind those eyes, something fixed and unyielding. What might a trashy nook like this one here mean to a war-scarred old guy like that, a bookish man of the kind who brooded about big ideas? Who could tell? The fact remained that, just meeting Larken's eyes as he'd emerged from that shed, Pat had felt like a trespasser here.

Marjorie was northbound on to 101. The three P.M. traffic was clotting and creeping around her, still five miles south of town, where she was already fifteen minutes late for coffee with Pat at Espresso Buono. When she reached him on his cell phone, she could tell that he, too, was carbound.

"Where are you, Pat?"

"One-oh-one. I'm just above Novato."

"Christ, you're thirty miles behind me. I'm just north of Rodent Park."

"Things ran late at the title company."

"It's kind of romantic, Pat, the two of us just cruising the traffic stream together, trading sweet nothings."

"Are you actually *cruising* that close to town?"

"Actually no, it's creep and crawl . . ." Should she tell him? On the phone like this? "I was just down in Petaluma. I had to go see the mother of the guy I told you about, Guy Blankenship. He had morphine patches, right? Well he, like, put on half a dozen of them last night. He overdosed. He's dead. He left a note, or he started a note. It said *tell Carl.*"

"Whoa."

"Right. Well, the police asked me about it. It's a wrongful death, right? I said I didn't know who it was. I said I'd look into it and maybe get back to them."

"Did you tell Larken?"

"He didn't come to work today, and he doesn't have a phone."

A little silence passed between them. Marjorie was picturing Carl Larken out for a run along some two-lane. She pictured the city ahead of her and thought of it semi-abstractly as an environment, as the habitat of Larken. That gaunt graybeard, implacable as Jeremiah. Picturing him like this, it seemed incredible to her that she had not seen his madness sooner. He was no longer a creature of civilization. He was like an animal that infiltrated the city by day, and returned to the hills by night. The man was almost auraed with otherness.

"Hey, Marjo? Tell the police. It's no harm to Larken. They'll hard-time him a little is all, and maybe he needs a little accountability check here."

Marjorie laughed, thinking of the vivid Mrs. Blankenship, whose ram-shackle house she had just left—the woman a bleached, cigarette-throated, leather-vested speedfreak. "No harm? If they told his mother, and she found someone smart enough to help her with it, she'd sue the corporation's socks off."

"You know I ran into him this morning?"

Larken lost himself in an endless patrol, beelining across the hills. He carried his little boltcutter for the stubbornest fences. He crossed pasture and vineyard and tree-choked streamcourse. Carefully void of intention, he chose his course as randomly as he could.

In these hills he had at last been shown, invited. Now, as Time closed in on him, these hills must show him his next step. He gripped this faith and patrolled them, hour after hour.

The sun had begun to wester. When he was startled out of his walking reverie, he was amazed to realize just how oblivious he'd been. Aware of nothing but these acres of rolling pasture dropping away before him, when close behind him, a voice said, "I see you have a bolt cutter there. Is that what you used to cut through my fence?"

When he turned, there was a frail old woman walking toward him from a jeep—the old-fashioned military-looking kind—parked a short way down the fire-break path his feet had been treading so automatically.

The lady wore khaki work clothes and a gray canvas hat with a little circular brim. She was so frail; hair as wispy as web escaped the hat. She was frail and there was something else about her—a scent he could almost pick up. "You've done it before, too, haven't you?" she urged, her voice very level, though age made it waver slightly. "You like to follow a beeline across people's property."

He smiled gently. "You've determined to call the devil by his name, right to his face, hesitation be damned," he said with admiration. "From now on you're not going to waste time with caution."

"I never have. You talk about caution. Am I in danger here from you?"

He had been honestly absorbed in her. She would be an omen, of course! Part of the answer he was after. But when she asked him this question, it stunned him for a moment, the alienness of the notion that he should lift his hand against her frailty. And in that moment he identified that faint scent she had. Chemotherapy.

"You are correct, ma'am," he was saying, "I do make beelines. I damage as little fence as possible, but sometimes I need to follow the route I'm feeling. You are in absolutely no danger from me. I'm afraid I might have a pretty uncouth appearance, but I'm a good person. I did two tours in Vietnam, a lot of them in-country, and I guess it's left me a little reclusive."

The slopes of dried grass below them were growing golder in the slanting sun. That rich light flooded her face with such detail. Blue veins across her forehead, the fine-china translucence of her wrinkled eyelid, her hair's sparseness betrayed by the looseness of her hat. She watched him as he spoke, not so much listening to his words as following her own train of thought about him. "You tell me I've decided not to waste time on caution. You seem to be telling me that I'm obviously someone with not much time left. Suppose that's true. Why should that make me care any less about vandalism to my property?"

"When I ventured that description of your state of mind, ma'am, I meant to express my admiration. I don't dispute the wrongness of damaging your fence. My trespass was totally impersonal, and I did no harm to your property—"

"Except to its boundary!"

"Except to its fence. May I guess, ma'am? Are you that little beef ranch, a hundred acres or so, triple-strand barbed wire?" Her icy look was as good as a nod. "I will of course pay you whatever damages you see fit."

Again she seemed, rather than listening, to be struggling to digest him. "I've seen you on the roads, you know, over the years—running, cycling. I've seen you running out of your driveway. You call yourself a recluse, and I've had exactly that thought about you as I drove past, that you were a kind of hermit. Completely in your own world."

"But aren't you completely in yours?"

"Are you hinting again? That you know I'm dying?"

"I'm just trying for an understanding. I'm dying too."

"Not as fast as I am." Almost wry here, her fragile, skull-stretched face. He could sense her mood exactly. She was partly lured by an unlooked-for understander of her plight, but equally was stung by his understanding. In the pinch, she reverted to legalities. "I called the sheriff on my cell phone as soon as I found the damage, and I told them I suspected you. I felt a little bad about that, not being positive, but then I took the Jeep out and found you practically red-handed."

Understanding flooded him. This woman was not an omen to him, she was more than that. She was *in herself* a gift, a token of passage. He understood now the garish Sign that had been given him, in return for his morning's offering: his right hand full of blood.

"I'm sure, of course," she was saying, "that the officers, after writing up a report, will let us settle it between ourselves."

All this golden light! It was beginning to shade over to voluptuous red-gold. Hills rolled away on all sides, and the two of them stood bathed in this ocean of light, and at the same time they were utterly unwitnessed by another human. Perfectly alone together in all this big emptiness, with the royal sun, alone, looking on. Larken, before setting out on his day's quest, had made and properly tied a bandage for his right hand, though the red stain had seeped through even this one. Perhaps because she sensed his own sudden awareness of it, she took note of his wound for the first time. "How did you hurt your hand?"

He smiled apologetically. "I was bitten."

"Bitten by what?"

"I was bitten by a god. A god who is about to break out from these hills. Is about to hatch from them. He has promised me . . . immortality."

He had her full, bemused attention. He pulled the bandage off his hand. Out of the deep tear in his flesh, black-scabbed though it was, the naked tendons peeked.

The setting sun gilded the trenched meat, and it glowed like a sacrament.

Deep night. The county road far below him had at last gone quiet and empty.

The darkness, even after these long hours of it, still felt like a balm to Larken, as if the bright work of bloodspilling that he had done today had scorched his retinas and made sunlight agony to them.

He lay far upslope under one of his oak trees, his own hillside rock-solid under his back. He lay perfectly still, wholly relaxed, so that the vast crickety sound of the night felt like a deep lake he sank in, deeper with each heartbeat into the creaking, trilling music of the earth's nocturne.

And then, woven into that vast music, it began to be faintly, sinisterly audible.

So far off at first, so sketchy: a jostle of leaves . . . a friction against bark. An approach. Something moving through the leafy canopy, something small and very far, picking its way from branch to branch. It meandered, finding its path through contiguous trees, but it was seeking him.

To Larken's ears this faint advance might as well have been thunder, for there was nothing else in the world but it. Because the earth was opening beneath him. This visitation he had bought with human blood would leave him changed forever, would actually begin his removal from this world and his advance toward eternity. He lay there, waiting as he had waited all his conscious life, to step off of the earth and into the universe.

It wasn't as small as it had sounded, now that it was working its way up the slopes of Larken's property. He began to hear a muscular agility, which had helped to mute its approach but, nearing, betrayed a solid mass laddering its way through the branches and boughs.

Just a short way down the slope from where he lay, his visitant came to a stop. In the short silence that followed, Larken felt an alien intent grow focused on him.

Sssssssst.

It was a summons, and its echo changed the air as it drifted up among the oaks and madrones. The night mist grew more spacious, its very molecules drawing apart, as if mimicking the separations of the stars themselves.

He got to his feet, and doing so took forever, his legs, hands, arms slow travelers across the interstellar emptiness that had entered each cubic foot of the night air. He threaded downslope through bushes—manzanita, scrub oak, bay, scotch broom—that were abstract silhouettes, like archetypes, but whose odors, rich and distinct, filled him with a terrible nostalgia for that mortal world that he was now abandoning.

He stopped, doubting that he dared, after all, all, all . . . to do this. It spoke again instantly, in answer to his hesitation:

Sssssssst.

Down he walked, dazed but foot sure, stepping down through eons of mist and shadow . . .

Here was the big oak tree that marked an arc of level ground where Larken's long-defunct compost patch lay. Up in its branches was where his caller awaited him. It seemed that from the tree's overarching mass a fine, impalpable panic rained down. As if the tree itself, that crooked old leafy mortal, radiated its terror at what this man was bent on doing. Larken stood in this faint rain of fear, like a warning breathed down by the tree.

Though his fear was dire, his hesitation had left him. His legs had carried him too many miles and years on this path to retreat from its terminus.

Its terminus, this compost patch—a sunken crust now which the oak's canopy overhung. A dried, sunken, vegetal crust that to Larken was terror itself, a patch of Absolute Zero. He came to the brink of the worst place on earth.

There was a small, energetic commotion in the oak's lower branches. Feet, shod in something like track shoes but gaudier, dangled into view from the lowest bough. These shoes were blazoned with stripes and chevrons in sweeping curves of some glossy material colored copper and silver, and dully luminous, burnished, giving off an inner light. Short legs followed, too-short legs sheathed in baggy cholo-pants whose excess material stacked in bulges on the shoes' tops.

This was the dreadful ripening of what Larken had lived to summon, and only the combined weight of his whole past life—though such a frail, slight weight it seemed now!—sufficed to hold him steady on his legs, sufficed to plant him to confront this strange fruit's falling, at long last.

The visitant dropped to the ground and stood entire upon the crusty mat. He was a natty little monster three feet high. The whiskered, 'gator-toothed snout of a possum was likest to the face he thrust forth with a loll-tongued leer of greeting. He was jauntily hatted with a snap-brimmed bookie's fedora of straw—or woven brass? For it glowed like dirty dull gold. The hat was cocked arrogantly over one beady black eye. His baggy black sport coat was hung up at the back on the upthrust sickle of his tail, a huge rat's tail, a stiff, dried tail, a comma of carrion whose roadkill scent Larken caught on the cold air of this eternity.

The visitant hissed, *Feeeed me*—its tongue, a limber spike of black meat, stirring in its narrow nest of canines.

Larken discovered at his side something he had not noticed: a shovel standing upright, stabbed into the earth.

Stepping out of an airplane into an alien night sky above Vietnam had been nothing to this, but Larken did it in the same kind of here-I-go instant: he took up the shovel and stabbed it into the scab of compost.

He dug, knowing without thinking exactly where to dig.

It was his own heart he shoveled out chunks of and spilled to one side.

The shovel was heavy and cold, did not warm to his hands. It was time's tooth, chewing up lives and spitting them out. It bit out his heart and dumped it to one side.

He had not understood. He would not have done it if he had known how they were to serve.

Careful, very careful he was near the depth that he knew. He knelt at the last and scraped the soil away with his hands.

He uncovered a little arm, the slender, bow-and-arrow arc of two bones, the flesh all but moldered away. He stood up and turned away, his tears streaming down for those precious bones, that little arm.

The visitant's steps crunched across the compost. Something much more massive than that dapper little monster it sounded like. The monster's littleness was so dense with greed, as dense as the heart of a neutron star.

Larken stood with his back turned, tears streaming, as the Messenger feasted behind him, as it ripped at the compost and soil in a horrid undressing of the precious bodies sleeping in their garment of earth. The sound of its feeding, the gnashing and guttural guzzling, long it lasted, and he would carry that sound into eternity.

When the meal was done, the visitant spoke again.

The price is two more. They are here.

And Larken heard a distant purr and crackle, car tires crunching up his drive. He turned and saw glints of headlights far below, and the beam of a patrol car's searchlight climbing the twisted ribbon of gravel.

The first officer said, "Christ. It's abandoned." Their headlights, as they pulled up onto the narrow plateau where the driveway ended, flooded against a little house walled in weeds and vines, its roof a thick sloping scalp of dead leaves a foot deep sprouting grass also dead now in the dry fall.

They got out and splashed their flashlight beams across windows opaque with rain-spotted dust. They approached the gaping front door and poured their beams inside, across furniture blurred by dust and leaves and cobwebs.

"Christ," echoed the second officer. "We're not gonna find him here."

The first shrugged. "Some indications of whereabouts, maybe."

They moved farther into the house, and the floor felt the same underfoot as the ground had. Their beams woke a startling scuttle and scramble of animal paws. They tried light switches that didn't work. Kitchen and living room conjoined with no wall between. The second officer began to search these rooms.

The first officer followed a short hallway farther inside. The hallway was festooned with dusty cobwebs, and behind this dust was walled with books, books, books, their ranked titles like muffled shouts and exclamations choking in the dark.

Insanity. Right here. If the guy's brain was packed with all these mummified shouts, then the missing woman was dead. The officer, though he tingled with this intuition, dismissed it as ungrounded, at least so far. There was no denying, though, that to leave a house like this, just abandon it with everything in it, indicated some kind of insanity—if it didn't prove homicide.

The door to the bathroom opened off this hall.

Tacked to the bathroom door was a drawing. It was clearly a very old one, done with pencils and colored markers. It was divided in panels on an oversize sheet of art paper. In each panel the father, small daughter, and smaller son appeared to be self-drawn. The panels presented a narrative: The trio find their cat nursing five kittens. The family dog licks the kittens while the mother cat stands by with raised hackles and fluffed-out tail. They carry the kittens in a box. They stand in front of a supermarket with the box, the little girl handing a kitten to another little girl. The kittens look like slugs with pointed ears and tails. Dad is clownishly self-drawn with big ears and wild hair, the little girl very precisely drawn with pony tail and bangs and a pretty dress, the boy drawn with barely controlled energy, head and limbs various in size from panel to panel, hair all energetic spikes.

The officer heard a shift of mass, a sigh.

"Ted?"

A big, sinewy shape stood in his flashlight beam. The officer struggled to clear his sidearm.

"I'm sorry," the shape said sadly and cut his throat.

Up before sunrise. Marjorie hated getting out of bed in the dark, but loved the payoff once she was dressed and rolling down the country roads in the first light, cruising and owning them almost alone. The countryside here used to be a lot more interesting, though. She remembered it in her girlhood—orchards, small ranches, farmhouses, each one of these houses a distinct personality . . . Money, she thought wryly, scanning the endless miles of grapevines, all identically wired and braced and drip-lined, mile after mile—money was such a powerful organizer.

As the dawn light gained strength and bathed the endless vines in tarnished silver, it struck her that there was, after all, something scary about money, that it could run loose in the world like a mythic monster, gobbling up houses and trees, serving strictly its own monstrous appetite.

But there was Pat and his crew ahead. A bright red Japanese earthmover—skiploader in front, backhoe behind—had already bladed out the wide strip of bramble and weed between the vineyard fence and the roadside rank of eucalyptus. The mangled vegetation had already been heaped in a bright orange dump truck that was now pulling out for the dump, passing Marjorie as she approached. The next load the truck would be returning for had not yet been created, but Marjorie could see what it would be. The earthmover, with its backhoe foremost now, stood confronting the cinderblock shed. The hydraulic hoe's mighty bucket-hand rested knuckles-down against the earth, like the fist of a wrestling opponent, awaiting the onset. Its motor idled while its short, stolid Mexican operator had dismounted to confer with Pat.

And instantly Marjorie forgave money, loved and trusted it again, seeing all this lustrous sexy powerful machinery marshaled to money's will. And just look at that cleanness and order it had created. Where there had been tangle and dirtiness and trash before, was now clean bare dirt, reddish in the rising light, beside the columned trees.

Pat stepped smiling out to the road. "Good morning! You look radiant!"

"I look that tired, huh?"

"Nothing some Espresso Buono won't fix when we head out of here. I didn't expect you'd actually come out."

They hadn't been able to make yesterday's date, Marjorie going instead to make her report to the police, but they'd agreed she might meet him for this morning's early business. Why exactly had she come? "I figured," she said sweetly, "that if we grabbed a date this early, we'd actually get to see each other."

He nodded, but added, "Did you have the thought that Larken might show up?"

"Yeah. You've had the thought too?"

"I guess I have. Look, pull off into that drive down there. This won't take half an hour. Come watch this Nipponese brute do its stuff."

She pulled off about a hundred feet downroad, in the driveway of the fieldhands' little house. As she parked she saw Pat in her rearview, lifting his arm in greeting to someone beyond him. She got out and saw, about a hundred feet uproad of Pat, Carl Larken come coasting on his bike, one bandaged hand raised in salute.

He dismounted still a little distance off, leaned his bike on a tree, and began walking toward the men and their machine.

Marjorie had to gather herself a moment before approaching. She must tell Carl simply and honestly about the report she'd made. It was not, after all, a criminal matter, but there would have to be discussions with the police. There were accountability issues here. She began to walk toward them, had taken three steps, when she felt a wave of nausea move up into her through her legs.

She froze utterly disoriented by the sensation. The ground beneath her feet was . . . feeding terror up into her body. She stood, almost comically arrested in midstride. What was this panic crawling out of the earth? It had something to do with Carl Larken down there, approaching the men from the opposite direction, something to do with the impact of his feet on the fresh-scraped earth.

Look at his slow liquid gait, all muscle up his legs and arms. He was so *here,* he pressed with impossible mass against the earth. Suddenly all this regimented greenery, this whole army of rank-and-file vegetation, seemed to belong to him, while Pat and his helper and their bright machine had a slightly startled, caught-in-the-act air.

Marjorie gripped the trunk of a eucalyptus, but even the hugeness of the tree against her felt flimsy in this radioactive sleet of fear that was blazing from the ground beneath them both.

Pat and the operator stood slack-shouldered beside the red steel monster. Larken came to within fifteen feet or so and stopped. It seemed to Marjorie, even at her little distance, that the mass of him dented the earth, putting the two lighter men in danger of falling toward him. His voice was gentle.

"Good morning, Mr. Bonds. Señor." A faint smile for the operator. "I'm really sorry to intrude. I have to make use of this . . . land you own. It is a purely ceremonial thing, and executed in mere moments. Would you bear with me, Mr. Bonds? Indulge an addled old pedagogue for just a moment?"

"You say you want to perform a ceremony, Mr. Larken?" It was odd how much frailer Pat's voice sounded than Larken's. The idling earthmover half drowned him out with a surge in its engine's rumble.

"A simple ceremony, Mr. Bonds. An offering, plainly and briefly made."

"You want to do it . . . in that shed?" Again the earthmover seemed to half erase Pat's words, his little laugh at the strangeness of his own question.

"This spot of earth, right here, is all I need. The god I'm praying to is here, right underfoot of us."

The man's utter madness was out, it loomed before them now. But in that moment it was the others who seemed unreal to Marjorie. Hugging her tree, melted by her terror out of any shape to act, she found Pat and the operator, the jeep and the dozer, all too garish to be real—like bright balloons, all of them, taut, weightless, flimsy. Pat, helpless before this perfect nonsense, made a gesture of permission that was oddly priestlike —an opening-out of hands and arms.

Larken unslung a small knapsack and cupped it in both hands before him, tilting his head back slightly, his eyes searching inwardly. Marjorie, stuck like lichen to that trunk, a limbless shape, a pair of eyes only and a heart with the earthquake-awe in it—Marjorie understood that the strange man was searching for the right words. Understood too now that it was the rumbling of that dozer's engine that was awakening the earthquake underfoot.

He chose his words. "I have been your faithful seeker, your faithful servant, forsaking all others! All others! I make you now your commanded offering. Open to me now the gates of eternity!"

He opened the knapsack, lifted it high, and sent its contents tumbling down through the silver air—two pale spheroids, two human heads, jouncing so vividly on the ground, their short-barbered hair looking surreally neat against the red dirt, their black-scabbed stumps glossy as lacquer.

Their impact with the earth set off the earthquake. There was a shrieking of metal as the backhoe flung its great arm in the air, a gesture galvanic as some colossal scorpion's. The whole machine came apart with the fury of this straightening, the steel sinews spraying asunder in red shards and revealing a darker sinew within, a huge, black hatchling of tarry muscle clotted on long bone. Two crimson eyes blazed above its black snout as its crooked paw, prehensile, seized Pat and the operator together. The men cried out, their bones breaking in the grip that lifted them up to the mad red moons of eyes, lifted them higher still, and flung them powerfully at the earth. They struck the ground, impossibly flattened by the impact, transformed, in fact, to roadkill, to sprawling husks of human beings, bony silhouettes postured as if they were running full tilt toward the core of the planet.

"Thank you! Thank you! Oh, thank you!" Larken's gratitude sounded as wild as grief—his wail brought the god's paw down to him in turn. In turn he was seized up and lofted high, and was held aloft a moment while the god's eyes bathed him in their scarlet radiation.

And Marjorie, who had not guessed that she had voice left in her, screamed, and screamed again, because the earth beside the monster was no longer earth, but was a ragged-edged chasm of blackness, an infinite cauldron of darkness and stars.

The brute god held Larken high above this abyss. She could make out his face clearly above the crooked claw that gripped him—he was weeping with wonder and awe.

The god flung him down. His arms windmilling, down Larken plunged. The god gave one furious snort that wafted like roadkill through the morning air and leapt after his acolyte, dwindling down toward the starfields.

The earth closed over them, and Marjorie hugged the tree, quivering, staring at that resealed earth. The soil seemed sneakily transparent, thinly buried stars trying to burn through it like diamond drill bits. The planet felt hollow underfoot, and the great tree sustaining her seemed to feel it, too. They huddled together, feeling the ground resonate under them, like the deck of a ship on a rolling sea.

She straightened and started forward, a starship traveler negotiating the gravity of an alien world. The ship had crashed . . . there were the twisted shards of bright red metal . . . right here was where it had happened, the red dirt solid now, supporting her, supporting the black-stumped heads like thrown dice, their dulled snake-eyes aimed askew of one another, looking in different directions for the sane earth they had known, she had known . . .

The sane world lay that way, didn't it? Down this narrow country road she could find her way back to freeway on-ramps that channeled predictably to shopping malls that sold fancy underwear and barrels of jellybeans, to Humanity Inc. with its computers and telephones and case-files full of muddled souls with painful childhoods and histories of run-ins with the law . . .

But how could the road lead there from such a starting point as this, here on the margin of the asphalt? These two sprawled human husks? She gazed on the distorted profile of Pat Bonds, crushed bone clad in sunbaked parchment. Older than Egypt he looked, the eye a glazed clot of mucus, a canted half-grin of teeth erupting from the leathery cheek.

Crazed Cubist face, yet so expressive. He stared with outrage, with furious protest, at eternity.

Go back down this road. Take the first step, and the next will follow . . . see? Now the next. You're doing fine, Marjorie. Soon you'll reach your car, your car will reach the city. Just keep moving. It'll all come back to you . . .

In Memory Drive Slow

I'm gonna give it to you totally, nothing held back. I just want you to listen. I mean record it, whatever, but hear me all the way, because I'm going to tell you absolutely everything.

OK. Straight out, I deal. Totally small time—grams, eighths, sometimes a quarter O-Z. Strictly minor-league. None of that nine millimeter/bricks of flake shit. I sell a little blow, a little crank to Joe six-pack when he gets his paycheck and that's all. I pay my rent. Got a nice '65 'Stang, and bottom line, I'm just a working stiff.

So here's how I met the guy. First time I set eyes on him was that same night. I stopped at the Willowside for a brew 'n a bump. It was early, a few old farts at the back tables, and this guy was the only one sitting at the bar.

One of those sloppy, half-tough guys. 'Niners jacket, Peterbilt cap, hair shaggy with a beard and 'stache which helped hide how his face was getting porky. He'd go, "Aw-*right!*" when one of the fighters on the tube landed one. When Lloyd picks up his empty and says it looks like he could use another one, he says, "No shit, Sherlock." Lloyd's half his size and could totally whip his ass. Classic chump, easy money from my point of view. I take a stool a couple down from him.

Lloyd shoots me a look, we read each other. I don't move action on his premises unless the situation's right, and I kick him back twenty on each hundred I make. You see I'm giving you total honesty here, right?

So when I know the chump will catch it, I pretend to sneak a sniff off the crook of my thumb, and then act startled to see him catch me at it. Chump says, "Hey bro, why doncha share the wealth?"

I act trapped. I sign him to be quiet and scoot over next to him. I fake recognizing him from somewhere and ask Lloyd for two bumps and beer backs, so the chump thinks I'm covering so Lloyd won't catch on. He thinks this is cool—I can literally see the thought in his blurry chump's eyes. We knock back the bumps and I whisper, "Chill, dude—not inside here."

We make phony talk and he plays along, feeling cagey. "I'm Jake," I tell him, and when we shake I give him a five-move hand-jive riff I make up on the spot. The spades are into a good thing with this hand-jive shit; when he can't follow the moves it humbles him, makes him feel like he's not in the know, right? Now the chump is definitely impressed with me, because I know the secret handshake and all. His name, he tells me, is Leon.

Pretty soon I lean close and say and hardly moving my lips: "You can taste if you're ready to buy—G-M's eighty."

Leon cocks me a nod—Mr. Cool, shooting careful looks at Lloyd, who's standing wiping glasses with his back to us and probably grinning like a fool. "Outside," I whisper to Leon. "Hang here five. Get another beer."

As I went out I palmed thirty bucks to Lloyd, a little joke, like a prediction I'd get a minimum three hundred from the chump. Lloyd winked at me.

In my 'Stang I put bindles and a flat pint of 100-octane Schnapps into my jacket pockets. I got out and looked up and waited over by someone else's ride. Leon came out and I watched him cross the lot toward me: this bulky zero on the beer-gut side of thirty, walking this weird stiff walk, pretending he was muscle-bound. The guy was so simple I felt like I oughta just phone in the shakedown. Cut it short, just tell him, "Look, Dipstick, just give me all your money now. Save us both time!"

I told him we'd deal in his ride. On the off-chance shit happens in my wheels I don't get involved that way, and I know Lloyd will look out for it for me in case someone gets hurt. Leon's ride was exactly the one I'd thought it would be—a dirty, battered old Dodge one-ton with a bunch of crappy tools heaped in the bed. We climbed in and he gave me a scuffed-up CD case to chop lines on.

I pulled a bindle and my short Buck. I cut some very fat rails. This was what I called my coke, you understand: about half crank, some mannitol, and a dash of real blow for taste. People who've been drinking, why waste real blow on them? Crank pops their clutch and gets them rolling cheaper.

Leon snorts. "Aww-*riiiight!*" he says. "That's some decent blow!" I take his money and give him his bindle, then cut some more rails out of mine—the party's on friendly Jake, right? He started chopping out lines from his bogus bindle, and I kept putting the pint back in his hand, milking him right along. How? By listening! By acting impressed. For numbnuts like him, substances are just a way to get some company. As long as they're chopping lines, people will sit there and listen to them!

I heard about the unbelievable bitch he was married to until the divorce a couple years ago. She had the house and the brats, thank god. She couldn't get her claws on what he made under the table, but her faggot lawyer had his unemployment checks garnisheed right out from under him. On and on and on.

It took less than half an hour. He asked me if I'd take a ride to his cash machine with him and he'd buy another bindle. "That's a big ten-four, good buddy!" I told him.

We took Occidental east. The Willowside's the only tavern for miles—it's all dark fields and trees and big lonely houses out there. Leon's loving it, gonna gut his account to buy bindles to bribe me to listen to him some more. The fields are spinning past on either side and Leon's driving way too fast, shouting me the story of his own dramatic life. Now he's edging up to something he thinks is a big deal . . . and here it comes: Leon mentions his "manslaughter beef a couple years back."

He looks to see if I'm impressed. I say, "Whoa! Heavy duty!"

What he wanted to talk about was his dramatic battle in court, but there was no way he could go on about these things without describing what the manslaughter actually was. What it came down to was, he was driving home from work DUI one afternoon, speeding down a residential street, and he killed a ten-year-old on a bike. Pathetic, and what else would it be with this guy? Hardly said ten words about the accident anyway—talked about his hard time in the joint.

You have to remember this was just a year or two before they made hard-ass vehicular manslaughter laws. His mouth was in such high gear he actually gave me the details: what his bit shook down to was about six months in county, and he ended up with a year's work furlough and five years' summary. His whole time in county he celled with a ninety-pound cross-dresser.

It was hard work for me to keep acting impressed with this, but we were already entering the residential streets on the west edge of Santa Marta. He was driving too fast, drifting across the center line on the curves. I was just deciding I would grab a cab back to my ride from this chump's cash machine, when something catches Leon's eye and he stops right in the middle of the street, staring. There's no other traffic—everyone's indoors watching TV—and I look where he's staring.

There's a homemade wooden sign wired to the pole of a street lamp by the curb. The letters were spray-painted through stencils, a little crooked, but big and clear:

In Memory
Kevin Cray
10 Years Old
Drive Slow

Well, I realized that I'd seen this sign before—one of those pathetic kind of things that stays in your mind, right? It'd been up there a long time, a year or two, maybe. One of those things that catches your eye, and then you look for it now and then to see if it's still there.

The streetlight put a kind of glow on the sign. I saw Leon looking at it, and something clicked. I realized I was sitting beside the *reason* for that sign. This Kevin Cray was Leon's Manslaughter Beef.

Maybe that was the point where things started to go so truly strange that night: the way I suddenly understood this chump so completely. Leon was definitely not a Noticer of what was around him. I somehow *knew* he'd driven this road a dozen times since that killing, but this was the first time he'd seen the sign—tonight, boozed and wired again, losing it on the same curve *again,* he finally recognizes this spot only because there's this sign staring him in the face. You wanted to laugh. You almost felt sorry for a fool this total.

But what happened next was *definitely* where the strangeness started, where something began tampering with my *mind.* Here's where it began, and you can hook me to a lie detector right now, whatever you want. Leon realizes we're at a dead stop, he guns the truck, we're hauling ass outta there, and as I sat there gazing at his big scared profile I suddenly got this picture in my mind—like it was a slide and my head was a projector and someone had just stuck it in there.

It was this little blond kid with a bike. His face was so clear to me! He had light, light freckles near his nose, his teeth were perfect and looked a little too big for him the way they do for kids that age, nine or ten. He had on these red baggies with yellow lightning bolts on them, was wearing a tanktop hanging off his skinny little arms, he had a little scab on his left knee, and a Bart Simpson button on his shorts that said "Don't have a cow, Man." And this whole image had an aura about it, an emotion like . . . sorrow.

It was all so sharp in my mind I was disoriented, and I blurted out: "Hey! Kevin Cray! Was that the kid you killed?"

I was instantly pissed at myself. Bad, *bad* technique! I had to be milking this chump. Talking about his manslaughter beef, fine! But *"that kid you killed"?* No way! Far too raw! Look at him—his fat cheeks were popping sweat right above his beard-line.

He notices we're dead-stopped mid-street, and he jerks us back into gear. As we lurch on down the road his eyes are wild and he keeps opening and closing his mouth. I realize he is shaping a Thought. His voice comes out rusty. "You know what? You know what the problem really is?" His eyes are growing shiny with pity for himself and his hard life. "I'll *tell* you. The problem is really those MADD bitches! Dyke Bitch Mothers Against Men Having One Fucking Little Beer! And those same bitches are the ones that send their spoiled brats out to play in the street! Go where you want, Sweetums! You own the street! Those kids are just plain death traps!"

We were speeding again, and on these residential streets sure to get popped. The image of that kid that had thrown me so hard was gone just like that. I realized that my chump here was a lot more emotional than I took him for, and I had to get a grip on him. There's a liquor store ahead, and I shout:

"Pull in here! This one's on me!"

I got a flat of Beam. We sat in the dark corner of the parking lot and took the top half off it. I chopped out some chubbies from my fifty percent stock and got those up his snout right quick. I could see right away that Leon felt this was much more like it. I got back to work, piping him some gee-wow rap about the heavy action he'd seen, smoothing his feathers. Told him studies had shown little boys were suicidal, that it was an instinct in them, Nature's way to control population.

"I'll tell you the long and short of it," Leon says. "He came barreling straight at me outta nowhere! He hit *me* head-on!"

Well, suddenly the weirdness happens again. Suddenly there's the kid in my mind, and he's so detailed it's unreal. He's like coasting toward me on his bike, and I can see the blond fuzz on his earlobes, can see how his left tennis shoe is just starting to come untied. I see him coasting toward me, then his eyes go wide and stark like he suddenly sees *me,* and it terrifies him.

It rattles me. I fight it, but I've got to say something, got to check it out. I ask Leon, "That Cray kid, was he blond? Was he wearing a tanktop and a Bart Simpson button when you hit him?"

What the fuck was I doing here, saying what I just said? Leon looks like I just punched his face. "How do I know? I told ya, he came at me so fast you would'na believed it!"

I tried to pretend I was making a joke—I mean, *all* little kids wear tanktops and baggies, right? I chop jumbo lines and give both our noses and throats the freeze that refreshes. I pumped him more strokes, tell him he's a dude that's truly seen the hard-ass side of life exsettera.

Here's Leon's Bank. We coast up to his ATM. But he's acting dispirited. He's slow pushing the buttons, hits the wrong keys, and curses. I realize I've got to change the mood fast or my chump's going to deflate on me. It was that goddamn *sign* that had queered the whole mood.

Right there, Inspiration spreads its wings in me. It lifts me up, and I know that the situation is saved and the rest of Leon's cash is mine.

"You know what really pisses me off? It's that fucking *sign,*" I growl to him. "You know what we should do, man? We should steal that fuckin' thing, take it out in the fields, and *burn* it."

Touché! This really nails my chump's G-spot. The deed is just his league. He would be too chickenshit to do it—even to think of it—alone. With me he's up to it, an actual adventure, and it means he'll have company that much longer. He keys his ATM like a maestro and gives me the cash for the rest of my doctored stash then and there.

We do more blow—*he* does a lot more, I fake it—then we slam more hootch and cruise back to the scene of his killing, and the site of its plywood marker. Now that I have his money, I would dearly love to get right back to my ride and be done with him, but the deed at least can be quickly done. I saw a pair of parrot-beaks in his truckbed that could snip the sign's wiring.

And so they do, though of course Leon does it like a numbnut. Standing on the roof of the truck, he snips through the upper wiring first, so that the plywood topples forward, and bruises and bloodies his forehead. Seeing that happen gave me the strangest feeling of . . . delight! Like he was the fighter I wasn't rooting for in some bout I was watching. *Ha! Gotcha!* was exactly the feeling it gave me. This feeling was so sharp it bothered me. I mean, I had what I wanted from him, the cash. He was easy money to me, nothing more. Why was I *giving* a shit?

We got the sign in the bed. I was getting this strange vibe of isolation—I mean out *here* in the middle of this huge suburb. Window lights were glowing out to the horizon, TVs murmuring within, but the silence was so total. Somehow I realized it was the signboard in the truckbed that was creeping me—as if it was a tombstone. No! As if it was a corpse itself. Those miles of people in their living rooms all around us seemed like . . . on another planet.

We started driving back out of town. Leon one-handed more powder in his snout and booze down his throat as he drove, a fierce humor in his glittery eyes, a gaze that got more fixed and more fierce as we wound through the ex-urbs and out into the open fields.

I was lulled somehow by the ride. The dark countryside seemed right streaming past, isolated houses, farms, hedgerows in moonlight, the big sign bouncing softly on the junk and tools in back . . . until all at once the landscape seemed alien. Definitely not the way we'd come in.

"Leon," I say, "where we goin' here?" I'm trying to keep it humorous, but I'm really pissed. There's only a few roads *out* there in that country stretch west of town, and this road didn't look like *any* of them.

"There's gotta be a crossroad up here—I'll hook a left." We were both feeling pretty disoriented. I grew up around here, knew every yard of pavement in the county, but not this road.

Then Leon goes, "What's *with* this bitch! I've got her *floored!*"

And I realize we're definitely driving slower. It's not just the truck. Leon's *voice* sounds slower too, slower and a little deeper. Then I go, "What the hell was that!"—and I realize *my own* voice is deeper and slower too but I hardly notice it because I've just felt something move—something weighty very definitely move back behind us in the truckbed, and Leon is gaping at me and I know he's felt it too.

"Stop, for chrissake!" I tell him.

We get out of the truck. There's not a headlight in any direction, nor a house—just trees and fields stretched out under moonlight so strong it throws shadows. We look back in the bed, keeping our distance from it. And I swear to you, swear to you, out of nowhere, there's no wooden sign in the truckbed lying on the heap of tools. There's a *naked body* lying there! A small body, a young boy's, and it's all smeared slick with blood that looks jet black in the moonlight. I swear to you here and now, a naked kid with his head half crushed.

I'm like hypnotized, watching the blood leak real slow down through the hair of one of his sideburns, thinking *Christ this kid's still bleeding*. Then I nearly wet myself because the kid *moves!*

Then Leon is shouting *Help me!* And I realize Leon is climbing into the bed, which is what makes the body move. *Help* this chump? I hold my hands up and step back. His eyes are wild. His face is like a pig's that's being slaughtered. He picks up the corpse, staggers to the edge of the bed, and pitches the kid onto the shoulder. It lands with a grisly smack and a knocking of the skull and joints like a quick little drum-riff.

"For Chrissake let's get outta here!" I shout, but it comes out slow and echoey and not like a shout at all. We jump back into the cab but it's not like jumping, the air we move through's like molasses. I pull the door shut and it's so heavy-slow to close. "Floor it, asshole!" I shout in my rubbery voice.

We start forward, but the field doesn't stream past us the way it should. The trees are going by one, two, three, four. I turn to shout again at Leon—it takes a long time to aim my face at him. I see his lips are hanging loose and spitty. His gasping blows the spit out into a bubble from one corner of his mouth. The bubble pops and I see all these glittery pieces of spit flying slow slow motion through the air.

I turn my head to look back through my window at the corpse, turning and turning my head like it's taking forever, and I see the corpse on the shoulder not two truck-lengths behind us yet—see the corpse *moving*, getting onto its feet, and starting to come after us!

One of its thigh-bones is broken and its end pokes out through the meat of the leg—pokes out and in, out and in with each stride of its running—but it's moving near normal speed, you see, while our truck and us in it are inching through molasses.

I start to turn my head to shout at Leon, but my head moves so incredibly slow I decide I'm going to just open my door and jump out of this fucking truck altogether.

But I'm still just turning, turning, only now getting my hands on the door, when the truck shudders. Something has jumped into the bed behind us.

Leon's gripping the wheel for dear life. His mouth starts opening, strings of spit growing longer, longer between his lips, and there's a rattle of something heavy being pulled from the tools in the bed—all these sounds happening at real speed, you understand.

WHAP-CRUNCH—the rear window sprays safety glass in like buckshot. My face is all cuts, but the blood has just barely started to slide out of them when a big pair of parrot-beaks pokes into the cab between Leon and me.

Nothing slow about those parrot-beaks! Two quick bites—*CLACK-CLACK*—and they bite clean through both his wrists. So swift that lopping! But so slowly, slowly do Leon's two wrist-stumps come away from the two hands still gripping the wheel, and so slowly, slowly do two fat mushrooms of blood sprout out of those stumps! So slow his blood, it has not sprouted two, three inches high from his stumps before two much smaller hands shoot into the cab, seize Leon by the hair, and haul his whole big body backwards out the window-frame.

I'm sitting still trapped in slow-time, watching the big fat blobs of blood still hanging on the air, gradually stretching out as they started to fall, watching Leon's fingers come loose on the wheel and his hands tumble onto the seat, fingers twitching like dying crabs, while meanwhile, back in the truck bed, things are happening in real time, to judge by the sounds. The sounds come thick and fast, ugly sounds, sounds of metal and meat, clicking and clacking and hacking and chopping.

Believe me, I jumped out and started to run—still in slo-mo, but actually getting two, three strides from the truck, when *wham,* I'm knocked flat on my face.

What cold-cocked me? I don't *know*! It *couldn'ta* been Leon, not with what was happening to him! It *had* to be that kid! Crazy as it sounds, it had to be!

I don't *know* where he went! I don't *know* from fingerprints! I was in the goddam truck, that's all . . . !

King Gil Gomez and Monkey-Do

"Gil Gomez and Monkey-Do" is a humorous novella, a twist on the ancient Sumerian Epic of Gilgamesh. As Enkidu dies in the original, Monkey-Do also meets his fate in this version. Gil Gomez mourns the loss of his friend.

Dedication

I dedicate this story to the anonymous poets I stole it from, feeling doubly safe in so doing, as there is no way they could possibly catch me now. And, as anyone must do who loves this tale, I gladly acknowledge a profound debt to the library of Assurbanipal in Nineveh, as well as to the generations of great and modest scholars who have grappled with its cuneiform treasures, not least among whom is N. K. Sandars, from whom I have benefited greatly, to put it mildly. But most particularly, I would like to give thanks to King Gilgamesh of Uruk and to his friend Enkidu, without whom none of this would have been possible.

—The Author

I

This is the story of the Great King Gil Gomez of Ureek, whose father was the Good King Giles Gonniff of Ureek, whose father was the Grand King Gulls Gimmick of Ureek, whose father was the Grim King Growlz Gimme of Ureek, who first *built* Ureek from the bricks of formerly environing cities, which the Grave King Growlz and his army energetically erstwhiled. This was a great dynasty, but all the deepest scholars of that era agree that the days of Great King Gil Gomez himself were the true Great Old Days of Ureek, and that he was the greatest of the many estimable kings of his line, as King Gil on his own behalf has so amply testified to posterity in the abundant monuments of brick and stone he has left behind.

Moreover, King Gil—with all his tremendous personal stature and charisma—was agreed by all the *gods* to be the chief of their subjects upon all of those river-braided plains. They admired him most especially when they saw him out driving his Ride through downtown Ureek at the height of the rash hour on Main Dragon Lane—when he sat the saddle of that prodigious vehicle, with its bossed razzles, chrome-edged swoops and platinum gaspers on all four squirts, just steering his casual way through the sunny din. At such times King Gil was splendour itself. You couldn't touch him for ease or flash as he tilted the wheel with lordly aplomb, and the immortal gods thought him the finest recruiter they had in the field.

Indeed, in the job of wreckreating their creation for them, King Gil was almost too energetic. True, he had enlisted his people in the raising of flatteringly prodigious monuments to the gods' divinity—votary mountains of zig-zag brick, and the like—but he was generally so amped up behind his projects for the city's glory that he showed signs of gobbling up his own population in the process. He had taken to funnelling oldsters past a certain age into the facile fuel vats, was plugging all the young sparks into the high-powered machinery of the army and state troopers, and was using them with such abandon that a serious shortage of that group was already impending, and he was even said to be claiming King's Rights and lube-ing the local nubiles with the royal oil on their wedding nights.

So the immortals agreed that the King's great potential had to be pulled into line, to gear him for some truly big-scale wreckreating they had in view for him. A way to trim his horns was thought up. The gods proposed a custom-made man to pose a counterforce to King Gil's friskiness, and no sooner had they proposed this than they set about custom-making him. They made him hairy. They built him big and broad. He had a spine like an I-beam and shoulders like unfolding wings. In either arm he had the shove of a bulldozer—though he wouldn't have known what a bulldozer was—and before his gnarled and wily feet the roughest mountain gorge was as a highway—though he wouldn't have known what a highway was either, as he was utterly innocent of humanity and the wonders men had wrought. He shared the world and ways of the animals, and elbowed in for his place at the waterholes with the hooved and hairy herds.

And that was precisely where one of the King's wardens, out protecting King Gil's animal, mineral and vegetable rights in the surrounding plains, first spotted him: jostling a small knot of Titanotheres out of his way in his eagerness to drink. The warden stood observing this simple-minded anthropoid ruminant for some time. When at length he drove back to his station, he had a faraway look, like a man just returning from a long cruise in the hurricane belt.

"Jake," he said to his captain, "I know what's been trashing our mammoth-traps in the south sector, and chewing through our barbed-wire perimeters."

The next day he took Captain Jake out to the waterhole. The brute came back, and they both watched him from inside their armored van. Captain Jake said:

"That's the biggest, strongest-looking, hairiest son-of-a-bitch I ever saw. We'd better go tell the King."

Now when King Gil came out for his look at this new man, he was impressed and delighted. He watched for a while, and then threw his arm around Captain Jake's shoulders and strolled him off to the side.

"You've done a great job so far," he said. "Outstanding." He tucked a bill into the captain's breast pocket. "Now I want you to get a good woman out here—get Scarlot from uptown—bring her out here and get them together. Then get him cleaned up and send him to town."

The King spun off in his ride and the captain got on the horn to Scarlot. Scarlot was a very good woman indeed, entirely up to the work, but when she got to the waterhole the next afternoon and saw the job she had cut out for her, she sighed.

"Holy shit," she said quietly. She took a deep breath and squared her shoulders. She ungirt her loins and other peerless parts, and advanced.

"Hey!" Captain Jake called. "You! Big monkey! You see?"—and he pointed vigorously to Scarlot, already wading out.

The new man looked, and then looked harder. A new light bathed his benighted face. His forehead bulged as new spaces opened in his brain. He looked back at the captain and nodded. A huge, rusty voice broke out of him:

"Monkey see!"

"Now," the captain cried, making coarse gestures with great vigor, "monkey *do!*"

And the giant nodded, slowly at first, then more vigorously as Scarlot waded toward him, parts softly joggling.

"Yes!" the monster roared, afire with new purpose. "Monkey *do!*" And he sprang to meet her.

And for three days Scarlot gritted her teeth, hung on, and purely copulated his brains loose. On the fourth day they slept. The captain came in early to wake Scarlot up. It was time to clean up this Monkey-Do.

Not only was Monkey-Do very big and very hairy—he wasn't the least bit hygienic in his ways. Far from it. He ate with his fingers, talked with his mouth full, never flossed his teeth and farted when it felt good. He was careless with property too, and anything he'd handled even briefly looked like it had been dunked in mud and then used by a pride of lions for a scratching post.

He had more than forty pounds of ticks and fleas distributed over his body and even at his best—downwind on a gusty day—he smelled like a medium-sized barn in mid-August.

So they sandbagged a bend in the river, made a small lake and dumped several truckloads of powerful industrial solvents into it, and then lowered Monkey-Do into it with a crane. After that they set him to run a few hours at 78 rpms in the tank of a cement-mixer they'd filled with TSP and boiling water. Then they laid him out and used a pair of rakes on him. Finally the woman sat down to him with some tinsnips and a five-gallon bucket of Brylcreem, while Captain Jake went back to town for some accessories.

When they were done with him, Monkey-Do was a dazzling sight. He smelled like a bale of begonias and looked like a walking pompadour. He wore a pair of two-tone, high-rise, neon platform shoes, contour-tailored flare-leg mink slacks with automatic pockets and noiseless magnetic zipper, a tigerskin top hat with a meter-wide brim, and a form-fitting moneybelt tastefully styled in velvet and ferro-concrete. Meanwhile, as she was decking him out, Scarlot enlarged him on servilization with all its concomitant wonders of sliced bread, bottled wine and facile fuel, and by the time the trio were road-ready Monkey-Do's jaw was sticking halfway out of his face with a noble resolve to advance and embrace this godlike race and its marvelous ways.

And so it was gladly that he finally stepped with his friends through the big main gates of Ureek—rejoicing in his heart to enter the splendour of their frame. The city was already assembled in bleachers on either side of Main Dragon Lane. A brilliant banner arching over his head proclaimed him—to a roar of greeting from the populace—"The Challenger." And, facing him from across the concourse, was King Gil Gomez seated in his Ride.

In short, the battle was on, and Monkey-Do rose to the occasion, exulting as he strode forth in the honor done him by proclaiming him a royal challenger—challenger to *this* king, no less, so dazzling in his shining, throbbing, thrumming Ride. And thus honest Monkey-Do advanced to combat with open arms, eager to embrace it. And neither did the Great King Gil flinch aside from this moment of encounter, but boldly gunned his Ride and charged bumper-on, fearless for his person in the impending fray.

They met with a thunderous concussion which shivered up through the footsoles and posteriors of the rapt populace. Monkey-Do actually staggered a bit at the impact and stood astonished at the power of this matchless King. But he would not play the poltroon and rejoined the fray. Again they met, again their fury was as thunder on the plains. Monkey-Do was even more staggered than before, and a deep impression of the King's splendid power was formed in him. He understood that this King of Ureek was verily a *king* of kings, and had been marked out to have a great impact upon the world of men. And still, after the shock of two encounters, the dauntless monarch was battle-keen, and wheeled and charged again. Monkey-Do, dizzy with admiration, leapt forth to meet him.

And for a third time their encounter was thunderous, and the people were jostled by the power of it, and the wine sloshed out of their cups. And now Monkey-Do was really moved. "Great King!" he cried, "truly your strength is beyond compare!" Then he fell flat on his back, sending up great billows of dust that covered the bleachers and set the citizens coughing. Thereafter, the partnership of those two heroes was sealed.

For from that moment on, Monkey-Do was completely devoted to King Gil. The more Scarlot showed him around Ureek, the more the King's set-up stupefied him. He swore his jaw would need a second hinge to sing the city's praises adequately.

"Scarlot!" he'd shout, snatching her off the ground and shaking her for emphasis. "Was there ever such a thing as this city? Whole rivers are sucked down to slake her thirst, then sewered back seawards to cleanse her giant bowels! Whole empires of grain are a snack to her threshers and scythes. And look at the hills—though of course the gods were their makers, they just left them out under the wind and the storm to be chewed down to dust. And see now! The dust has been bricked, the hills are built back up into the sky! See Ureek, bone of their bones, and framed as well from the bricks of a hundred lesser cities, shaped in their turns from even more ancient hills! And the plains? The gods left a desolate ocean of nowhere sand and soil, but now a thousand leagues of King's highway reclaim the waste, net it and tie it together, force it open to millions of godly men and women ardently urging their majestic rides, all roaring and regal, all going somewhere! What a city, Scarlot! What a King!"

As for King Gil, he was extremely partial to Monkey-Do from the first, and he immediately made him the Royal Sidekick. For one thing, he liked Monkey-Do's attitude. For another thing, he could make good use of Monkey-Do's strength. Because Gil was a working king, a real go-getter, full of projects. He had a trick, which Monkey-Do came to love, of staring at him dead-level for a long, pregnant silence, and then thwacking him on the shoulder and saying zestily:

"Doody, we've got a *job* to do!"

A *job* to do! To Monkey-Do it was like a high, sweet horn-note blown through his spine, for when King Gil sounded it, then the two of them would go down to the Royal Arsenal. There, it was always the same—they took off their tools. King Gil backed out his awesome battle-ride, which was named Doom-Buggy, and under whose treads the earth groaned aloud as at the grinding weight of seven catastrophes. And the valiant Monkey-Do took down his pickaxe, which was of the weight of seven bulldozers and which was named Wall-Wrecker, and Death-of-Cities; and likewise he took down his mighty wrench, whose torque was the torque of seven cyclones, and which Monkey-Do (and everyone else) called Loosener, and Death-of-Locks.

And then they and the troops set off down one of the royal speedways to wherever it was they were scheduled for some executive action in the foe-realm. Once they got there, there was much to be done. First, contact had to be made with the local intransigents, their reservations had to be overcome, their objections razed and their defenses lowered and all the obstacles they presented to the sackcess of the King's mashion had to be smoothed out. Altogether it was noisy, dusty, bright red work, and it wasn't over even when Monkey-Do had unbolted the last gate and leveled the last gatepost. There was still the local citizenreap, who either had to be baled to feed or chained to tend the facile fuel vats in one of matchless Ureek's smognificent refumeries, and both the mulching and the manacling were equally gruelling dirties.

But Gil was a can-do kind of King, and his Doody was doughty, and in the busy days of their heroic teamwreck some fine, proud cities of those river-braided plains came to dust and rivered—brick by brick along the speedways—back to ever-loftier Ureek, that ever-more-peerless-pearl of cities.

II

But good King Gil's heart was unquiet. One evening he and Monkey-Do were up in the penthouse of the ziggurat, and while Monkey-Do was busy exclaiming over the magnificence of the city-wide view they had, King Gil was inclined to be moody about it. Monkey-Do was enthusing over how there were so many people in so many strange get-ups performing such a multitude of bizarre tasks, pumping such a diversity of goods and services through such a variety of streets, alleys, canals and conduits throughout the vast labor-inth. But the King just waved it away.

"A city, Doody, is, after all, anything you want to make it. As long as it gives everyone something to do, some things to get and some to get rid of, and gives everyone some people to obey and some others to boss, why, beyond that just what you *make* of it doesn't matter—just whether you make it a bigtime or smalltime operation, and by the gods, Doody, at least no one can say I haven't made Ureek into a bigtime town!

"Because after all, Doody, our basic *job* in this world is to carry on the work of the gods. I mean, they made the universe, sure, and I have the most total respect for their accomplishment. But you've got to realize that they didn't make a thing which hasn't broken down into something else since they made it—mountains to meadows, world-capping ice-lids to high, warm, summery seas. And they made *us* to carry on with the remaking of things which they so obviously intended to continue.

"And that's just what's been eating me, Doody. What have I done that's really *new?* Ureek's bigtime, sure, but it's still made of dust—still the same old trite, brick-baking, slavish imitation of the gods, who made the world out of dust to begin with. . . ."

He broke off and looked down at the river, and both of them watched a little logjam of paupers' bodies drift by the city wall, buoyed by cheap cork floats spray-painted black, and festooned with tawdry wreaths from the mortician's bargain shelves.

King Gil snorted and said: "That's what I'm talking about! Look what a trashy end the gods assigned mankind! To go wheeling willy-nilly, chilly-nullity all floatsam-jetsam down the world-sewers! A great man has to soar *above* such dirty triviality. I mean, after building the walls of Ureek so high, I'm standing too far off the ground to just complacently pull it over me like a blanket when my so-called time comes!

"So by all the appropriate gods, I'm going to do something new, something really big. We're going to rise above this trashy conclusion everyone else is facing, Doody. We're going to get a new material to build with, and build a new kind of power with it—build two new wings to Ureek out of splendid new material so that our fame will outsoar the most immortal name any city has yet made! Doody, we've *really* got a job to do. Because we're going to the everliving Mountains and we're going to bring back from them every last everliving tree from old Lumberdaddy's everliving forest!" And the King pointed as he spoke to the great mountains just visible on the darkening horizon, at the very rim of the world of the riverplains people.

Monkey-Do jumped to his feet and said very earnestly:

"Oh my! Gil-boss, I truly wish you wouldn't set your mind on that particular plan. Oh I really do! I've *seen* that forest, Gil-boss, and it is a bad-ass forest full of the biggest, gloomiest, twistedest, most ancient trees this world ever saw. And I've seen Old Lumberdaddy too! And Gil-boss, he, most verily, is the biggest, gloomiest, gnarliest titan you could possibly imagine. He's got *standing,* as old as the earth! I honestly think that we don't want to mess with him, your Majesty."

"Doody! This isn't like you! Aren't you even *indignant* when you think of the wastefulness of this monster? How does he use the tremendous power the gods gave him? He's a tree-shepherd! Those mountains of material, those splendid green dynamos of power at his disposal—all he does is pump their energy up into the sky, spewing it into the void to stand as numberless and useless as the stars! All those trees do is stand and loaf in the sun! They should be *accomplishing* something for us! Be barracks or billyclubs for our troopers, or basinettes, potty-seats and cuneiform blocks for the babes of Ureek. Cut him down and truck his power to town, I say!"

"But Gil-boss—consider the power you're talking about! The power that pumps the forests out of the scaly bellies of the hilly heavenfloor! Old Timberfather is prodigious! Every leaf in the forest is a nerve of him. Every twig that a bird settles on is a delicate little muscle of him, flexing. Each toadstool of the clammy, covert billions of them is one distinct drop of his sweat. The cliff-cracking might of his Power Plant, his engines of vegetal fission, is kept humming in perfect harmony by mere governing glances of his sovereign eyes. And consider the multiplicity of his vision! All the quick, silver rills of snowmelt that stitch the green steeps, every treecrotch full of captured rain where sunwarmed larvae squirm to life—these are also his ever-wakeful eyes, that witness his infinite green text's unscrolling, and each leaf's particular self-declaration!"

"Bah! You are suffering, Doody, from exaggerative paranoia. This Gloompoppa isn't even a god! He's one of their mere subcontractors, an Elemental! Believe me, our boys up in Know-how have already been clued by divine Smashcrash himself. They've developed a special axe that will split him head to toe where he stands. I mean, this is no time for you to turn chicken, Doody, because this is the grandest job we've ever plundertaken!"

Needless to say that settled it. The new slogan—Fell the Foe-roosts—went city-wide, and the troops geared up for the expedition. They rolled off down the speedway in fine style, a hundred thousand big reaper-mills in the lead, and when they got to the end of the speedway the graders moved up front and extended it as they pushed till at last they reached the foot of the foothills of the Everliving Forest.

III

The reaper-mills deployed along the edge of the forest and idled there looking at its making a deep, foggy, restive music like a pack of faintly doubtful dinosaurs. King Gil and Monkey-Do likewise regarded the forest, and the King had a curiously emotional look on his face. For lo, the pitch of this hill was steep, and the earth of it was scabbed with ice-torn rock, and the trees grew dense and tall. High above, their tangled top-branches held aloft huge, ragged masses of darkness, like rude, paleolithic weapons poised to drop on intruders. And, as this was but the first of three foothills that lay between them and the *truly* huge mountains where Old Lumberdaddy was laired, every man of that army was much moved by the sight of it, as King Gil and Monkey-Do were likewise much moved, gazing from the bridge of the Doom Buggy.

Then the King woke from his revery. He whooped into the riot-horn and gunned his mighty battleride through three hurricane doughnuts and a cyclonic figure-eight, sweeping the chain-saw snarl of its engines out across the murmuring green steeps that affronted them. And the King's face glowed like a coal when he addressed the troops from his bridge, the bullhorn seeming to amplify his breath along with his voice and waft along the endless line the sweetness of that royal exhalation, an intoxicating scent like five-star brandy.

"There before us loom the foe-roosts," cried the King. "There, all massed and waiting to be possessed, are Ureek's vast new wings, ready to spread themselves and lift her renown aloft. Since we'll be starting with the bones of those wings, set your mills for big-gauge lumber first—headers and stringers are what we'll need, ledgers and rafters, beams and joists, pilings pillars and ridgepoles. It's time for us to get whacking, cracking and stacking. So now, in the name of all the applicable gods, we've got a *job* to do! Let the line advance and reap at will!"

So the reaper treads pawed the piny loam, and the royal army grunted and munched its way up into the forest. Their advance was slow. Each few yards, each mill must needs squat and grunt out big, steelbanded bales of four-by-twelves or the like from their bumbay doors. And on that first day they surmounted that first hill of the three that lay between them and the mountains where the giant skulked in his fortress, and when they had stopped at day's end, King Gil sat gazing at the sunset, and at the *second* hill of the three, and once again his face showed great feeling, as in fact did the faces of the whole army as *they* gazed at the forest before them.

For this hill's steepness exceeded that of the hill they had reaped on that day. Moreover, its trees were *very* big, exceeding the bigness of those they had ripped that day. Raftered up high in their monstrous, leafy arms, they held whole crooked catacombs of dead-cold darkness—snarled, whispery tunnels like the web of a nightmare vast enough to wrap a thousand royal armies in—as snug as a straitjacket—if ever it fell on them.

"You know, Doody," King Gil said to the Royal Sidekick, "this is really one bad-ass wilderness we're getting into."

"It truly is, your Majesty," Monkey-Do nodded vigorously, "as you said once or twice before."

King Gil nodded absently. "Mmm. And you saw Old Lumberdaddy when you were here before?"

"I surely did, Gil-boss. I saw him, no mistake about that."

King Gil again nodded absently. "What do *you* think about it, Doody? Because I get the feeling that this Lumberdaddy is going to be one truly big, bad-ass Elemental. What are your thoughts on it?"

"Oh my, I'm glad you brought it up, Gil-boss, because truer words were never spoken. Old Loambreeder, Old Timberpoppa surely *is* one bad-ass Elemental."

King Gil nodded mournfully. "Fix us a pitcher of cocktails, Doody. We don't want the men to think we're getting dispirited."

The next day the royal rippers advanced again. Their great cleated tracks chomped on the snake-scaled earth and their snout-scythes whickered, and the geared saws in their bowels grunted prodigiously, and the lumber bales flopped from their bumbays and whacked down coffin-flat, to lie in tidy churchyard rows on the stump-pimpled slopes. On that second day they traversed that second hill of the three that lay between them and the truly big mountains where the giant hulked and hammered in his tree-forge. And when the army stopped at the end of the day and the King sat back with a pitcher of cocktails to look at the sunset and at the *third* of those three foothills, he felt, as did every one of his men, even more moved than before by what he saw.

For the pitch of this hill was yet steeper than that of the previous two, and the earth of it was fairly dragon-scaled with rock. Moreover, the bigness of its trees surpassed that of any the army had ripped thus far, while down from the vaulted darkness that was caged in their uppermost branches came the sounds of an eons-vast zoo, the mumble and purr and creaking tread of every shape life ever took, restlessly rattling their leafy prison, waiting for full dark to descend and roam at large.

"Boy, that sun sure is sneaking away fast behind those hills," said Monkey-Do.

"Mmmm," said King Gil. Now that the mountains had bitten off more than half the red disk, the darkness was creeping down from those higher branches, and the King watched it with appalled fascination.

"And you feel how fast it gets cold up here too, Gil-boss?" Monkey-Do went on. "It's what I was trying to tell you about this place—it can really give you the creeps in a big way, right, your Majesty? What are you doing, Gil-boss?"

The King was getting up—carefully, to keep his balance—but with a great air of purpose. "I think I'm going to give Mom a call."

The King got on the horn to his royal mother back in Ureek, where she was chief of the priestly staff. "Mom? Gil. Listen, Mom, I thought I should let you know that this is one enormous, big, hairy, dark forest we're into up here. I mean, words cannot actually convey—"

"Calm down, Gillums dear. I've been checking it with the appropriate gods. Smashcrash, Sun of Know-how, has promised me that you've absolutely got the green light with that Axecelerator he gave you. *Don't worry,* he said—his precise words. Just go in swinging and you can't miss."

"Well, all right, Mom, though I still think—"

"Hush now and put Doody on for me."

"OK."

Monkey-Do took up the horn. "Yes, Mom-boss?"

"Doody, I want you to really get in there and do your job on this one, do you hear me? I want you out there in front of Gillums at all times doing what's called for."

"All right, Mom-boss—you can count on me."

"All right then. Goodbye, dear."

"Let's have another pitcher of cocktails, Doody," the King said. "I just can't shake this feeling that Old Lumberdaddy is going to be one bad-ass customer to deal with."

On the third day the royal reapers advanced yet again and began to traverse the third hill that lay between them and the truly monstrous mountains that gloomed beyond, where old Beampoppa skulked and puttered down in the deep Power Plant of the Everliving Forest. On this third day, their advance was yet more arduous than it had been on the previous two. On the other hand, it was far more abbreviated. For just at noon, at the forwardest point of the reapers' line, Old Lumberdaddy appeared.

He came out dead-on to the lead-reaper—prow-to-prow with it, so to speak, and his vast dimensions overwhelmed those of the usually huge machine. And as his head thrust out of the shadow-caves under the crests of the trees, he spread those enormous trees from his path unconsideringly, as a woman presses the reeds aside to ladle a drink from the river. His grey, glacier-savaged brow loomed down upon the reaper to inspect it. Out of those wind-rocked, oceanic trees his hugeness pressing forth was like unto the prow of the great Arkbarque of Old Float-on-past-the-tomb Tim—that ark which the whole (remaining) world lived in. In comparison, the reaper-mill looked like one of those little reed rowboats paupers go fishing in. The giant's eyes—two moons in total eclipse with fine, faint fire-lines around their rims—rose from the lead-reaper and scanned the semi-circling host of its fellows, and the wide slopes of locust-work that fell away behind their line.

All the reapers went mute in mid-grunt. The black steam of their sternpipes stopped, the last mass-blast of it lazed up into the blue noon sky and left the whole field frozen there a moment in unsmudged, sunny silence. This silence lasted while Lumberdaddy gazed, a stress-line forming in his jaw, creasing and crackling the millennial lichens bearding him. It lasted while the giant brought his hand into view, blazoning forth in the bright air the cyclopean grandeur of his make, for his fingers budded and branched, writhed and ramified like souped-up roots taking their purchase on the air. But the silence ended when he wadded the lead-reaper—with one curt squeeze—into a wrinkly lump of steel and damp, red splinters which appeared to be very little larger than a sarcophagous, or two average-sized fuel drums—an estimate confirmed when the giant hurled it at another ripper a mile down the line and put it right through the view-port of the pilot's cabin without damaging the viewport's frame.

Then the army raised a roaring and a grunting and a tail-smoke such as it had never raised before and, undauntedly regathering his wits, King Gil boldly blared the battlecry through the horns of his ride, while skillfully changing his pants with his free hand. Monkey-Do unbelted his wrench, Death-of-Locks, and goosed the engines of his battle-skiff, but though he did not shrink from the fight, sweat and tears in equal parts freely drizzled off his face and splashed onto his matted shoulders, and he was sorely dismayed.

"Oh dear, holy, sweet, simmering shit," he groaned. "Now we're going to eat it—oh now we surely are! I really wish you'd listened to me, Gil-boss, with all my heart I do. Look at him! The bones of his frame are like millstones—whatever he embraces is as good as dust! His mouth's the deepest death-swamp in the world—see the breath of it blasting our men's flesh all shaggy with mildew and rot! One gust of it makes garbage of our fiercest troops!"

The King nodded vigorously. "And see there, Doody? When he gets those sunflares in his eyes, see what one glance of them does to whole squads of reapers! They're rusting! Cracking and exploding in an instant into ancient trash, and their crews are turned to dungbeetles scuttling out of the debris!"

King Gil's face was also moist, dewed with the regal perspiration of a kingly concern for the troops. At least his large-souled agony was brief, because before he knew it—before they could move, really—the surviving tenth of their army had wheeled and retired, making remarkably good time over the newly-cleared ground behind them, rumbling vigorously downslope and away over the fresh-cut stumpstubble.

IV

For a long awful minute old Lumberdaddy just watched them go. Then his eyes flared—two flame-rings etched his pupil's rims—and the whole clattering retreat stopped dead, and every last reaper of that vigorously retiring remnant froze and fell mute in mid-grunt, then collapsed into piles of rusty scrap, whereafter the only sound left for the noon breeze to waft across the stubble was the dry-legged scrabble of the big beetles' panicked exit from those piles. Old Lumberdaddy scowled. He nodded once with satisfaction, slid back and seemed to disarticulate in the touch of those billion leaves, each one delicately erasing a single atom of him, till only the numberless leakages of sunlight occupied the vacancy he left amidst the trees.

King Gil was already on the ground, afire to be ready for any extraordinary personal heroics this might require of him, and now he knelt and hugged the soil with mournful fervor. "Doody! Another pitcher of cocktails!" Monkey-Do stuck a pair of straws in the pitcher and they partook, dispensing with glasses. At length King Gil was moved to pray—more loudly than distinctly, but in earnest:

"Oh you gods! You two-tongue-ing devenomtease! All this goat-grunt and bullspizzle about how we had it clobbered with one hand tied to our behinds! Lies! You *lied* to my *Mom!* You mated her meek me make this corpsed axeperdition! How about a liddle stinging reas*sur*agement? An auspecious dream—with some troothing sooths about how we're gonna get out of this alive?" And then he thudded gently into slumber.

Monkey-Do stayed awake. He did *not* want a dream, because he could sense the one he had in store for himself—a wormy, pestering sensation in the back of his skull. So he made another pitcher and spent the night pouring its contentments in a steady trickle down his throat.

Next morning, when the King woke up, Monkey-Do said: "Well, Gilboss, we've seen enough, right? We've already got enough wood for four new wings—let's pick up our stakes and go cash in our chips."

The King looked baby-fresh and bright as a daisy. "Ah, Doody, you're so charmingly, disarmingly naive! What's mere material to the power that *breeds* it? To get that, we push on to the Power Plant, as planned. Oh boy, Doody, you should have seen the dream I had last night! Our worries are over. I got the gods' go-ahead. So Doody—" King Gil looked him long and meaningfully in the eyes, then smacked his left arm round Monkey-Do's shoulders and dramatically pointed his right forefinger upslope—"We've got a *job* to do!"

To tell the truth, some of the old thrill was gone from this routine for Monkey-Do, but he nodded and gunned the Doom Buggy uphill.

"There I was, Doody," King Gil said, mixing another pitcher of cocktails while Monkey-Do drove, "on the ground, crying and kicking my heels against the dirt and shouting for some help from the gods, and lo and behold Smashcrash himself strolls right up to me. So I bellow: 'Oh great Smashcrash, god of know-how, go-how and glow-how, you can't let me down now! I mean you were the one who pumped up my ambition for this axe-ploit.'

"He looked so fine, so *sharp,* Doody! He was wearing these silver mirror shades that I'm going to have a copy made of for myself as soon as we get back to town, and he was wearing this really jazzily-cut asbestos toga, and he said to me in just the mellowest, friendliest voice you could imagine:

"'Hey now, Gil-dumpling, don't get steamed! Stew no more, I'll see you score. Old Smashcrash will splay some rays on this situation for you. Pop me your clutch and I'll get you rolling—I mean I *geared* you for this gig, did I not?' And I reached him my hand and he pulled me to my feet."

The Buggy had made short work of the last slopes footing Lumberdaddy's mountains and now was shouldering up the flank of those granite-father giants themselves. The size of the trees here put Monkey-Do's mind into a kind of stupor—the twist of their fissured trunks spiraled up like wind-scrolled flames, or huge slowscrews tightening deep into the sky. Up in their shadow-ceiling the wind rambled and gusted and muttered in every mood, and at the same time seemed like one stupendous inhalation of the forest's green lung. And always as he drove the buggy in its dodgy gallop amongst the giant's calloused shins, dead leaves rained—lead-grey, mud-brown—around them everywhere, like wornout pieces of the ancient gloom itself.

"He was marvelous, Doody—there's no describing this perfect sincerity he radiated—not the least bit conceited or phony to me. He looked at me with his easy smile of wonderful compassion and said:

"'Smashcrash reads your needs, gumdrop. Dim is grim—who wants to park in the do-nothing dark, unheard of, right? You want to sound your horn and shine and I've got the watts it takes for you, a sky-size beam-machine. Is that winurgy for energy eating you? Well, I'm gonna snap some switches on you—lend me your antennae and feature this transmission, and know that the glow will grow all over you and yours.'

"And then I saw this mountain and this big axe swung down on it and knocked it clean in half and the sun popped out of it—rose straight out of the halves and floated over towards Ureek, which I could see far off just as clear as a bell. I mean it hung right over the city and just flooded it with light till the city blazed like it was just one big pile of radiant energy! Then before I could even express my thanks, Smashcrash took my arm. 'There's yet more, sweet Gillypop, a further haul. The city needs expansion and you crave to spread your wings, but pine for new resawrces, right? Brick's hick? Plank's top-rank? Well, if lumber's your number just roll your globes on *this!*'

"And then, Doody, I saw this whole huge forest rip its ankles out of the rocks and start marching together down to Ureek on the plains. What a sight! They moved with this tremendous pomp and dignity, like legions of elemental volunteers, like an army of living seigetowers all gathering around Ureek to attend my disposal. It was all so marvelous it made me feel kind of . . . smallish—almost humble! Can't you stay in tenth gear, Doody? After all, you did put new brakeshoes on her before we set out."

Monkey-Do banged it up to tenth and, as they were plunging into the first of the high dark valleys of the giant's mountains, did some steering of their plunge that was all the more remarkable for his keeping one eye always on the Mightmeter, which monitored the root-thunder in the earth below their treads—the deep, slow drumrumble of bedrock broken by the probing vegetitans. Monkey-Do did not seem to be so enthused by the dream as the king was.

"So the forest surrounded the town, Gil-boss? How close did they gather around the walls?"

"So close, Doody, they could lean over and look inside the walls, which all of them did, or jostled and shoved for a chance to do, and some ran their leafy hands testingly over the walls, as if marveling at the prodigious city into which I was going to enlist their huge bodies!"

Monkey-Do nodded, flashed the King a glint of unease from his eyecorner. A little later he asked:

"Just how close to the city was the sun hanging anyway, Gil-boss?"

"So close that the city almost wore it like a crown, Doody! And the ziggurat seemed almost to be on fire with the pride and glory of it!"

The Mightmeter's needle began to thrash itself back and forth across the dialface.

"Fire up the root-router, Doody!" King Gil whooped, "and take us down."

They stopped the Buggy, got into the router and battened it down. Monkey-Do gunned it down the Buggy's bellyramp and rammed its snoutscrew into the earth.

Down and downer it gobbled them, termiting through a skein of huge and huger convergent roots. Down there, the earth glowed green and its loaminescence limned the sinus of their weasely way. Down there, the forest's anchor chains twisted, always tighter, toward the mountain's centerbone. Down there, the lesser roots soon coalesced to the primeval few, roots of the true gargreentuan leafiathans, and it seemed an awesome obscenity, nakedness so huge as theirs straining with the force of slowed-down tidal waves against the blind, wet, mulish density of Grandam Earth.

Then, as a rat might fall from a rafter into a roaring factory, they plunged through the rootweave roof of Great Lumberdaddy's Tree Forge, the Power Plant of the Forest itself. Monkey-Do hit their 'chute, and as they sank toward the floor, the heroes gazed upon Lumberdaddy. Furiously and soundlessly in the all-swallowing thunder of that vast machinery—he moved his hugeness in a dozen labors.

"Oh my," said King Gil Gomez in a deep, slow quaver, expressing a kind of tender woe. "Terrible is the glory of this giant."

"O terrible in deed," said Monkey-Do, his voice hoarse with mournful reverence. "See how barbarous beauty grows rampant from his vast arboreal frame! His brambled brows drip vines all gemmed with fruit—velvet molds and gold-haired mosses thatch his shoulders! See his craggy sinews strain to turn the torque-wrench, tightening huge roots into bedrock—such a wrench—it dwarfs a thousand Death-of-locks. And see him thrust like dipsticks into earth the ramifaction of his fission-fingered hands, root upwards to set with infinite precision the spark-gaps between the green electric blades of grass that blaze in their legions high over us under the sun? With them he oils as well the pistons—surging in their stony sockets—that drive the grarather trunks into the sky!"

"Yes! Even as he regulates the stuttering pumps engorging them with their green blood!" cried the King. "What rude globe-cracking vigor moves through him, Doody! What granite-splitting splendour swells his thighs, and cords with strength his forearms, python-sinewed! Are not his tropic loins bejungled with every form and hue of fruit and bloom? His musk is the smell of the tomb and of coitus, of rain and of warm wheaten bread!"

Monkey-Do had gotten the Axecelerator wheeled out of the router and set up to fire, moving dreamily as the two of them marveled. But now the moment had come. Lumberdaddy noticed them and stared outrage at them, and now the axe was ready to fling. King Gil stepped forward and returned the titan's stare with wide, astonished eyes. He raised his right hand and drew a mighty breath.

"Oh Smashcrash!" he bellowed. "You stinking lump of embers! You *conned* me—blew smoke in my eyes with that dream! You lied to me and now we're going to be annihilated! So all right! So you win! We'll forget about taking the giant and the power plant—just save our lives and we'll let all the rest go!"

Monkey-Do, seeing that the King was blinded anyway by his copious tears and perspiration, fired the Axecelerator and flung the axe into the base of the giant's neck, splitting open his chest down to the middle and laying him thunderously upon the earth.

King Gil heaved a sigh and thwacked Monkey-Do on the shoulders. "We've got one hell of a dismantling job ahead of us now, Doody," he said, indicating all the awesome machinery around them. "I recommend just chopping it to pieces that we can handle, and not worry about reassembly until we get it back to town."

Well, Monkey-Do was strangely taken with the beauty of those huge pumps and pistons and generators, and he decided to start with his wrench so he could touch the machinery and figure it out a little. But he'd no sooner laid his hand on it than he gave a howl and pitched off the scaffold down to the ground. King Gil helped him up and dusted him off, but Monkey-Do was shaken, and somehow not quite his old vigorous self.

"Ye gods, Gil-boss! You know what that machinery did? It punched a hole in my life! It tore a leak in my life through the palm of my hand! I tell you I can *feel* it, Gil-boss. My life is leaking out of a hole in my hand!"

The King comforted him as best he could. To try to distract him from this silly notion he asked him, "So now, Doody, what do you think we should do with old Lumherdaddy here?"

At this, the giant rolled his head to one side. Though his cheek was against the earth, his eyes seemed still as high as moons above them. Sluggish with injury, his jaw stirred, his voice fell out of the depths of his broken chest, and words tumbled toward the heroes, like spent boulders at the landslide's limit.

"You can't run my plant as I do. Heal me, don't hack me."

"You know, Doody," said King Gil, "there might be something to that—we could chain him to the ground to manage the plant where we rebuild it, harness his—"

"Take him back?" Monkey-Do howled, completely forgetting the royal prerogative. "Never! You know what kind of power is in him and his machine? I'm telling you, just touching that life punched a hole in my littler life, and it's draining away right *now!*" Well, King Gil could be big about things, and seeing that Monkey-Do already had the Axecelerator in hand he helped him with it, and together the two heroes chopped Old Lumberdaddy to cordwood, and then chopped up his powerplant and carried it piecemeal back to Ureek.

V

No sooner had Gil gotten these stupendous spoils back to town than he had the boys from Know-How all over them, thicker than flies on a midsummer mule-pie. Snouts down to suck up details, they scrambled and zigzagged all over it and then converged and caucused till the drone of their confabulations drowned the gunfire-and-chainsaws-sirenade of Main Dragon Lane downtown at the height of the rash hour.

At length they swarmed back uptown to their complex on Know-How Hill for a final sniffing and fingering over of each other's findings. They adjourned after designating a committee for the Preparations of the Preliminary Report on the General Drift, and a few days afterwards this chosen band of savants repaired to the royal ziggurat, where the King received them. It happened that there was, infesting every inch of the old Vegehemoth's machinery, an exceedingly vital mix of microflora which, in their chthonic metabolic elan, found a highly congenial medium in human skin and aggressively colonized it. Thus the savant who stepped up to the foot of the throne was not unscabbed on face and hands with eerily lush crimson and aquamarine lichens, nor were his brows uncrusted by phosphorescent orange algae, which lent his deepset eyes a faintly lunatic glow. He accompanied his handing-over of the written Synopsis with a brief spoken summation of his committee's findings.

"Some ways to use it, My Lord, we see. How the whole thing works is a mystery."

King Gil gave the savant and his fellows a long look of absolute candor. The King was widely and justly famed for his candor and sincerity in matters of policy and procedure. "Fellas," he said, "I am just as certain as I can be that you are going to go back up to Know-How Hill, and that there in less than two weeks' time, using this valuable set of insights you have gathered so far, and working as though your very lives depended on it, you are going to achieve a degree of development and productivity that exceeds my most wildly optimistic dreams. Here is an outline of my requirements."

Scant weeks later the city had half-a-dozen new projects rolling full speed ahead, fully utilizing these latest and greatest of all the natural Ureeksources the King had ever brought home. He had been very busy getting things going and suddenly one morning he realized that he hadn't seen Monkey-Do in a while, and that he now had a great number of things to tell him about. He headed straight over to the Sidekick's suite on the other side of the ziggurat.

He was unprepared for the spectacle that greeted him within. Monkey-Do lay on his bed looking terrible—big and jumbled as a train-wreck he seemed, with stale grey eyes and wearing a rain-shrunk skin from some ragshop. His best-loved comics in sloppy, futile heaps environed him, while a nauseous medley of smeary cups and glasses (antennaed with mangled, leaky straws), and vials of gem-bright pills and tinctures, dispensed the harsh, antiseptic perfumes of whores.

"Boy, Doody, you look like the skidmark in the devil's drawers! What's got you moping in bed like this? You missing dozens of tremendous new developments. I mean hey, do you *feel* OK?"

"Oh Gil-boss, dear Gil-boss—" Monkey-Do bleated in a voice of earnest anguish. "I feel like the dingleberry that hangs drying for all eternity in the devil's crack and which, when the world was young, *made* the skidmark in the devil's drawers."

King Gil laughed heartily and pounded Monkey-Do's shriveled shoulder, which, sluggishly, Monkey-Do rubbed with his rickety, stark-tendoned hand. "Wait'll I bring you up to date on the scope of these new goings-on, Doody!" Warm in his eagerness, the King spun the air-control knob to 'light frost.' "You'll be seizing your socks and raking your locks and kicking your sweaty bed a mile into the air in your eagerness to be out and about and see it all." Stoically Monkey-Do pulled loose comic books around himself as paupers will gather dead leaves for a fall night on the riverbank.

"Now I don't really want to drag you too far into the detailed theoretical bagatelle and the hired mathematics of it, so let me just put it as simply and clearly to you as I know how. First of all there's our whole new Farmed Forces, all made possible by the Breeder Repeater Know-How tinkered out of Lumberdaddy's gear. Essentially what it does is to make zygotopes—to engorge these ordinary, vacuous vegebubbles—engorge them with the power of fetusynthesis. Then once the soderasts and podomites have them planted, their multiplication starts and they produce endless numbers of tractorable vegetuplets—all stout-limbed and true, growing row on row and field on field. At last we can say that every plantoon of every branch of our forces is composted of troops who are grounded in the rootiments of Ureekian servilization, with deep grasp of her marls, manures and herbitage.

"But that's not all we've done with guided vegetal fission—now we've got the lumber-orchards going too! The trees have an abridged development cycle, edited of leaves. From their squarish buds thousands of yards of finish-grade millstock sprout straight as rulers—from one-by-ones to twelve-by-twelves, lapping, siding, tongue-and-groove all growing to lengths precisely preterminated by the calibrated pressures of their sap. Ureek's new wings are spreading up and out like sixty! Tens of thousands of neat, marvelously compact habitations for Ureek's new millions! Doody, it's simply . . . Doody? Hey, Doody!"

Monkey-Do was asleep. Though it was deep it wasn't a healthful sleep. Sweat ran off him in rivers while his tremblings and groanings set the statuary rattling and tapdancing out in the corridors.

King Gil was alarmed. By the time, hours later, that Monkey-Do awoke, he had his medical staff on hand and all the help on the whole floor tiptoeing around in felt slippers and shushing each other.

"Oh Gil-boss," Monkey-Do bleated, rolling his waxy eyes to meet King Gil's. "What a rotten dream I've been having! It was dark and cold and a stinking wind blew ashes in my face—thunder tumbled out of the sky like huge boulders that jounced on the earth and made it roar with pain. There I was on the ground, but I was *different*—a weightless, raggedy thing—and above me, with a clattering wing-noise, there came the Man-unmakers settling down towards me. *Whap-whap-whap-whap*—down they came, driving such an icy wind against me! They gave off an ancient, greasy, big-lizard stench from the wrinkled flesh of their working wings.

"They had claws as big and cold as the bumpers on your prime ride, and with these they crushed hold of my brittle little stick-legs—because I'd been turned into this meager carcass—a buzzard's carcass, with paperthin bones and parchment skin and dung-crusted tailfeathers, and with this terrible icy lump of hunger at the very center of my being. They grabbed me and snatched me up after them—I flapped in their grip like an old blown-to-rags umbrella as they whipped up and up through the blackness, and then down, down and down through a greasy, brown, smoky sky—down and down till we'd dropped to a naked brown world of dust and dunes and stony dirt. And there sat hideous old Crusherkillghoul, Gil-boss, crouched on a dust-dune. They flung me down at her feet. What a terrible sight she was! She gave me the horrors, truly she did! She wore a kind of glove that hid the top half of her—the skinbag of a woman's upper body, with two bristly feelers reaching out through the eyeholes—and they touched me and probed my scrawny, muck-crusted heart while it squirmed inside of me—but below her empty dugs you could see she was a huge, black, filthy fly, though a fly not all developed yet, because she had only stumps of wings, and her thorny black-staved belly paled and tapered down to a wax-white maggot's hinder half. Other maggots were there too—big as wolves—her squirming brood that nested near her.

"'Monkey-Do,' she said—her voice was boomy and buzzed at the edges. 'Monkey-Do, your new world partakes of you.' And one of the Man-unmakers tore the left drumstick off my scrawny body—I didn't even *feel* it, Gil-boss, just the tug of it. He threw the drumstick to Crusher-killghoul's brood and it sank from sight into their slippery wrestle. They snatched me into the air again.

"'Now, Monkey-Do,' she cried, 'you will partake of your new world.' And they swept me out over the plain and flung me down on dunes of dust with millions of other souls all frantically gobbling the ground they sprawled on. And I mean millions, Gil-boss! All the men and women that ever lived flinging the smoky meal into their gullets, all the kings that ever were, their crowns on crooked, tearing the earth's dry flesh and guzzling to beat the band, and I guzzled there with the rest, to smother an agonizing hunger like a dirty lump of unmeltable ice at the very center of me.

"Oh Gil-boss, I'm going to eat it! I *knew* it. I just knew what it meant when it first happened! The living, unbroken powerplant—it tore a hole in my lesser life when I touched it! I'm dying! My life's leaking out of the hole it made in my hand!"

"Aw come on now, Doody, you can't let these morbid fantasies get the— Doody, come on now! Doody!"

But Monkey-Do had passed out again. Even deeper this coma seemed—he didn't stir at all. All the rest of that day he lay without so much as a twitch. King Gil was frantic. He called his mom and she brought in her whole staff of meatmenders, all of whose nostrums produced no effect at all. That morning King Gil and his mom decided to employ emergency measures, and for the next three days they plied Monkey-Do's dreadful, spongy-grey inertness with their most potent available remedies.

On the first day they brought Monkey-Do's Treasure Chest out and enticingly deployed its contents around him on the bed. His chrome wristrocket with the surgical-tube rubber and the sling made of one of

Scarlot's G-strings; his skull-and-crossbones code-ring with the secret message compartment; his stomp collection of flattened, plasticized enemy heads. These they laid near him, along with innumerable other impedimenta particularly dear to Monkey-Do's heart—and yet their nearness caused not the slightest palpable stirring of that organ.

On the second day, they brought out his *Special* collection of comix, from the safe which he had marked 'Secret' in black paint. But these included several of the earliest issues of *Crunch the Barbarian* and *King Kaboom*—and nearly though King Gil wafted them before Monkey-Do's face, no slightest breath from his nose or lips stirred their pages.

On the third day, by which time Monkey-Do smelled very pungent, King Gil tried his most potent ploy. Leaning his face close to the spongy grey face of his Sidekick he cried in his most vibrant voice:

"Well, it's time to get up and at 'em, Doody, because, by all the gods, we've got a *Job* to do!" And he gave Monkey-Do a great thwack on the shoulder. Monkey-Do did not move, but instantly King Gil snatched away his hand and bellowed:

"Yow! Mom! Doody's shoulder isn't hard and solid at all! It's all *puddingy* and it's got *worms* in it! Ye gods, Mom, it's—it's so *graphic!* Doody's dead! Dead as a shitbug!"

"There there, Gillums," his mom said. "Come away now. Better Doody than you, at least."

"But that's just *it,* Mom!" King Gil shouted, flinging wide his arms to show the enormity of the concept—"Sooner or later, it *will* be me! Because we're all going to die, everybody, and that means *I'm* going to die too!"

King Gil was desolate. He gnashed his teeth, and pulled his hair, and wrung his hands, and didn't eat, and drank too much. His mom tried to comfort him but he was inconsolable. Then, just when she was getting afraid that he was really going to pieces, he turned to her with an air of great resolution and thwacked his fist into his palm.

"There's only one solution, Mom, and I'm going after it. Not *everybody* dies—Old Float-on-past-the-tomb Tim, who rode the Ark through the Deluge, *he* never had to die. He still lives with his whole family on the Faraways in the sea of death! I'm going to see him and get the straight poop on avoiding death."

"But Gillums, that means you have to go to the underworld, I mean, while you're still alive."

King Gil looked solemn. "Mom, the way I see it, I've got a *job* to do." The thwack he gave her shoulder unbalanced her a little, but she listened attentively as he went on. "I want to take off right away but I can't leave without giving poor Doody a fitting ceremony. Assemble the City Holdsters and the Board of Wrecktors, I'm going to deliver a beautiful lament. Oh, and get someone from Know-How Hill to write me a beautiful lament."

Thus it was that King Gil came to deliver his justly famous Lament for Monkey-Do before an assembly of all of Great Ureek's men of substance. Though every schoolchild knows those lines by heart, it would not be amiss to reproduce them here.

King Gil's Lament

Oh Doody, you're so undone, so derelict!
I'm wrecked with grief—with grief all Ureek's racked!
Could all your big life leak out of so tiny a crack?

Oh Doody won't you
Your undoing undo?
The Elders and I are a weepy crew,
All the Townsfolks' hearts are torn in two—
We're all crying our eyes out for Monkey-Do!
The Putrefacts tending the facile fuel
Almost forget to stir the gruel—
They wretchedly rend their rubber suits
And let the hot slop fill their boots,
They just don't give a hoot, they feel so blue!
All crying their eyes out for Monkey-Do!

Oh Doody please do
Your undoing undo!
For the Drainspectors down in the watercombs too

Crouch mourning on their re-hinged knees—
Their eye-nubs leak and mouldy lungs wheeze,
While the Ventlurks up in the airshafts grieve—
They're so busy bawling they can't work the flues,
The monoxides back up and no air is pumped through—
All Ureek is gasping and sneezing for you,
All crying their eyes out for Monkey-Do!

Oh Doody can't you
Your undoing undo?
In the Hoardhouses, Coinpimps and Cashpanders groan,
Distractedly granting mere paupers a loan,
And allowing defaulters to keep what they own,
While the Meatmenders fumble their scalpels and shears
And flood their client's incision with tears,
And must double the bill for his repairs,

(Stand crying their eyes out for Monkey-Do)
While down in the stations the city Po'lasbers
Still clutch by the collars their most recent captures
And dolefully drum on their skulls with their bashers
While in court the Cantsellers, Feeturners-at-law,
The Grabvocates, Liehards—all dangle their jaws,
Their jargon gets jumbled and sticks in their craws,
While the Fouluns and Offals and Refusees,
The Gorebags and Glandroids and their torturees
Incarceraped in our Penageries
All howl with one voice, "Oh Doody, oh please!
Dear Doody won't you
Your undoing undo?"

For we're groaning and sighing and crying and crying,
All crying our eyes out for you!
All crying our eyes out for Monkey-Do!

VI

So King Gil, in his tragic turmoil of mind, took to wandering the face of the earth, following his errant anguish over the wide unrulered land and uneroaded hills and plains. But even in his grief King Gil remained a gogetter at heart, and he knew that no matter how long and how wide he wandered the gods were not likely to guide him to his goal if he behaved like some moping do-nothing, just scuffing along with his hands in his pockets. So from the outset he was determined that he wasn't going to duck any challenges, or fail to make his mark on the world, even while he was searching for the gate through which to make his (temporary) exit from it. Thus it was that no wild beast that menaced his wandering path—indeed, got anywhere near it—found the DoomBuggy's royal guns either slack or slow in dealing out a kingly retribution. And thus it came to pass that big-shouldered Lions tawny as wheatfields, Tigers onyx-eyed and ermine-chested, Eagles whose wings flashed brazen, and Gnus and bulky Bears with the gait of wrestlers, Ibex and blunt-browed Bison, Oryx and Peccaries, gamboling Grazelles and slim-ankled Canterlopers, Shrikes and Shrews and Kestrels and ponderous, seamy Gonadons, Kites and Pronghorns, gliding Anacondors plumed with majesty, limber Lemures, Capybaras, ghoul-eyed Hyowlas, slothful, sinewy Pythophants, pig-tailed Torpirs, all banana-snouted, sadly shambling sly-eyed Sardonosaurs, Hippos and Jakals and Wildebeest, fugitive fleet Fanxes on their black silk paws, Kudus, Kimodos and Cakledires and sociable Chumpandas dangling like garrulous fruit in the trees, and ring tailed Slythes—radar-eared-hugging the boughs—that of these in their bestial presuming pride—of all these and many more besides King Gil's dauntless artillery made short work.

And how heartened he was to learn, when at last he did stumble on that awesome black gateway from the living world, that he had chosen the right policy to gain his passage through it. He was in need of heartening as soon as he'd seen it. So cold and rotten was the black breath that vented from that gateway's jaws of moldy stone that it raised every hair on his neck and left scarely any room for qualms about the two great man-scorpions guarding the gate, though the one now approaching him stood big enough to look him in the eye through the DoomBuggy's viewport.

"So *you're* the one that's been sending us all this *traffic,*" the guard said. "What are you doing with all that game? It's been a *stampede* through here lately. Have you got an army in there with you that you're *feeding?*" His stinger-bulb, bobbing cobra-like on his bead-string tail, stabbed toward Gil on the emphases, while the man-head cocked quizzically, torquing into a galaxy of wrinkles the gasket of throat-skin attaching it to the vast thoracic end-plate of the body.

"Well heck," King Gil chuckled with a modest shrug. "I suppose you could say that I ran into a little *trouble,* a little opposition out there, but it was nothing I couldn't handle. I guess I'm just not the kind of guy who likes to walk away from a challenge, no matter *how*—"

"I just can't get over it," said the guard, advancing. "I mean, what do you want here? You're still alive. Are you *sure* you're alone in there?"

"All too alone," cried Gil, his voice cracking. "Oh, the pain your innocent question probes! You see, I just recently lost my—"

But the guard, appearing not to feel the least bit dependent on King Gil for an answer to his question, had reached his two vast pinchers forth even as he asked it, and now he plucked the Buggy into two pieces, and both of these—very neatly—into several smaller pieces. Having completed this experiment and seen that no one besides Gil fell out of the vehicle, he nodded, satisfied.

"So what on earth do you want *here?*" he asked the King, who was still dusting himself off. "You're still alive."

"Oh magnanimous Gate-guard! I have to go down anyway. You see, mine is a heartbreaking—"

"Whatever," the guard nodded curtly. "You've done enough for us to rate a favor. Come on in. Mind your step going down—all the way there it gets darker and darker."

"You mean, just *walk* on down?" King Gil asked, allowing himself a rueful gaze at the tatters of his defunct ride.

The guard looked bored. "Well, we could send you down the usual way if you really can't stand to walk."

"I wouldn't dream of imposing! Actually I'm an avid walker." And with a brisk, firm step, King Gil walked through the gate and down the staircase.

The stairs were mossy, their masonry was ragged and gapped. In the darkness they gnawed like malicious, senile teeth at his sense of balance. Teetering, tottering, paddle-wheeling his arms for equipoise on a thousand invisible verges of vacancy, plunging down tip-toe a half-step ahead of falling, precariously capering, stiltlegging storklike, or pouring like a snake most intimately along a wall wherever his blind reach found one—in these ways King Gil made his downward passage through those utterly eyeless miles of feverish steepness. It was a staggering experience, but not half as staggering as the blazing barbarous plentitude of color that flooded him when he pitched out into the world the gods called home.

"Ye Gods, what a landscape!" he hoarsely honked, feeling yokelish for the outburst, but unable to bite it back. For all those hills and meadows were lushly brocaded with vines and shrubs which gemstones fatly freighted, wrought gold and clustered pearls. Everywhere he looked this lucre-fruit flourished, flashing and smoldering with lubricious light. The trees that towered here were ivory all inlaid with veins of silver, while over everything a swanky breeze luxuriated; surcharged with frankincense and cedarbalm, it gracefully dispelled the stench of the plenteous dungheaps of dead that reeked and festered everywhere beneath those latticeworks of jeweled verdure. King Gil, his face a study in bemused—nay, stupefied—cupidity, gorged his eyes forgetfully. Smashcrash, god of Know-How, Glow-How, and Go-How, stepped into the meadow with him.

King Gil jumped, then shouted with pure relief. "Yow! Mighty Smashcrash! Am I glad I found you! I wasn't sure how I was going to. You see—"

"Gillypop! Well *yow* yourself, your Midgetcy!" The god was all amiable concern. "You're a mess! What's happened to you?"

"Oh thank you for asking, Magnanimous Smashcrash! I'm all ground-down looking because I had to walk all the way down here because your guards just annihilated my ride up at the gate—"

"So you *walked* all the way down! My, how you get around, Gillums! Busy busy busy!" The deity's voice had a strange crackly hum to it which

King Gil could have sworn he was feeling on his skin, like insect feet. The god was inexpressibly charismatic-looking, standing there in his dazzling white asbestos toga, his calm, warm smile, and his shades dispensing from their fine-beaded half-globes rainbow flashes of the jeweled meadow. King Gil felt tremendously encouraged.

"O Smashcrash!" he cried. "The last few weeks have been just awful for me! You see, it's because Doody just died, as I'm sure you're aware—I mean died and festered right there on his bed! It was so *graphic,* Smashcrash! I mean I always *knew* about death before, but till then I just never *realized!* Nothing could make him stir! Finally I even thwacked him on the shoulder and said 'Up and at 'em, Doody—we've got a *job* to do!'—and not only did he not even move *then,* but his shoulder wasn't hard any more—it was all *puddingy,* and it had worms in it! It was *awful!* My mom said to me, 'Well, dear, better Doody than you, at least.' And I said to *her,* 'That's just *it,* Mom! Sooner or later, it *will* be me!' I'm sure you can imagine how I felt, Smashcrash, so finally I just decided the only thing to do was come here and explain to you immortals that I just honestly don't feel that death is for me, and to get the straight poop from you about avoiding death altogether, and getting immortality, like you gave to Old Float-on-past-the-tomb Tim and his family."

"Ah, Gillypop." Smashcrash's smile was a shade sad now; the prickly mellowness of his voice felt to Gil like a caress of eerie consolation. Strangely, the fragrant breeze grew murmurous and fitful as he spoke, and seemed to tug his words slightly out of shape. "It's just prepostumous, Gillums, this morbid festernation with your dustiny. You've still got plenty of time left. We're still in Dismember, right? Septomber, Sarcophagust, Marchuary, Ossuary, Mulch, Decaypril, Clay—yes, heaps of time for your disposal! Why worry?"

"Oh but Smashcrash, that's the thing! You see, once I really got to *thinking* about it, after Doody died, it *hit* me: no matter *how* long I have, once death *comes* it won't matter *then* all the time I had before! All that time that's *gone* won't be any consolation at all!"

"I can see you've really been clodgitating on the matter," murmured the diety, who fell to a musing study of his mortal companion. King Gil found that the breeze was taking on a hard-to-breathe quality—a subtle way of eluding his lungs when he tried to inhale it. And as, moreover, it didn't seem to cool him either, a copious perspiration began ripening on his royal visage. Smashcrash, his smile faint and meditative, reached forth a finger, scooped a dollop of that dew from King Gil's brow, and licked it up. His tongue had a surprising shape—bell-like, a fat, inverted blossom of flesh that engulfed his finger, sucked it dry and retracted in one quick flicker.

"MMMMMMMM," said Smashcrash with delicate gusto. "You know, Your Mudjesty, I really wish I could accompostate you, but Old Tim got an absolutely one-shot deal as far as I know. My sincerest advice is to just keep carrion on, do as you rotter, and you'll maggot through all rot. This little matter that engrosses you will come to an easy soilution."

"But Smashcrash, what about the fine job I've been doing for you gods, carrying on your work of—"

"You've been wreckeating things just splinteredly, Gillypops! We look down on your neighborhood these days, we hardly know the place! But you know I think maybe that's just your problem—you've been working *too* hard. What you need is a good stiff drink! See down there on the beach? That's Sister Sottery's place. I think you need to go in there and relax with a cool one and talk things over with her."

"Well, I just don't feel that I've gotten across to you—"

But in the very same moment that Smashcrash had indicated Sister Sottery's bistro down by the black-foaming surf, he had also transported (or rematerialized, for Gil couldn't tell which it felt like) the king down to the very doorstep of that establishment. Since he had no other immediate prospect but the black, rhythmically slobbering waters of that sea on which only one mortal had ever embarked alive, and since he definitely felt like having a good stiff drink anyway, King Gil went in. Sister Sottery was sitting in a big, well-stuffed armchair behind the bar, which was empty. She wore a hat composed of two green half-globes that clamped on halfway down either side of her face—fine-beaded, shiny half globes that threw off incandescent blushes of all the somber blood-to-honey-hues of the bottles ranked around her. She was very smartly dressed in a strapless, snug-fitting sheath-gown—an ample tube for her solid girth—made up of strung-together bones.

King Gil still had on him his standard field-kit of four lightweight artillery pieces strapped to various parts of his body, and with anybody less than Smashcrash himself he was in a mood to deal summarily, but he felt that in this particular situation, charm was the way to go. He took a stool.

"Greetings, Sister Sottery. Smashcrash just—"

"I know," she foghorned. "King Gil Gomez, am I right?"

"Yes! Then you *know!* Oh Sister, I tell you I've been just *so*—"

"Wait up, Gilly. First I want you to cut the dust with some of this." She rapped a flagon of wine on the bar between them.

"Oh my, thank you! Oh yes! Mmmm. That was delicious!"

"That's the spirit! Now here's another to get you started with. Just get yourself outside of this one now."

"Well actually I don't mind if—wonderful, thanks! Mmmmm. Ah yes!"

"Bravo, Gollypops! So now. Tell old Sis. What's the haps? Here, take another, you can work on it while you unfold your woes."

"Thank you! Wonderful hostess! Mmmm. Well, in a nutshell, Sipster, I'm just about at my wit's end over a problem that's been driving me grief-struck and half-bananas over the face of the world, and finally all the way down here. You see, my soulmate and sidekick Monkey-Do just died! It was awful! He just lay there for days and wouldn't get up, wouldn't *move!* I emptied out his treasure-box on the mattress beside him, and he didn't even twitch. I spread all his most treasured comics in front of his nose and his breath didn't even stir a single page of them! I thwacked him on his big meaty capable shoulder that was always just as hard as a brick, and it was all *puddingy* and had *worms* in it!—oh thank you! Mmmm."

King Gil paused thoughtfully. "Now I *knew* about death before of course, Saucer. Everything dies except your immortal selves etcetera etcetera. But with Doody it was so *graphic.* It really hit me then, you see. Mom said, 'That's all right, Gillums, better Doody than you, at least.' And I said right *back* to her, 'But that's just *it,* Mom. Sooner or later it *will* be me!' And to be perfectly candid with you, Souser, I really don't feel that death is for *me.* That's why I've come down here, to see if one of you might be able to give me the straight poop on the situation, or at least set me on my way to talk with Old Float-on-past-the-tomb Tim so that he can give me some pointers on how to get out of my dilemma."

Sister Sottery shook her head and broadly chuckled. She rose, marched to the shelves, and brought an amber jar and two shot glasses back. She poured the shots and sat saluting King Gil for a silent moment while the rattle of her gown chittered softly to extinction.

"Look here now," she said good-naturedly. "Death'senescence a mere formlaldehyde, your Moldjesty. If your memorial services you well it's the way we made you. Develop a sense of humus about it and carry on. Exsoil-sior! Above all don't get over-cryptical—at this stage of your life, what remains but the well-urned enjarment of your spoils? Try this now—a sip'llcureya. Skull!"

"Skull!"

They hammered back the shots, Sister Sottery's disappearing with a curious single slurping noise. In a mere second or two Gil felt the necessary eloquence to answer—which otherwise he might have despaired of—blossom like a spherical mushroom of thermal energy within his brain.

"Right, of course! Absolutely right, Sotster Saucery! That's how you *made* us. But then what about what you made us *for,* hey? I mean let's face it, you made us so that we could carry on with wreckreating the world for you so you all could take it easy, as we all know you had every right to *do* and more power *to* you. Do let's just look at what I've been been doing for you along *those* lines. Have you checked out Ureek's mighty walls and towers lately, her two new wings, her breeder reactors and the new radically loyal legions of vegetuplets they've made for us, hey? So what about *that* angle?"

"Now just listen, Gilly." Sister Sottery reloaded the shotglasses. Her cheeks glowed with ruddy goodwill. Her eyes lingered lovingly on the heroically molded features of the King. "What we need to concentrate on *here* is what really *is* the lot of mankind? My philosophy is, in your situation, descant, imbibe, enjoy, get paralyzed, and sleep it off. Look at the good sides of life. What about women, eh? Having a little woman to haul your ashes, and cook you up some nice worm grub, and wind you up in nice clean sheets? And breed you some little rug-rats too, so you can pass on to them and *their* decedents after them your putrimony, down to all pusterity! Hell, Gilly, you're a man inhume we place the deepest coffindents, a king of the most absolute extinction, and I've been very slab to meat you! I don't even care if you take my advice or not. You want to go see old Float-on-past-the-tomb Tim? See Urchin the Cabby. You can't miss his boat—it's just down the beach there, and I'll see you on your way."

Sister Sottery was on her feet and around the bar in no time. Rattling and chuckling, she flung an arm around Gil's shoulders and steered him out through the door. Pointing expansively down the beach, she thwacked him on his way, starting him off at a stagger.

"Straight ahead, you can't miss the boat! Fester luck to you, your Maggotcy! Warmest regards! Just remember that no matter how offal you feel you're going to maggot through just swell!"

King Gil found that, indeed, he hadn't far to go, but it happened that when he came to Urchin the Cabby's watertaxi, the boatman himself was up in the undergrowth answering a call of nurture, crawling over a corpse-heap in a copse. Hence when Gil approached the boat he was unprepared for the startlement which its meater caused him by darting snakewise at him from the stern with a clashing of its serrated jaws—for a bite of flesh was the fare immemorially ordained for all those who boarded the craft. King Gil's reaction was in quick accord with the vinous melancholy of his mood. He unclipped his belt-fed racket-launcher from his hip and reduced the meater to a few twisted shards of smoking steel.

Urchin came running back down to the beach. He was a small, stubby individual with fat red eyes and prickly black stubble all over his rubbery jowls.

"What have you *done?*" he came howling. "You big dim *shit!* You hulking dildo! That was my *meater.* Oh, why do they all come to *me?*" (This he howled to the underworld at large.) "Why does every dick-with-ears in the jungle have to come to *my* boat? I no sooner turn my back for a second than some bozo shows up and junks my ride! The fucking tub won't *go* now, so how do I get back to the boss? You better be good with a pole, chump, or your ass is trash."

"Oh 'steemed Urchin," King Gil said with an endearing smile, "howrya doing? Sorry about the damages, but you know it's sort of a lucky coincidence that you need someone to pole your boat, because it happens I've come all this way to *see* your employer, and I'd be happy to pole your boat, and as for being good at it, well just wait'll you see me in action!"

Urchin the Cabby stared at the king. His eyes didn't blink, but vari-colored smears of light flashed off them as his little round head, tight-mouthed, scanned the king up and down.

"Swell," he said. "Here's an axe. There's some trees. Go cut some poles."

VII

So King Gil poled. It was a very long journey, and the labor sobered him up considerably. A yet more sobering factor was that the poles he used had to be very long to reach the ocean floor and he found working with them to be tremendously wearying. Long and long across the inkblack swell he rammed the boat along, lurch by lurch. Urchin the Cabby, for his part, just steered and stared at the sea. At one point, when they were half an eternity or so from shore, he looked sourly at King Gil.

"I suppose you know you've lost me my job."

"Why that's. OK." King Gil gasped. "You lose. Your job. Come work. For me!"

Urchin looked at him morosely, then turned back to watch the inky swell.

Long and long Gil poled and panted, poled and panted, groaned, and poled and panted. And when at last they drew up to the Far-aways, there on the largest of those little islands, just as the legends said it would be, was the family encampment of Old Float-on-past-the-tomb Tim. The camp had a hobo-jungle look, all wedged-in as it was amongst the huge, bleached ribs and sprung planks of the long-beached Arkbarque.

As Gil poled them keel-deep into the beach, he saw Old Tim paused by a smoky driftwood fire, an empty tin can in one hand, watching their advent. He also saw Old Tim's wife—who had just stepped out of a narrow shack with a crescent moon on its door—similarly paused, and watchful. She had a long-handled fork in one hand, with several sausage-like objects impaled on its tines.

Old Tim was somewhat gaunter-limbed than Urchin, though just as prickle-whiskered. He was giving particular red-eyed attention to the pole in King Gil's hand but, after a moment, turned his back on his visitors. There was a small, rattly, liquid noise. He turned around again as the pair drew near, and set his can on the coals to boil.

There were plenty of the old couple's offspring sharing the great, gloom-vaulted derelict with them. Many of these were hanging around in the highest ribs of the crazy-tilted wreck, clasping their dizzy perches with an uncanny, seemingly effortless adhesion. King Gil's eye lingered on them as he took a seat on an overturned tub near the fire.

"Old Tim!" the king said with ready fervor. "It's really you! At last! I mean, at last I've *found* you! You know, I just can't help remarking how exactly like you all your kids look, I mean *exactly,* just younger is all." He was looking particularly at a young couple copulating not far overhead—she clutching with hands and feet the underside of a great keel-rib that formed part of the vaulted roof above them, and he clinging to her back. Old Tim's wife, a very gaunt and somber old woman, spat into the fire and watched it sizzle, scowling. Old Tim shrugged modestly.

"Oh, they're our spit and image all right. I mean they grow up to be our identicals, with even their thoughts in sequence with ours. And hell, they're all such breeders, they'd clutter up the islands with a pack of our simultaneous selves so fast it would make our heads swim. So most of them, just as soon as we have them we tie rocks to their ankles and drop them offshore. Can't kill our stock of course—there must be billions of them down there by now. Take a tea?"

"Sure," King Gil said uncertainly, taking the tin can that was thrust into his hand.

"Have a sausage," snapped Old Tim's wife. It didn't sound like a request.

"OK." King Gil took it by the stick it was spitted on, and with which she almost stabbed him. He sniffed the tea appreciatively. It smelled so nasty it made his eyes water.

"So. You got all this way alive, have you?" Old Tim asked. "Oh, by the way, Urchin, you're fired. You can stay to finish your lunch and then you can clear out for good."

Urchin, having just received a tea-and-sausage as firmly offered as Gil's had been, glared first at this snack and then at his ex-employer.

"Do I have to eat lunch first?"

"Absolutely You Bet!" Old Tim and his wife said simultaneously.

"Shit!" roared Urchin. He jumped up and kicked the log he had been sitting on almost a half-mile out over the ocean. Then he spun and kicked King Gil and, comparatively small though the Cabby was, his blow launched the monarch off his seat and rang his head against the broken hull of the Arkbarque some yards distant.

Dazedly, the King returned to the fire, gaping at Urchin who, his face screwed into a pucker of loathing, was sipping tea. King Gil was groggily remembering his racket-launcher, with which it seemed appropriate that he should chastise the bumptious menial, but then he had to take a sip of *his* tea, which Old Tim thrust on him anew, and the experience drove all else from his thoughts. He had never tasted anything fouler. The entire snakish tube of his innards—inch by inch—rebelled against the dram's descent. Tears coursed freely down his cheeks.

Old Tim drained his can and set it down smartly on the sand, smacking his lips. Thumbing at Urchin, he told King Gil:

"You know, he's always lived on it like the rest of us, yet he's *never* acquired a taste for it. I always knew that was a sign that he wasn't quite up to snuff—he was a stowaway on the Arkbarque in the first place, you know. I mean hey—it's a living, after all. We lay no changes on it. Our bellies just keep re-borrowing it to give our fingers and mouths something to do. How do you like the sausage?"

King Gil, after a brief, desperate consideration of strategy, swallowed it whole, and answered Old Tim with a convulsion and a pallid smile.

"Right," Tim said. "Now you can just spare us your preamble, Gilly. Your aim here is plain. You want to know how to steer clear, right? Evade the shade and circumnavigate the bier? Well, I'm afraid I've got—"

"He's right, you know?" cried Urchin, leaping up. "I've *always* hated the taste of putrescence! And now that I'm fired, you old fart, I'm damned if I'll eat this shit any more!" He flung down his spitted sausage. "Just go ahead and tell your everlasting old floodstory to him so he can pole my ass back to the mainland. I'm going to go on up and get laid, and have a decent meal for a change."

Old Tim was already beaming on King Gil the rapt smile of a man with a story all ready to tell. The King had a feeling that Old Tim was setting out to discourage him. He wanted to speak up, to steer the old man's discourse to more profitable channels, but he was still so unmanned by nausea that he dared not try his voice. Old Tim took up Urchin's discarded sausage and meditatively crisped it in the fire.

"You see, Gilly," he said, "your problem is you don't quite appreciate the immortals' attitude toward the question of your—or any man's—death. Urchin mentioned my well-known experiences in the Deluge, and I think you might find them apropos to what I'm getting at. Now I'm sure you're thinking that here I am, looking just like you or anyone else, a regular guy, and yet I alone in all the world am enjoying the leisure and pleasure of immortality. How did I manage it?

"Well, I can tell you that when I first got the word about the flood I didn't stop to *ask* 'Why me?' Oh no! I was taking it easy in my house when old Ea himself came hovering down above the roof and spoke to me. His voice came buzzing through the walls, rattling the rafters, saying: 'Tear down your house, Tim. Seven days from now it won't be any shelter at all for you. Tear it down and make a boat, a *big* boat, with the lumber. Get oil, asphalt and piny pitch, and caulk it tighter than a tick's ass. Fill it with your kin and kine and corn, and get inside and nail the hatch down after you. If anyone asks you what you're doing just say you're getting ready to move your family down to live by the sea.'

"Now, as to why the gods were sending the flood, at the time that was obvious to any man with a brain in his head. Since those days I've heard people give the damndest explanations, but the real reason of course was that mankind was just making too much noise. And it was a terrible racket, it truly was—as bad as the noise you people are making today, except that then the gods figured that the most direct solution of the problem was the best; that they'd had too much of a good thing and it was time to do away with us altogether. In the end they were glad Ea had spared me, and at the time I was so glad that I didn't ask any questions, as I say, but got right to work.

"We finished it with no time to spare. We were scarcely inside when the gods set things off. They kicked down the dykes of the nether waters—these waters here around us. Nasty, black and endless they came vomiting and geysering up to the overworld, churning out of every crack, sinus, shaft and fissure of the doomed earth, and licking in monstrous black tongues across the plains and into the valleys, swallowing nations like gnats and smashing their cities like cheap crockery. At the same time the Manunmakers crowbarred the locks off the cyclones' cages, and rolled back the huge hangar doors of the thunderstorms' pens—we could hear the wheels of those doors rumbling across the sky as we crouched in our tub, and we felt the rain start avalanching down. Rain in waterfalls! No man could stand upright, the strongest oxen's knees buckled beneath its downslaught and the Arkbarque was roaring like a drum around us. Soon her keel lifted and she began to float, and already the hills around us had begun to melt, and all life was erased from them.

"Well, the gods themselves didn't realize what they were letting loose. They fled in terror, all the way up to the ridgepole of the world-roof, and clung there shivering, astonished at the vast, ungovernable and uncreating power they'd unleashed. When the calm returned at last, and they could see again, there was a whole world-full of their disinherited servants, all bulgy and buoyant—whole, slow-jostling shoals of them aimlessly trafficking with the gilled and scaly plunderers of their erstwhile empires. They gaped aghast, and what they'd done began to sink in.

"Picture it, Gilly. When the Arkbarque finally settled on the mountainside, and we all came sloshing out onto that vast, smooth muck, the dead lay as thick as dates on a fruit-loaf, all curiously sprawled and plastered on the universal mantle of mud, clogging the ravines and decorating the naked branches of the trees. A feast for the gods all right, but a *one-shot* feast, and after that, very slim pickings for a long, long time! So when they found out Ea had saved us, why, you should have seen how greedily they gathered around us." Old Tim—involuntarily, it seemed, traded a look with his wife, and the old woman darkly nodded, looking to the fire. Tim went on: "And when we performed the rites of thanksgiving, and set the necessary suckerfices on the altar to cook, they swarmed over the meal as thick as . . . as *flies.*"

His voice rendered the last word with a curious buzz that made Gil's nape feel crawly. He struggled to clear his throat, and almost took a sip of tea to help, but stopped himself in time.

"Anyway, Gilly," Old Tim went on, munching his sausage thoughtfully, "what the gods learned from that was that it was much better for them to let life unmake itself, however slow and noisy the process might be. Let's face it, Gilly, the gods love suckerfices. They're carnographers and sarcotects. They made us wreckreators in the first place because they like novelty and variety in their suckerfeasts. You see what this means, of course, for your case. It's true that you've done some great things with your capital and all, but the gods are always looking for *new* infestors. And who can these new infestors infest in, if not your own—their predeceaser's—substance?" He paused to finish his sausage, and resumed in a rising, somewhat histrionic tone:

"For after all, Gilly, the world by itself is fingerless to unravel the still-nonexistent from its own fabric. Spoilers are needed to unzipper the limbless sphere and unwomb its embryonic future! Mortals such as we—or rather, such as you—have their proper defunctions and their—"

"Enough of this crap, Tim." Urchin was on his feet again. He looked at King Gil. "The drift of all this, dum-dum, is that it's no soap. Now I'm leaving. And if this yokel is coming with me," he told Tim, "it's now or never."

"Listen, Old Tim," King Gil managed to croak, "I really don't feel you—"

"Stop right there, Gilly," Old Tim said. He was looking scornfully at Urchin. "The wife and I have decided that we're not going to send you away entirely empty-handed. Urchin here, as the last act of his divinely commanded service to us, is going to take you back to the coast to the Sweetwater Rivermouth, where you'll find a little consolation prize waiting for you, for down under the water where the river empties into the sea is where the Juicy-Root Blossom grows. You just eat a few bites of that, Gilly, and your lost youth will be restored to you. Now how about that? That's fair enough, isn't it?"

King Gil beamed, clapped his hands and rolled his eyes. Urchin the Cabby also rolled his plum-red eyes, though not rapturously.

"You give me such a pain, Tim," he said. "You've always given me such a pain. Right. I'll take the Rube to Sweetwater and you can kiss my ass goodbye. Rube, grab your pole and come on."

VIII

So once more King Gil poled and panted, poled and panted, groaned, and poled and panted. He talked as well:

"Ye gods. Think of it. I won. Beat Death! Wonderful! *Hell* with death. Who wants it? The dark. The cold. Give *me.* The sun. That's what I. Wanta look at. Just look and look. Till my eyes. Burn out. I *did* it! Did it!"

To these and many similar effusions Urchin did not respond. He was sullen all the way back to the coast where they found the broad Sweetwater Rivermouth. This spread a great silver fan of sweet, upperworld waters a mile out into the inky onslaught of the Sea of Death. In the middle of this, without bothering to tell King Gil to stop poling, Urchin dropped the taxi's anchor. To Gil—as the latter was picking himself up from the deck—the Cabby handed two big rocks, and a leaky rubber hose.

"Tie these to your feet and breathe through this. Yank it when you wanna come up. It's down there. Jump."

King Gil was tremendously refreshed by that dive, or at least the first part of it. The water—cool and cleanly—bathed away the sour accumulations of both alien and personal substances that will, with time and toil, encrust even a royal epidermis. Speedily, however, he sank to where the pressure caused him serious discomfort. He hit the bottom and his hair splayed out like seaweed as he scanned with popping eyes the smoke-boil of sand he had kicked up. From the gently settling murk, the Juicy-Root Blossom emerged, as if sprouting before his bulging gaze. He seized its stalk and ripped it free, firmly embedding in his palm the numerous long steely thorns that decorated the marvelous vegetable, and thus ensuring his grip on it during his reascent. This he effectuated without delay, with a voiceless howl and a powerful tug on the hose. Urchin hauled him up without ceremony—or, indeed, any thought to the niceties of pressure-adjustment, and, three seconds later, had thwacked the King down on the deck. Gil, bleeding colorfully from his nose and ears, bent glazed eyes upon his plump, fragrant, dazzlingly polychromatic prize. Wonderingly, and not without gasping, he pried it out of his palm.

"I've done it," he gurgled in an awed voice.

"Right," said Urchin, poling them in toward shore. Coolly, he regarded King Gil's feet. "We've got a lot of walking ahead of us, dum-dum. You might want to take off those rocks."

"Actually *done* it," said King Gil, absently untying the rocks. "I've succeeded! Who would have thought? Who would have *dreamed?* I'm going to take this little beauty right back to Ureek. I'm going to walk right into the throne-room with it—"

"Watch your step, Gildo," Urchin said, as the King fell getting out of the boat. They started walking inland, upland.

". . . the throne-room of the royal ziggurat," King Gil said. "I'm going to proclaim officially the boon I've brought back to the city. I'm going to eat the flower myself of course, but first I'll get the boys in Know-How to whip up a synthesis for everybody else. Everybody. I'm going to *share* this boon with my people. Then, when I'm young again, the first thing I'm going to do is study all the classics, yes! This time around I'm going to master all that important stuff that I didn't appreciate the first time around, because Mom's certainly right about that one. And I'm going to have the whole Watercombs system re-engineered too, of course—I've put it off for too long now because it would have taken too much time. . . . And should I pick up Mechanics and Math too while I'm at it? Yes, I'm going to get a tutor in Mechanics and Math too while I'm at it."

But, measured on a universal scale of durability, what are the fondest hopes of humankind? King Gil proposed a great many other projects to himself in the course of that day's journey, and in fact talked unceasingly for the entire day, though Urchin set him a pace intended to discourage his conversation, such that they had covered thirty leagues by sundown when they made camp. King Gil took a seat by the fire Urchin had conjured.

"In fact I'm going to do away with the whole damned network," he told Urchin decisively. "I mean as long as we're re-wiring Main Dragon Lane we might just as well re-wire the whole downtown area while we're at it, especially since that fleet of air taxis we're going to build will need a whole system of re-charge platforms anyway. Now I think that's the right perspective to take on the job, don't you?"

"If you tell me one more thing you're going to do," Urchin replied, "I'm going to blow an eardrum. I've got to get some sleep. And," he added with an odd note of scornful emphasis, "so do *you.* So shut up and let us sleep."

Once he had fallen silent, King Gil himself fell asleep as quickly as Urchin. And here it was that ruin entered his fast-sprouting garden of dreams. For, as they slept, a serpent soundlessly produced its shining length from the waters of the creek they were camped by. It waved its lifted head in slow, lateral sweeps, like a bright-polished finger stroking the texture of the darkness. Its sweeps narrowed, and then it poured toward the snoring King, the ineffable scent of whose prize had pierced the reptile's nostrils like a needle, and strung it to its target. Thence it silkenly flowed through the dozen switchbacks of its zigzag stealth. Moonlight lacquered the fixed smile of its scale-shod jaws as these delicately pinched the loose-clutched stalk (and well might the slumbering monarch's clutch be loose) and plucked it free.

Darting away, it gave the Juicy-Root Blossom a triumphant toss and engulfed it, thorns and all. King Gil awoke in time to witness, with a howl, the serpent's meal. Its skin split open and, glowing with new luster, it slid from the husk, poured its rainbow length into a gopher hole, and was gone beneath the earth, whereon the King flung himself and pounded, as on a locked gate.

"Urchin!" he roared. "Help! A snake stole the Juicy-Root Blossom! Quick! Give me a shovel!"

The Cabby raised his head and gave King Gil a brief look. "Right," he said, and went back to sleep.

Long and long King Gil lamented. Long and long he cursed and pounded, cursed and pounded, groaned, and cursed and pounded. He did not see when, at length, a fine brown smoke began to issue from a small vent in the moonlit earth. Some feet above the ground this smoke cohered, gauzily, into the shape of a man—of Monkey-Do, in fact, all tissue-thin and full of gaps which the heavens showed through. He stood there, still and somber, on the air. King Gil, pausing in his curses to catch his breath, became aware of being watched. Looking up, he gasped to see that starshot simulacrum of his friend brooding over him, all smoky-eyed.

"Doody! It's you! Oh ye gods, what luck! You can help me! A *snake* stole my Juicy-Root Blossom, Doody, which was going to restore my lost youth to me! You're one of the dead, you can go down after it in the earth and get it back for me. And by the gods, when I get my hands on that fucking snake"—the King made vigorous strangling gestures—"I'm going to eat him whole! I'm going to—"

"You moron." The ghost said this slowly, wonderingly, not yet fully roused from his trance of meditation on the King's dusty, distracted person. "You dim, dribbling idiot. Do you *realize* what you had in your hand? Do you realize what you just let that vile little, no-legged, ten-cent string of snake-shit wriggle *away* with?" Monkey-Do was growing more animated now. His eyes glowed and the smoke of his substance curled round their fire like stormclouds bathed by sunsets. "You know, after all this time, after all I've been through with you, you royal zero, I've just come to *realize!* You're a *re*tard! You couldn't find your own ass with a search-party! And I *followed* you! *You!* Ye gods, what a blunder! Where was I *going?*"

"Doody! This isn't like you! You were going where *I* was going."

"True enough. So then why did I get there first?"

"Hey, Doody! What's the point of quibbling? I'll get there myself soon enough, now that I've lost the Juicy-Root Blossom. Come on, Doody, what do you say? Why don't you get it back for me? Hell, I'll *give* you a bite of it—maybe it'll help your . . . condition."

"Oh of course, your Midgetcy! Lay hold of it with hands of smoke—wrestle it from living jaws with my sinews of dust? Thanks, but I'll leave that to you when you have the same equipment I have, which will be, as you say, soon enough."

"So why are you rubbing it *in* like that, Doody? It's bad enough you can't help me—or won't help me—without rubbing it in like that."

"I'd like to rub it in so hard you shone with it! I'd like to *wax* you with it! But such are my present powers, I can't even do that much. My time's run out and I've got to get back to eternity. I'll see you there. Some job we did, eh hambone?" His shape burst—its hazy substance drained out of the air like fine sand—and funneled back into the ground.

Epilogue

Events had pretty much wrapped things up as far as King Gil was concerned, and he recognized this. On his melancholy journey back to Ureek he practiced getting used to it, but it never seemed to come any easier with trying.

Still, Ureek found him changed after his return. His movements were less sudden, his gait seemed slightly joint-sore. The bloom of his vitality was looking crinkly and octoberish. And, undeniably, from this time on King Gil's deeds rang with less clangor through the world. None of his later works rivaled those accomplishments that lay behind him now. Scholars of this period concur in marking at this point the end of the really Great Old Days of Ureek, and it seems proper to withdraw and leave him here. It will be enough, in speaking of his latter days, to see him as he is so often pictured in many fond memorials of his declining years, for he was often to be seen then, conducting Urchin—his new Sidekick—along the battlements and loftier promenades of the city, exhibiting Ureek's marvels to the saturnine stowaway.

"I mean, isn't it kind of *poignant?*" Gil would cry, gesturing down upon one of his favorite views of Main Dragon Lane at the height of the rash hour. "I mean that a man like myself could create all this power and glory, and still find it makes no difference in the final wrap-up? I mean just *look* at all that!"

"I've *looked* at it, Gildo, a million times! You dragged me up here just last night, remember?"

Such, then, were the exploits of King Gil Gomez of Ureek. He sought and, seeking, did not find—unhappy fact. But let no man deny, at least, that King Gil did wreak mightily. No man ever left his world less like he found it than King Gil. No man more unfailingly valued his fellow men for their innate worth, nor more unfailingly used it to good advantage. Of course at last, regrettably—all his great qualities notwithstanding—he *did* die. Old Numbtar at the last lay on him like a ton of bricks—heavy old Numbtar, who has neither hand nor foot; old Numbtar, who drinks no water and draws no breath. Then King Gil, as others have done, lay stiff and clammy as any hooked fish, drowned in an ocean of air that he couldn't make use of.

Oh, lay the suckerfeces to smoke in plenteous piles to do him honor, for he was a can-do kind of King!

Oh, set the flames to those sarcofeasts—so agreeable to the gods—for he was a go-getting King, till the gods came and got him!

Verse

The Younger Shea

Shea wrote these two short, starkly eloquent pieces sometime during his early college years.

The Greek Plowman

The war has walked away, horizon-hungry,
To paint farther fields with men
And decorate the wind's crooning ennui
With raw, fresh groans and tangled cries.
It is time to plow again, to clear the scattered crop
Of silent swords, and take my turn
With this indifferent earth.
But I tell you my plow stops wherever the stones wear
Blood splotches like careless robes,
And my mind scurries into itself
Like a rat in an empty granary,
Scrambling, whimpering for the nourishing morsel,
The granule of myself that makes me mine.
But there is only knowledge
Of how my sire's blind, thoughtless seed
Stung my mother's womb, and how I swelled to stand here
Where the wind calls the water to my eyes,
Where my breath climbs out to join the breeze,
Where the salt sheen of my sweat
Chills my back in the cooling dusk,
Where my hair lolls like grain in the wind—
While in the tomb beneath that field
The Rat scans the shadows

For the morsel of myself that makes me mine
That I might rise to wear my being like a crown.
But see how the stones wear the scarlet badge
Of man who hoped to hoard their blood.

I will carve furrows for the willful soil;
I see how the earth wears garlands of bewildered poets—
How she crowned herself with armies
At Thermopylae.

Two Nights

Somewhere among nights past
Humped heaven's mass of black;
Thick planes of stars
Were vastly bladed through it—
Cold swarm, biting the idiocy of void—
While broad in jelled thunder substance
The deep brute sea was flat under all the stars.
There were the beaches hard with starlight,
The ghostly sands
Numb with desertion at the edge of loneliness—
In hollow forever
Where fate marched endlessly in from the sea,
With the waves, endlessly. . . .

In from the plains of cold grey slate
Came the waves
Missing from the frigid desolation
The waves
Sweeping stately from infinity to die strange
On the beach
Charged, icy-boiling crystal sheets
Seethed up

Toppling, crushing sharply on hard sand
Into grey planes licking wide the beach—
Smoothly bellying back.
On night beaches the pulse of time . . .
Eon after eon,
Cadenced eons swelling from deep eternity
To gasp into past on cold beaches;
With the rhythm of recurring death,
Mourning emptiness.
Somewhere among nights past
There was a sea that had forgotten the world
And all the shivering stars hung afraid
Over the iron sea.

II

But tonight there is wind in the stars
And the sea;
The empty black scream
Towers into the chasm
Where the stars are stiff and braced in its blast
Lest they shower,
Sharp-cracking,
Onto the roaring cliffs.
Tonight the earth came up to the sea
And stopped afraid in sudden cliffs
While dark, hump-backed boulders
Ponderously crawled out from their feet
To stand
Paused massively hating waters,
Pondering black drowning;
And behind them the bitten cliffs slope out beckoning in the wind
To the scaly backs of their brute children,
For the black water is in fast mountains—

The shadow mountains thunder
From prisons of endlessness
To storm the petrified world.
The water titans surge to a world that waits,
To shatter arms and shoulders
On the ignorant bulwarks
And the wind howls into mist
The savage instant of waves
That crash and tower white from the rocks.
Tonight there is cold hell
And no death.

From the Novels

From *A Quest for Simbilis*

In this novel, written in homage as a sequel to *The Eyes of the Overworld* by the great Jack Vance, the rogue Cugel the Clever, in the course of his peregrinations in search of the great Mage Simbilis, encounters a narrow bridge across a bottomless chasm. The toll for crossing it is a game of glyfrig played against the gatekeeper. This is an ensorcelled monster (a Banded Hoon) whose task is to unmask card-sharps by playing a crooked game that only crookedness can beat, and then to slay the card-sharps thus unmasked. He has been installed here by a bereaved Mage whose son was slain by gamblers. The only way to cross the bridge is to lose everything to the Hoon.

Cugel cheats, of course, but eludes death.* As he sprints across the bridge, he beholds an inscription left by the Mage:

Though now you face a cheerless waste,
You are alive to see at least,
Your blood pounds, you can hear, and taste,
You're free to dance till the sun's decease,
If dance you will.

You've thus won more than one before,
Whom cardsharps stabbed in a den of lies
And robbed of what is not restored.
From him they took heart, ears and eyes.
Thus have I wrought to publicize
That cards work ill.

---

*An allusion to the river Styx, and perhaps also to Procrustes.

From *Nifft the Lean*

The book comprises four novellas: "Come Then, Mortal, We Will Seek Her Soul"; "The Pearls of the Vampire Queen"; "The Fishing of the Demon Sea"; and "The Goddess In Glass."

The Fishing of the Demon Sea

The Thieves, caught thieving in the capital of a cattle empire, are offered their lives by the Herdmaster if they will descend to the Demon Sub-world to rescue his adolescent son who, dabbling in magic, has gotten himself seized by a demon and taken below.

The Thieves enter the sub-world via a mine shaft that collapsed when it accidentally pierced the demon-world realm. Their rocketing ride down an old mining cart hurls them into an odyssey through exotic monstrosities. In the Demon Sea they must dive for the captive lad, with the help of a shapeshifting sorcerer.

The Pearls of the Vampire Queen

Vulvula, a beautiful immortal vampire, is Queen of the Pearl Swamps of Fregor. In its waters giant polyps live. The pearls grow like blisters on their tentacles, which must be heroically wrestled to harvest the treasures and escape death.

The Thieves, harvesting pearls, discover a more lucrative venture. Vulvula drains the blood of her Year King each midwinter, which now approaches. Her youth and beauty are perpetually sustained by this yearly infusion, but she must have all the king's blood for the charm to work. With exquisite strategy and daring, the thieves penetrate the royal pyramid in the center of the busy metropolis of the swamp, and they steal a cup of the Year King's blood as he lies sedated in his chamber on the eve of his sacrifice. A harrowing escapade flows from their blackmailing of the Queen, who begins to age the morning after her renewal ceremomy.

Nifft and Barnar Hammer-Hand have come to Fregor Ingens to steal the Pearls of the Vampire Queen. Queen Vulvula is heard here intoning the liturgy of her Elevation of the Year King, that annual ceremony in which she devours her consort.

Your sons have fattened in my rule.
Your rafts go laden with peaceful trade.
There's no man's wife need fear the ghul.

Your pearls are spared the poacher's raid—
They're farmed by laws that spread their worth,
And keep ensheathed war's wasteful blade.

You've had what Good men get on earth—
Now grant your Queen does nothing cruel
Who, dead with craving, ends her dearth.

Her year-long lord, with year-long Heaven paid,
Comes now to see her year-long thirst allayed.

Rise to me now, my love, a king,
And descend from me as a God.

You will sit in Eternity with your line,
And rule the ever-after-living hosts.
You will wield the scepter of the shadow-kind.
You will be the judge and shepherd of the ghosts.

Rise to me now, my love, a king,
And descend from me as a god.

In Kairnheim, Nifft and Barnar are sent to the Sub-world to retrieve a lad kidnapped by demons, an exploit which involves the Fishing of the Demon-Sea. Before their unwilling descent, Barnar recalls a relevant poem by the learned Parple.

Man, for the million million years
He's shared the earth with demonkind,
Has asked why they, in their ageless lairs,
So lust for his frail soul and mind.

Whatever hands set the clock of stars
Wheeling and wheeling down through time
Also sundered those two empires
With barriers both now over-climb.

That men should go down to those sunless moors
Where Horror and Harm breed deathless forms,
Or to the Demon Sea's littered shores,
Or its depths, where riches breed like worms—

That men do this (as the Privateer
Gildmirth of Sordon did in his pride)
Is no surprise, save that they dare
To sail that shape-tormented tide.

But why are netherworld nets flung here,
And men snagged out of their mortal terms—
Trawled kicking down from life in the air
To immortal drowning in monstrous arms?

When at last the thieves have reached the Demon Sea, they encounter the adventurer Gildmirth mentioned in Parple's verses. This bold privateer has endured long centuries of bondage to the sea he came to plunder, for a Spaalg, a demon predator upon the will, has held him captive there. The Spaalg regales Gildmirth and his guests with a mocking eulogy to his "lover," the prey of his parasitism. The privateer's limitless riches in a realm where they are meaningless is the Spaalg's first taunt. Gildmirth, through stolen magic, is a shape-shifter, and this is the subject of the demon's jest in the second stanza.

What man in wealth excels my lover's state?
He hath no cause to dread lest others find
Where all his mountained spoil doth fecundate,
His breeding gold that spawneth its own kind
And sprawleth uncomputed, unconfined!

For what vast fleets of argosies,
Though numberless they churned the seas,
And endlessly did gorge their holds
With loot from his lockless vaults of gold,
Could make him rue their paltry decrement?
His eyes these dunes of splendors desolate—
They've parched his palate for emolument,

And make him term a "tomb" his vast estate.
In beauties what man is my lover's peer?
For, as in gold, so is he rich in graces.
None hath a form so various and rare,
Nor charm that shineth from so many faces.

Mayhap another's eyes are stars—both clear
As diamonds are—still they are but a pair!
My love's as constellations blaze
Wherefrom a host of figures gaze
Whose features are so manifold,
That tongue must leave them unextolled. . . .

The Spaalg has a further taunt before it parts company with the humans. Here the demon adopts Gildmirth's voice.

I once was a man with a heart and a face,
And while this heart and face were mine
I had two eyes that I lived behind
In a place for hoarding the things I'd seen—

And I had two ears that I lived between
Where the things I heard could be brought to mind.
But now where my heart stood is empty space
Where sights lack anything to mean,
And my ears' reportings echo to waste,
Lacking a place for taking place. . . .

At length, after perils not briefly describable, the thieves come to Sazmazm, a demon titan from the secondary Sub-world, whose attempt to erupt into this one caused the explosion of his colossal body. His living but everted anatomy forms a towering landscape on the primary Sub-world's plain. The thieves confront the heart, a living mountain whose aortal blood is gathered by Sazmazm's insectoid minions, who burrow back down to the lower world, returning their master's essence drop by drop to its natal hell. Barnar, viewing this eon-spanning, incremental toil, recites part of a nursery rhyme he knows.

And that Neverquit Bird, though small and weak,
Lights again and again on the Neverend Strand,
And he packs into his narrow beak
One little bite of that infinite beach,
And recrosses the sea till he reaches that land—
That land of his own he is building to stand
In a sun-blessed place beyond harm's reach,
That land he is making with stolen sand
And a will that will not be denied what it seeks.

From *In Yana, the Touch of Undying*

In this novel the portly, bookish Hex abandons the academic life on a gamble for a life of vaster horizons. Misadventures sweep him halfway across the world, in the course of which wanderings he encounters Sarf, an old school friend. The pair join an insurrectionary force, striking at a powerful maleficent capitalist by capturing one of the cities of his financial empire, Slimshur, and putting its populace to the death they inflict on others. Two of their captives work as Encouragers on the walls of Slimshur for the Harvest. Giant sea slugs are sung ashore by these Encouragers and their orchestra. The slugs emerge to devour the "criminals" shackled on Slimshur's stony slopes. They leave a vast blanket of slime both coming and going which, when dry, becomes a supple fabric much prized in textile markets throughout the Southern Sea. One of the captive Encouragers, about to taste the fate over which he has so often officiated, sings Hex and Sarf's Encourager's Song. It addresses Shlubb the Primal, the mythic progenitor of the slime-producing slugs.

Advance, great Shlubb, both Dam and Sire
Of all that thrives ashore!
Ascend! Embrace what you desire
Of fruit your own fruit bore!

For all thy spawn are but at pawn
Beneath the open air.
Some now reclaim of those who've ta'en
Their life from your deep lair!

Several misadventures later, Hex and Sarf, crossing a grassy uplands, encounter an Ogre pasturing his flock of hill-plods. They dive to cover before they are seen by the prodigious brute. All unwillingly, they witness an amorous interlude between the Ogre and one of his beasts. The grotesque shepherd, with his great throat-bag adding resonance, and fingering from his shamadka a trilling accompaniment, is a gifted singer. He regales his chosen one with an initial coy lyric.

Oh cease to dissemble! Thou loves't me not!
Though hotly thou swearest, thou carest no jot!
Wherefore woe is my lot!
Aye, woe, bitter woe is my lot!

To deceive me thou needs't more than swearings and sighs!
To hoodwink me thou must undrape thy pale thighs,
Add thy paps to the lie—
For such breasts can give weight to a lie!

And if thus thoul't dissemble, I'll credit deceit
So long as thou give'st it both body and heat,
And thy lips make it sweet,
Then good sooth! 'Tis a dish I will eat!

The Ogre then proceeds to a more exhortative ditty, which gathers urgency with each succeeding verse, till, concluding the last, he flings his shamadka across the meadow, and comes to grips with the object of his ardor.

All day in fragrant toil we've filled
Our arms with flowers of every style.
Now forbear to judge me bold
If—pressing still our harvest goal—
I beg: "Do not, do not withhold
The choicest blossom of the field!"

Oh let it be now as I so long,
So ardently have willed!
Dispread thyself the grass upon,
And yield, yield, yield
To me that chiefest blossom of the field!

Successive Flower Queens have crowned
Thy hair, thy breasts—each was cast down
By some more splendid potentate.
A Zarl made Quimsey abdicate,
Then fled thy brow, her honored seat,
Before still-reigning Fairy's-gown.

Depose her now, for she's surpassed!
Thine own bloom unconceal!
Enthrone thyself upon the grass,
And yield, yield, yield
To me that choicest blossom of the field!

Still farther down the shore of the Southern Sea, death in new forms narrowly evaded, Hex, in the ruins of a once-mighty port, encounters the Riddler, and death in its worst form yet. He answers the riddle by accident, and narrowly survives.

I'm each salt ocean's other shore
Where tasteless tides of drought don't roar.

Defining all like daytime's light,
I'm all-concealing as the night.

Fuel that feeds all urgent fires,
Extinguisher of hot desires.

I raise all wings of Enterprise.
I am the Gulf where nothing flies.

What am I?

Their craft sunk at sea, Hex and Sarf are rescued by a beautiful giant, Kagag Hounderpound. This Apollonian colossus swims them ashore, asking as recompense a small favor: the slaying of two shore-witches who bedevil the giant with spells they utter from the safety of the strand. The grateful travelers set in motion the slaying of the witches, when, almost too late, they overhear the witches' curse, and grasp that this magic is the only force that keeps their gigantic benefactor (whose true nature the curse also reveals) from coming ashore.

Curse you, Kagag Hounderpound!
We damn and ban you from this ground!

On ruin, Hounderpound, you gloat,
And under swarming shipwrecks float
To see the dead rain dreaming down;
The storm-broke hull
Soon crowns your skull;
In your museums of the drowned
Long galleries of trophies bloat.

Curse you, Kagag Hounderpound!
We damn and ban you from this ground!

For in the wrestling sea and storm
All crafts or lives escaping harm—
All such survivors wake your hate!
All ardent wills
Whose ships and skills
Whose dwarfish toils outstrip their fate,
These gall you, these unbroken forms!

Curse you, Kagag Hounderpound!
We damn and ban you from this ground!

Withhold your huge, unmaking hand!
This patiently wave-hammered sand—
This smithied gold—won't feel your touch.
No, nothing that breathes
Outside the seas
Will strangle in your envy's clutch,
Nor shall your claws unshape this land!

From *The Mines of Behemoth*

Behemoths are giant ants whose nests open, not on the surface of the earth, but under it, in the Demon Sub-world, for Behemoths forage below and feed on Demons. Humans drill down to the Behemoths' larval nests from above and drain the larvae for their exceedingly nourishing body-contents. This "sap" is used to nourish crops and feed cattle.

But if one can penetrate the nest more deeply, to the chamber where the titanic Queen gives birth to new Behemoths, some of her "pap" can be—with peril—taken, and this makes giants of all who ingest it.

Nifft and Barnar are commissioned to penetrate to the Brood Chamber of a Nest. Halfway down they fall on the back of a foraging behemoth and are carried through the Demonworld where it feeds. At length they do reach Brood Chamber, ascend the colossal Queen, and carry back to the upper world the giant-creating pap, with huge consequences.

The Mines of Behemoth, because of its initial serial publication, has been reduced to heroic couplets. This verse summary is in three parts.

Mines of Behemoth in Heroic Couplets

I

Barnar and I to tedious toil were bound
In Kairnish sap-mine's gloom far underground
To delve on Barnar's nephew's young behalf.
(The mine had been mismanaged by that calf;
His mother urged us on to set it right.)
Just off the Angalheims, Kairnheim in sight,
A benthic brute devoured us, craft and crew.
His over-hasty feast the feaster slew.
From his dead maw we did retrieve our lives
And crawled ashore. Those isles, abuzz with hives,
Are honey-troves, distilleries of mead,
Their heights all blossoms where the bright swarms feed.
There Bunt we met, mead-magnate, keen for coin,
Who us with bags of same hired to purloin
A certain ichor, only to be found
In those same sap-mines whither we were bound.
These mines that pierce the mountains' roots are nests
Whose tunnels tortuous and chambers vast
A giant race have wrought. Their entries yawn—
Not skywards—but below, where demon-spawn
In tides of turmoil, wrath, and deathless spite
Their sub-terrain beswarm in red-lit night.
Here the giants forage. Demon-kind
Their endless feast is, demon blood their wine.
With these infernal viands once replete,
The giants to their nest, and Queen, retreat.
Their feast, disgorged, her royal maw receives,
And they, in turn, the eggs that she conceives
Receive and tenderly do bear away
To nursery chambers. Royal progeny

Are every nest's chief treasure. It is they
Around whom all Behemoth's labors turn.
From egg-troves, grublike hatchlings next are borne
To larval vaults for feeding. Here men feed
As well as larvae—here our mine-shafts lead,
For sap's no other than what larvae bleed.

Our gory work there Bunt paid us to quit
And seek the chamber where the Queen doth sit,
From her to steal a certain exudate
Which, lapped up by her babes, doth stimulate
Their growth to that great hugeness they attain.
So slipped we out—our goad a greed for gain—
And trod those mighty tunnels in our quest
To find the Queen, and do rich Bunt's behest.

But paltry human purpose ever stumbles
Upon mischance. Behold! The tunnel rumbles!
We face the onrush of our giant hosts!
We climb the wall but, thence dislodged, are tossed
Upon the back of one as it speeds past.
Our flea-weight by our mount is undetected,
And we, from our set course, are thus deflected
Down to the demon kingdom far below,
Where our insatiate bearer's bent to go.

II

Behold! Two parasites are swept along
Astride a brute whose breed they preyed upon.
Barnar and I, I mean, who spiked and bled
Behemoth babes within their nursery-bed,
Until greed for a greater theft us led
These babes to quit, the mazy shafts t'explore
In quest of the nest's Queen and her Ichor . . .

Then chance did mount us on this Forager
(Most dire of all the royal myrmidons)
Who, unaware, to sub-world bore us down.

Our mount a host of sisters joined in plunder,
And scourged the sub-world plain, their tread like thunder;
Their scything jaws a demon harvest lopped,
A bleeding yield which crammed their giant crops.
(Upon this carnal turmoil still looked down
The blood-red eye of Heliomphaladon,
A mega-demon long immured in stone,
His disjoint orb this hellish region's sun.)
Our sated Forager turned home again
To render up her takings to the Queen,
And thus the Royal Sanctum we attained
That had our venture's foremost object been.
With awe, we viewed the nursling multitude
That drank the pap her Regal flanks exude.

The Monarch's milk proved past our power to steal—
Her hugeness past our power even to scale!—
But when again our bearer bore us out,
And Luck dismounted us, we'd learned the route
Between the Nursery—whither we repaired—
And the Royal Mother in her lair.

We'd learned the perils of the Ichor's source,
And the Unguent of Flight seemed a resource
With new allure, although a demon's bond
Was all our surety it could be found.

Accordingly, when Costard, and the Bunts
Descended on us, keen to join the hunt
For Royal pap, we led them to the Queen.

There, when the task's immensity they'd seen,
They vowed—unwelcome allies!—all to go
With us to seek the Unguent below.

Again (though lacking now a giant steed)
We trekked the sub-world, and obtained our meed!
The Unguent, a magic oil, besmeared
The claw of great Omphalodon, interred
In hell-floor by the selfsame spells that bound
His mighty eye, from hell-sky glaring down.

A demon guard controlled the catacomb
That reached the claw within its stony tomb.
In slaying this, a human thrall we freed,
Whose warnings 'gainst excess we failed to heed,
So that, when with the Unguent we emerged,
So did the Claw, with a colossal surge,
Erupt at last up from the sub-world floor,
And sent us tumbling—flying—out before.

Indeed, we flew! We trod that blood-red sky—
Barnar and I, I mean, for fate denied
Our friends a share of those air-striding powers,
Though generously we lofted them with ours,
And all together, winged back to the nest.

There soon enough, we set ourselves to test
What flight could do to gain that Royal pap
That Behemoths from their vasty dams do lap!

III

The Queen's pap-pores, from whence doth trickle forth
Her giant's Ichor, ranged about her girth,
Are every one by thirsting spawn assailed,

And their approach the direst risk entailed,
Whilst parasites beswarming her vast back
Our perils multiplied with their attack.

All this despite, with milky plunder soon
We to the Bunts returned, whose golden boon
We found our lust for gain did not assuage.
For why should we, with such an equipage—
With power of flight, with demon many-eyed
The paths of pelf to point, our captive guide—
Why in Lord Lucre's richest, vastest trove
Should we not deeper probe, its wealth to prove?

From Queen we'd seen a queenly scion spring,
Who, with attendant lords, had taken wing
For demon-flesh to plunder, far and wide,
Her nascent Nest with nurture to provide.
In the wake of this vast pillage we did fly,
Where Wreck and Ravage, under the red sky,
Did roofless, gateless, strewn and bloodstained lie.
Here a clockless time we soared at will,
And did our nets with nameless riches fill.

From hell emerged, and with our pelf in train,
Barnar and I trod sunlit earth again
(Though discord over how to spend our plunder
Worked like a worm in us, our bond to sunder).
Dry-Hole we reached, a thriving cattle-town—
Or had been last we saw. Now, coming down,
A ravaged wreck we found it, crushed, bedunged
By titan kine who trod its streets among!
Costard these colossal bovines bred
From cattle on Behemoth Ichor fed.
Nor did that feckless dunce himself elude

A like fate: his own flesh the pap imbued.
Gargantuan, deformed, and mad, he dragged
His hugeness through the hills, to coastal crags
Nigh Kairngate Harbor, whence he cast him down,
And in the foaming Agon, seemed to drown.

We bought a ship, the Bounty, stuffed her hold
With all our demon booty and our gold.
Our wealth afloat, the open main us beckoned,
But a fifty-weight of gold from Bunt we reckoned
Was owed us. Thus to Dolmen we returned
(Oh, would that we that luckless port had spurned!)

The harbor swarmed, the steep roads to the heights
With traffic seethed, for all was not aright
Amidst the hilltop hives: Bunt had his queens
Fed the Ichor, till, behemothine
And even huger now had grown those swarms
The which, though flightless, worked colossal harms
Upon the frenzied Dolomites who toiled
With flame and blade and barricade to foil
The giants' irresistible onslaught.
I—greed-mad I!—the embattled heights now sought
The paltry debt from beleaguered Bunt t'extract.
Even as I climbed, the mountainside convulsed.
A monstrous queen, her assailants all repulsed,
Had dragged her hugeness to the mountain's brink.
I scarce had time our ruin to bethink
Ere it befell—the titan insect tumbled
Adown the slope, and with an earthquake rumble,
Drove half of Dolmen Harbor her before,
And half the anchored vessels by her shore,
All in commingled ruin to the deeps

Where, even now, our mangled Bounty sleeps
In moldering weedy murk amid the host
Of other fortunes men have won, and lost.

Behemoths are immense colonial insectoids whose nests honeycomb the roots of the mountains of southwestern Kairnheim. Their anfractuous burrows open on the First Sub-world. The Behemoths feed on demons, and mankind, from amidst the mountain peaks, sinks shafts to feed on the Behemoths' larvae, which contain a nutritive ichor, called "sap," that has a thousand uses in the markets of men. Behemoths are among earth's greatest benefactors, for they convert the swarming, poisonous energies of Demonkind into wholesome sustenance for humankind.

Hadaska Brood, in his lines of homage to Behemoth, introduces to us the beneficent titans.

What dread being dares to farm
Where every breed of demon swarms?
Who dares till there? Who shall go
And scythe the harvest row on row?
Who in that sunless gulf of harms
Could drive the plow? Would dare to sow?

Behemoth's jaws alone the share
To carve the flinty furrow there.
Behemoth's strength the reaper's blade,
Her bowels the barn where harvest's laid.
To hers, what husbandry compares,
That has half demonkind unmade?

The "mines" of Behemoth are the larval chambers of her labyrinthine nests. The men who mine them are called "tappers," because they insert the spike-nozzles of suction hoses into the vast obesity of the giant larvae, and tap them for their sap. Those tappers who venture from the larval chambers to scout deeper in the nests for demon treasures, or for precious exudates of Behemoth more difficult to obtain than the sap, have, rarely in humanity's long predation on the titans, found their way to a nest's Brood Chamber, where the immense Queen gives endless birth.

One such legendary venturer was Scroffle Smalls. A thoroughly venal man, wholly lacking in spiritual dimension, his chance encounter with a Behemoth Queen changed him forever. The wonder of that fecund colossus awoke his soul to the grandeur of Life. He abode thereafter on her body, a worshipful parasite on her hugeness.

Smalls is chronicled in a fragmentary ballad, which Shag Margold reports to us. It is his commentary which introduces the ballad and bridges its lacunae with his conjectures.

(The text is a "roguerie," a ballad form used by the Lulumean skelds to treat of common men in uncommon situations. Here follows, then, the first fragment of "The Apotheosis of Scroffle Smalls.")

The Apotheosis of Scroffle Smalls

Scroffle came to tapping drunk,
a-snoring on his battered trunk
that rattled in the teamster's wain.
Crapulous, with throbbing brain,
Smalls to chambers subterrane
Repaired to tap for lawful gain.
Full many crafts he'd underta'en,
But nary one did he sustain.
He'd been a wicker, whiffler, weaver,
A thatcher, tapster (and a thiever
When out of work and no one looking).
He'd dabbed at grooming, brooming, cooking,
Had tree-jacked up in Lebanoi,
Mucked stalls in Cirque as stable-boy . . .

In all did aimless Smalls endure
A week, a fortnight, but no more.

For Ale Smalls' aim was, Mead his mission,
And Aquavit his chief ambition.

In grub-nest deep in mountain-bone,
Smalls got his first shift tapping done.
He lacked that awe some tappers feel
For the titans they despoil,
Lacked reverence too for Miners' Writ,
The which forbade tappers to quit
The larval trove whence sap was mined.

For on just this Smalls set his mind,
Seeing that he could not find,
Wherever he might turn his eyes,
The "egg-sheen" that Perfumers prize.
Thus from grub-trove Scroffle slipp't,
Beseeking now a hatching-crypt
Whilst his fellow-tappers slept!
Through tunnels vinous Smalls did wind—
His coin-lust no trespass declined.
Thus sneaked Scroffle, greedy-wary,
Looking for an incubary
Where the Queen's eggs lay enchambered,
All by tireless Nurses pampered . . .
But even so, a bit of hose
The poacher with his prize endows.
Careful Scroffle midst the eggs
Must be lively on his legs,
For when the Nurses "turn the trove"
That poacher's crushed who's slow to move.
A little keg of twenty gills

The venal Smalls intends to fill.
Eggs nigh a score for this must bleed—
Each plundering moderate indeed,
Lest any egg show hurt or feeble—

(Here ends the first fragment of the ballad. At the opening of the second fragment, we find ourselves miles from the Incubary. In fact, we find ourselves in no less a sanctum than the Royal Brood Chamber, where the Queen lies a-breeding, circled by the tides of her countless spawn.

Not only is Smalls in the Brood Chamber, he's astride a Behemoth—on a Nurse's back. We can only conjecture how this happened. In the tight fit of the tunnels, men in danger of being crushed underfoot by a Behemoth's passage will climb the walls for safety, and thence might fall upon a giant's back. Indeed, that very mischance befalls Nifft the Lean and Barnar Hammer-hand in this present volume. By some such accident, then, Smalls no doubt found his perch on a Nurse's back. Behemoths have fleas and ticks [and worse] as big as men, and such passengers go unnoticed.The Nurse caste of Behemoth has the task of conveying the Queen's incessantly extruded eggs up to the Incubaries where they are tended and turned and groomed for parasites until the larvae hatch from them. Thus Small's accidental mount is bearing him right up to the planetary flank of the Nest Mother. But long before he reaches that living shore, he has been smitten by the titan's glory.)

Smalls' mount speeds the throng between,
With rapture doth he eye the Queen.
All wary wonder and wild surmise,
He crouches twixt the Nurse's thighs
And views the massif of the Mother
As the Nurse brings them together
Through the tides of sister-giants
Streaming round the titan Parent.
And nearing, still stares raptured Smalls.
The Mountain Mother him enthralls.

A revelation in him grows—
His clenched face seems in labor's throes,
Til he, transfigured, cries aloud
His vision to the multitude:
"Queen, thou art great, and I am null!
I see thee, and abhor my soul!
My Days and Deeds—all small and foul!
My Queen, though subterrane thy throne,
Thou has me Sun and Moon just shown!
Til now, my soul was dense as bone—
The sky was just a painted stone,
The sun a link-boy without pay
Who twixt taverns lit my way;
In mutant Moon did I discern
No god's eye, ope'd and shut by turn,
But just a month-clock sots might mark
(A-staggering homeward in the dark)
To 'mind them soon their rent is owed,
And they must sooner go abroad!
Great Cosmos kissed my lips, ears, eyes,
Its grandeurs glowed on low and high,
While I, unknowing, earless, eyeless,
An ale-housed ghost, went worldless, skyless!
This lesser Smalls thou now hast slain,
And slewest by merely being seen!
Thyself, in majesty arrayed,
Art Being's glory stark displayed!
Thou mountained Isle, thy brood a sea!
In wave on wave thy progeny
Flood to thee, from thee, to again—
So spendthrift of thy splendor, Queen,
Whose loins these mountains countless
Populate with legions dauntless . . ."

In the course of the novel, we learn of a theory that holds the race of Behemoths to be the creation of ancient wizardry. By this tradition, a vengeful Magus fashions them to repay an injury he suffered from demonkind.

Hermaphrod's Vow

A mage of days forgotten
By sub-world spawn assailed,
His left arm sundered, eaten,
Escaped with sore travail.
Then he knelt and swore a vengeance
On the sub-world's savage legions:
"Dire jaws that my art fashions
Shall make of ye their meal!
At this endless feast of titans
Your flesh shall be the meat.
Your bones shall hell-floor whiten,
Still my giants ye shall eat.
They shall your limbs dissever
And imbibe your blood forever.
Naught can ye from them deliver,
Nor shall their jaws abate!"

When Nifft and Barnar enter the subworld astride their Behemoth, they first behold Heliomphalodon Incarnadine—an immensity from the Tertiary Sub-world who sought the light of the sun, but whose eruption was aborted far short of its goal. His blood-red eye is the sun of this region of the Primary Sub-world.

Heliomphalodon Incarnadine

Sunken in his Dark did long repine
And craved to clutch the splendor of the sun

Whose glow and grandeur, legended in lore,
The mighty demon ne'er laid eye upon
'Mured as he was in his Third Subworld lair.

Crouched where fang-tormented myriads moan,
And Universe is but a rumored light,
The demon gnawed Forever like a bone,
Whilst solar phantoms scorched his murky sight.

Till was more real this storied star to him
Than were his world's inexorable walls.
His molten hands did through the world-bone swim . . .
Now behold where all disjoint he sprawls!
On sunless hell his eye forever shines,
Heliomphalodon Incarnadine!

When, at the story's end, all Nifft and Barnar's vast wealth has been sunk in the sea, the doleful pair hold a kind of funeral service for it on the shore. They intone a lament composed by Passerolle.

Hymn to Having Had

How you gleamed! How you dazzled me, shone in my arms
When I hugged you and had you for mine!
But all things that live must at length come to harm,
If it's only the harm of their ceasing to shine!

You blazed when we loved! You were both flame and wick.
How meltingly glowed you your body away!
And all our sweet nearness, we lived it up quick!
Now somewhere, the still-fleeing light of our days
Wings shining along with the lie we still love,
Though long have our hands and our hearts ceased to move!

Introductory Stanzas to Selected Chapters

VI

I met a Titan in the earth
Where Mountain Queen gives endless birth,
And though so terribly she glowered,
Her hapless babe I half-devoured.
And then (I am afraid you'll laugh!)
I met what ate the other half.

X

Who goeth to the Mother's breast
Of greater Life to sup,
Oh, tread ye nimbly through the Nest!
Oh, firmly grip thy cup!

XI

Now saddle my mount, I am riding to plunder
The Ur-hoard encoffered in caskets infernal!
Swift my mount bears me, her footfall as thunder,
Where hell sweats its lucre in fever eternal!

XIII

Behold them kiss their mother's side
A-suckling of her pap.
They wash against her like a tide
That at its shore doth lap.

XXVI

Oh let me and my fortune ride the sea,
On Ocean's bosom know—at last!—repose!

There nor flame nor thief need dreaded be,
And lapping swells lull weary lids to close . . .

XXVIII

Where wild winds shepherd their cloudy kine,
Where lightning's unborn sleep sheathed in blue,
That's the bright country that I would call mine,
And there would I do what the winged ones do!

From *The A'Rak*

Big Quay, in Northern Hagia, is a bustling entrepôt of trade, a rich city capitalized by the gold that its god, the A'Rak, a giant spider, brings up to it from under the earth. The A'rak and his sons feed on Hagians very sparingly—only the poorest and most marginal feed the god, and at the annual lottery only a score or two draw the lots that make them A'rak's food. The ghoulish covenant keeps the rich very rich, and all well.

But the A'rak was driven here from his own world by a pursuing nemesis, Pompilla (an immortal tarantula wasp). The witches who inhabit the islands around Hagia have resurrected this nemesis, and Nifft has unwittingly become part of the expedition that sneaks Pompilla into the heart of Hagia.

Sensing his danger, the A'rak, at the annual lottery, consumes the whole ten thousand assembled in the stadium, molts, and grows even more gigantic. The city is locked in a climactic battle with the God and his spawn when Pompilla arrives.

Margold transcribes Targvad's A'Rak-on-Epos, as rendered from the High Archaic by Roddish the Minusk.

A'Rak-on-Epos

Through a crack A'Rak crawled through the sky of his world
Out to oceans of space where the great star-wheels whirled;
He tiptoed across this white pavement of stars
And up through the floor of his new world—ours.

The first world he'd feasted on festered and bled,
A charnel house heaped with his harvests of dead,
Till his undying hunger was driven to flee
By the scourge of a Foe more immortal than he.

Now lowly he lurks here, a tenant discreet,
And sparingly, modestly sups at his meat—
Sends his spawn out a-hunting and hides 'neath the soil,
Then devours his sons and possesses their spoils.

But once he ran rampant, and will never forget
The untrammeled slaughter that fevers him yet
In dreams when he rears up his gore-crusted jaws
And feeds at his will without limits or laws.

Now pious he crouches in churches and whispers
Of riches his vassals may reap from their vespers,
And devours them in nibbles, by alms and by tithes,
Though worlds were once fields that his fangs swept like scythes.

As he once in abundance of butchery bathed,
When from his greed escaped nothing that breathed,
Howso pious and sparing he shepherd and shear thee—
Forget not! His lust is to slaughter and tear thee!

Nifft has come to Hagia, whose vaults are groaning-full of the God-given gold, at the stimulus of a prophetic poem. It is fragmentary at first, but seems to hint at danger to A'Rak, and thus at the vulnerability of A'Rak's vaults. The poem in its entirety is at last assembled:

Let the A'Rak's web be woven,
The ghost-web that he's wont to weave
Of souls torn from bodies cloven
By his fangs that all things cleave.

Let him slay, and slay, and tear them,
Souls alive from bodies slain,
Let him weave those ghosts and wear them—
For one doth come to work him pain!

Heap the smoking meat thou'st plundered,
Weave the soul-stuff, weave it strong!
For such soul-stuff can't be sundered,
And thou'lt need its shield ere long!

When thou'rt clothed in slaughter's garment,
Wil't thou not be bravely clad?
Staunch the fabric spun from torment,
And bright the dyes by victims bled!

But 'ware that thou be not the garment
Of one whose style out-braves thine own!
One who does not dread interment
Where thy murdered prey have gone!

For howso thick thou be appareled
In thy woven web of woe,
Thou may'st find thyself ensnarled
At the onslaught of thy Foe.

When the wing-song of her hunger
Serenades thee from the sky,
And the bright barb of her anger
Seeks thy life (thou knowest why!)

Then, oh A'Rak, thou might'st cower
When thy shield becomes thy chain,
And Pam'Pel in all her power
Shall thee slay—At last! Again!

Whilst Nifft is aprowl in Big Quay, sniffing out his advantage, he encounters Dame Eelritter in a tavern. This witchly adept, in a friendly spirit, shares with Nifft a Hagian folk-ditty, which captures that particular horror that always must lurk in the bushes for Hagians who share their land with A'Rak-spawn:

Something Unspeakable Followeth Me

Clawtip by clawtip, so gingerly-daintily!
Advancing now two steps, now one step, now three. . . .
Hark there! Canst hear it? Though ever so faintly?
Hear it tiptoe from thicket to gully to tree?
Something unspeakable followeth me!

What stayeth when I stay, and when I go, goeth?
It hasteth when I haste, and when I slow, sloweth.
To advance I'm afeared, yet to linger am loath,
Such tickle-foot terror attendeth on both!
Doth the boskage there stir? I search, but naught showeth. . . .

Crickle and crackle old Crooked-Legs speedeth,
And under my footfall, concealeth his own.
Hast ever happed past some copse where Crook feedeth?
Heard his paralyzed prey—as he's drained—feebly moan?

Ye zephyrs that fluster the foliage, stand fast!
What was it, just yonder, that just whispered past?
What pursuer so leisurely-sly giveth chase?
Ye gods! Let me not feel that thorny embrace!

Ye breezes harassing the high grass, desist!
By little and little, degree by degree
Thy rustle and bustle the monster assist—
Lest I be seized, let me harken! Oh list!
That delicate stealthing, what else could it be?
From a footfall so multiple, what hope to flee?
For scuttling from thicket to gully to tree,
Something unspeakable followeth me!

The Spider God grants a long and eerie audience to Nifft, in which he describes the destruction of his natal world, Arthro-Pan'Doloron. His planet was devoured by the vortex of a colossal black hole. A poem survives from this event, a nihilistic paean to the consuming Dark.

Galactivore Imperator
A wheel of suns to tatters tore,

And at one stroke, its denizens
Drove from their earthen tenements.

These denizens were myriad,
Un-wombed from loins unwearied.

All their host a-marching came
From Chaos toward the beckoning flame.

All sparked to life by starry fire,
Some were dainty, some were dire,

All were random, none were pointless
Bent on being, gargoyles dauntless,

Each clung to its borrowed stuff
Until its flesh was vortexed off.

Their borrowed stuff was repossessed.
Their every shape at once unfleshed.

(Their shapes survive one nano-tick,
Like candleflames without the wicks!

The pure design hangs there a blink,
Before it back to Nothing sinks!)

Hail mad contrivance! Yeasty dust!
Winged, finned, footed, on ye thrust!

Contraptions! Pushing snout, maw, muzzle,
Each in its bit of the puzzle!

Eyed, antennaed, tongued, and fingered,
Barbed, tusk'd, horn'd, clawed, fanged and stingered. . . .

For those black millstones, Null and Void,
Reclaim all dust in lives deployed.

(Woe that lives should coalesce!
Woe that dust should effervesce!)

Grind them out, and grind them back,
To dust a-vortexing in Black!
Tyrant ghouls, and martyrs crimeless!
Genocides, and saviours timeless!

Grind out gallows bravely mounted,
Dungeoned innocents uncounted!
Implacably all dust reclaim

That found a shape, a wish, a name.

Those black millstones, Void and Null,
Grind the thoughts from every skull. . . .

Grind out stars, then grind them back
To dust a-vortexing in black. . . .
Grind out sinewed wings a-winging,
Grind out corded throats a-singing,
Grind out gem-bright, brimming eyes,
And ardent tongues in colloquies,
And hearts engorged with little hoards
Of suns and moons, of touches, words. . . .
Grind them out, and grind them back
To dust a-vortexing in black. . . .

(Ye ghostly hordes of lives that were
In starry cauldrons once a-stir,
Even echoes now ye lack,
In the unreporting black
That reclaims thee once again,
When your sprites have had their spin. . . .)

Oh, have mercy, Void and Null!
That is empty which was full!

Grind abysses overleapt!
Grim peaks conquered, death-vows kept!
Grind out mourner and bewept.
Grind out deeds, and deeps they dare,
Heroes and the Hells they harrow . . .
Grind out Plague and wondrous cure,
Ambition's bow, and Conquest's arrow,
Saints, and torments they endure. . . .

The Spider God's Scourge, who has pursued him since the end of his world, is the wasp Pompilla, who paralyzes him and makes him the host, the living meat, of her larvae. His Huntress's daughters become his possessors, time without end. At the last, the Spider God lies immured with the young of his conqueror implanted within him.

Pompilla's Taunt

In the gulf of a past whereon other stars shone,
And another sun beamed than doth beam on this earth,
In a starwheel that spun till its eons were done,
Our troth was first plighted, thy death with my birth.

Betrothed and then sundered! Oh Bridegroom, thy terror
Made thee flee—fruitlessly!—far from my touch!
But at last of our offspring shalt thou be the bearer,
And I thee impregnate! My daughters shall couch

In thy silken entrails, and nurse on thy meat,
While thou liest reposeful as corpse in its tomb,
And long wilt thou, living, endure as they eat—
Conceiving them, knowing thyself as their womb!

Though thou seek remote suns by planetoids girdled,
And those asteroid torrents thou plunge in and ride,
Though hid in such welters of world-rack thou hurtle,
My nurselings still bowered in thy bowels shall abide!

Then down Time's abyss that yet yawneth before us
They'll go hide-and-seeking, our numberless brood.
The cries of thy stricken sons rising in chrous,
Wherever they flee by my daughters pursued!

From *Epistle to Lebanoi*

(unpublished)

Epistle to Lebanoi is the fourth Nifft novel, yet unpublished. We find Nifft in the port town of Lebanoi where he goes to seek out demon spices from the infamous spice swamp. Nifft is quickly swept up in a pending demon war waged by the narn-son Gothol and his father, the mage Zan-Kirk, against the warlock's lover of yore, the witch Hylanais.

Shag Margold introduces the text with a history of The Witches' War- the sundering of the amorous relationship between Hylanais and Zan-Kirk- enacted with such force as to simultaneously sunder the Great Rain Bowl of Lebanoi.

She swung her staff against the stone
She bruised and broke the mountain-bone.
All Lebanoi below did hear
The mountain's stubborn substance tear.
"Be witness here, thou sundered tor,
Of kingly love that is no more!
The riven state depict my heart!
Faithless warlock! Would'st depart?
Would thou lie with loathed Narn
Mere power to prove, then claim the bairn?
And curse me with the tainted yield
Of your foul tillage in hell's field?
Should'st thou do me adultery
what spawn thou has in bastardy
Shall choke its life out of my grip
And I thy bitch's bowels shall rip!
Are we not in our powers' full bloom?
Do not the years afford us room?

All wide earth to over-soar—
Abysses, mountains, skies explore?
Whence this lust for darksome trade
In smithies where Mankind's unmade?
In smoky Magor's molten bowel
Where hellspawn on the anvils howl?
Ah, Zankirk, had we not a vow?
That all-encircled us, as now
This sky, these green-clad mountains do?
Thour't all to me . . . Not I to you?
Go then! Rut as suits thy will!
But know, therewith our vow dost kill.
Thereafter, from un-plighted troth,
I fly bird-free, and nothing loath
To try the love of any man
That please mine eye, where-e'r it scan.
And should I choose conceive, I shall,
And so, of all we've shared, ends all!"

Zan-Kirk and Gothol have enslaved demons to people their army. Hylanais' army, in contrast, is comprised of the risen dead heroes and warriors of yore.

The flagship's a galleon of seventy sail
Sea-rotted to cobweb, like gossamer veils;
Bright coral corselets bejewel each hull.
And the rigging is seaweed that sways as they roll
Upswell and downswell o'er the billows' broad back
Where the Narrows at midnight run foam-white and black.

Their splintery mainmasts like barnacled bone
Sway seven times seven past the late-rising moon,
Their bowsprits wear beards of millennial moss

Grown shaggy whilst drowned in the seas they now cross
Upswell and downswell o'er the billows' broad back
Where the Narrows at midnight run foam-white and black.

The cavern-eyed steersmen that stand at the wheels
Gaze rapt at the stars flung in dazzling fields—
Gaze ravished to see them, so long having lain
Blind to their blazing in Death's black domain
They surge upswell and down o'er the billows' broad back
Where the Narrows at midnight run foam-white and black

The gristle and bone of them's all that remains,
Their breastplates hang knocking against their stark frames,
As they harken to echoes of thunder and pain,
Their last battles haunting the dark, plunging main.
In the ocean's wet clamor they still hear the cries
Of dying batallions awash in War's tides;
They remember War's visions, the dust-storms of steel
As cavalries thundered to meet on the field.
They see ghostly batallions surge forward, fall back
O'er the Narrow at midnight all foam-white and black.

In the culmination of the Witches' War, Hylanais sent her unfaithful lover to his watery grave. Gothol, the son born to Zan-Kirk and the Narn mentioned in Hylanais' poem to Zan-Kirk, must first raise his father from the dead so that they may together call the demon army.

Father who art sunk in sleep
who art shepherd of the drowned—
Bestir thy flock to quit the deep
Come sound the Bell thou soughtst to sound.

Recall the lofty shrine of stone
Whence giants of our race adjourned;

What sea of stars have they o'erflown?
What whirling worlds of wonders learned?

Their ark sails incandescent floods
Past archipelagoes of flame!
Unto what power have these, our blood,
In all these wanderings attained?

Unto what wisdom have they grown
That left us wisdoms we have lost?
What Rescue might to them be known,
Whom vast galactic gales have tossed?

Lest Heyna-Dag devour the moon,
Lest Sod-wrag cleave the bosomed hills
Lest Bone-Bane cause the stars rain down

Long hast thou lain in dreams of war.
Lift from the sark your eyeless gaze!
Stand beneath the sky once more,
Where seas of suns spill all ablaze.

What archipelagoes of flame
What wonders have they given names?
Still crowned with powers we since have lost
that vast galactic gales have tossed.
Let us, bestriding soil and stones
and greet those who've bestridden suns . . .

From *Mr. Cannyharme*

(unpublished)

Mr. Cannyharme, resident of a cheap hotel in the Mission District of San Francisco, is the immortal ghoul whose predations H. P. Lovecraft first revealed to the world in "The Hound." Cannyharme preys now, not on the dead, but the walking dead, the drugged-out lowlifes in the inner-urban jungle. We are introduced to him at the outset of the novel, by the following verses.

In Netherlands did old Van Haarme
A vasty boneyard till and farm,
Did plough and plant a funeral field
Where gnarled lich was all his yield,
And parched cadaver all the crop
That e'er the ghoul did sow or reap.

But it's Carnival Row in latter years
That the canny hound now scythes and shears.
The boggy graves of his natal fief
He's abandoned for Carnival's shadow-strife.
It's Poortown's earth that he seeds now, and tills,
Where the shambling shadow-folk drift without wills.

Jack Hale, a writer who night-clerks at a Mission flophouse, is recruited by the ghoul to become one of his undying servitors. The recruitment is sly and indirect. Jack receives a pamphlet, a wacko religious tract it seems, with Cannyharme's first lyrics of seduction.

My ancient lust was to enslave the dead,
And up the brittle ladders of their bones
To climb to zeniths thick with stars bestrown,

Against vast, cold Eternity to spread
My sinewy wings; to press my taloned tread
Upon the very pinnacle of Time.

But now it is quite otherwise I climb,
For, not long past, my lust did learn to know
Through living flesh a readier way to go
To oversoar the mortal phantomime.
Now I empower those who would be mine
To imbibe a deathless vintage, red as wine,
And—ever unentombed—run wild at will,
And breach Time's very walls to seize their kill!

Jack, through a means which his own confusions with whisky and speed have obscured to him, finds that the wacko tract received from Cannyharme days before has changed its text . . . hasn't it?

Where the lich in the loam has lain mouldering long
And the maggoty minutes gnaw meat off his bones,
There Time is a monster that mows down the throng
Of once-have-been, gone-again, featureless drones.
And that lich's coffin to me was a door
Through which I went nosing Eternity's spoor.

But the living dead's doorways, once opened, gape wider.
Through these you may go where the galaxies sprawl,
And up through the star-web dance sprightly as spiders,
And dart quick as rats through Time's ceilings and walls!

There we go feasting and rutting at will,
And Time is a wine we imbibe when we kill!
There we conjoin with Gods older than All,
And preside with them over the Eons' slow crawl!

Jack's third message from the ghoul comes through his own fingers, meshed with pages of gibberish he types. When the letters are unthreaded from the rest, Jack confronts the following claims.

Through all the human stockyards you have trod
Where your bestial bretheren broil and bleed,
Beseeching brute Predominance, their God,
To grant them scope to blunder, bray, and breed—

Here you have wandered, haunted by a will
To weave from words a world more rare and bright,
Outreaching death, to shed its radiance still,
When you have sunk to dust and endless night.

But I, who lay so long entombed below
That abattoir by your brutes tenanted
(Oh, how their hooves did teach my soul to know
The living deaths by which they're tormented!),

I who now long have walked among that herd,
I am unroofed by Time. The eons sprawl
Like open fields I pillage undeterred!
My feet outrace the centuries' slow crawl!

Know, wordsmith, that it is my wish to shower
This grandeur, this forever, this deathless power
On your rare kind that strive for vaster views—
You hard and hungry ones whom the Abyss
Excites to try their wings. You sterner few
I lift up to the plane where I exist.

From the Short Stories

From "The Angel of Death"

A "Son-of-Sam" type killer, with psychosexual issues, is terrorizing the city. An interstellar scholar of sentient races, a kind of anthropologist, arrives in the city on a Friday night and assumes human form. He is a good, but not infallible, decoder of (to him) alien consciousness. He makes himself conspicuously attractive, like a Nordic Pimp, and seeks a mating experience, this kind of interaction being among the richest in information about a new species' relationships. He meets an equally statuesque young woman, a sweet kid who has trouble getting men because of her height. As they mate in a car on a midnight roadside, the Killer comes by and shoots her through the head. The anthropologist instantly repairs her telekinetically while seizing what he can telepathically from the mind of the killer. In his misunderstanding of the psychotic images in the killer's brain, which he takes as a fantasy the man wishes fulfilled, he assumes a monstrous form and devours him.

Those sniggering bitches
Out scratching their itches—
All steamy and sticky,
All teases and twitches—
I shatter their skulls into
Spatters and tatters—
I slug and I slug them
To jumbled red matter!

From "Fat Face"

A Hollywood harlot is wooed by a shoggoth. This simple, soft-hearted young woman is innocent of H. P. Lovecraft, and of *At the Mountains of Madness,* where shoggoths were first shown forth to the world. Since Lovecraft's day, their polymorphic skills have much advanced, and they move among men now, unrecognized. When Patti, not much of a reader, scans the tender missive the monster has penned her, most of it, like a gust of bats, flies right past her understanding. It leaves her uneasy, though. Perhaps it's the two little poems embedded in the text.

Shun the gulf beneath the peaks,
The caverned ocean black as night,
Where star-spawned gods made their retreat
From the slowly freezing world of light.

For even star-spawn may grow weak,
While what has been its slave gains strength.
Even star-spawn's will may break,
While slaves feed on their lords at length.

Epithalamion

Your veil shall be the wash of blood
That dims and drowns your dying eyes.
You'll have for bridesmaids Pain and Dread,
For vows, you'll jabber blasphemies.
My scalding flesh will be your gown,
And agony your bridal song.
You shall both be my bread,
And, senses reeling, watch me fed.

* * *

Oh swiftly let us two conjoin!
Speedily her loins unlace!
Tenderly her paps annoint,
And bare unto my seething face!

From "The Recruiter"

In this short story adapted from the novel *Mr. Cannyharme,* the Ghoul God makes an intimate contact with Chester Chase, an old man who has tenanted the hotel for twenty years. Small checks from an elder sister have long sustained him; she has died now, he is penniless, and he lies starving in the safety of his room, from which he dreads to be evicted. Several nights into his terminal fast, Chester, increasingly detached from his body, is touched by the Ghoul, who speaks within his mind.

A series of small poems making up a narrative of Chester's reanimation

Sometimes a god might choose out a mortal to mate with.
Sometimes for prey might a god seize a man to devour.
And some gods there are who consume the doomed mortals
they meet with
In both ways, for theirs is the hunger, and theirs is the power.

Not long after, the Ghoul plucks Chester's soul from his body, and carries him across the sky of the night-stilled city.

Faster, Chester! Chase, make haste!
Let's go where they rest and fester,
The hustlers finished with the race.
All lie low now, slow with faster—
Let's fly down and scope the place!

They plunge into one of the graveyards of Colima, the "stone city" south of San Francisco. The Ghoul plunges Chester's soul into one of the graves.

Upsy-downsie, in and out,
Let's see what this town's about!
Chester, what are you afraid of?
Let's see what this city's made of. . . .

Oh, look where they moulder and crumble away—
How rank-and-file orderly is their array!
An army of underlings, mine to control.
Let's do some recruiting. Come down! Lend a soul!

The mannikin of parchment and bone stirs in acknowledgment. Chester is snatched out, and away, and returned to his body.

Two nights later, the much-weakened Chester suffers a seizure. His flesh in crisis, he is again plucked out by the Ghoul and swept back to the graveyard.

On this occasion, Chester's soul is the vehicle of the corpse's actual reanimation—along with a shadowy host of others. Chester is interior to the lich's piecemeal leakage upward through the earth, to stand reassembled in starlight again.

Let reanimation start!
The butting skull's the bulky part.
So let it, Chester, lead the way,
And ram your passage through the clay.

Then from its rack, unjoint each bone
To climb the rathole one by one,
Each rib and radial, ulna, femur
Scuttle limber as a lemur!
What rags of flesh that may remain,
Worm after in a snaky train!

When the sleep-besotted troops in their mouldering cerements stand regathered, Chester steers his charnel vehicle at their head and leads them down to a ghostly yellow bus that waits to transport them.

Captain Chester! Ten-shun!
Pull yourself together, man!

Let us stroll down to the bus-stop, old buddy!
No-one will squawk that you're smelly and muddy!
It's your own private coach, and your fare is pre-paid,
And no one will notice you're slightly decayed.
Give them the signal, Ches. Lead the parade!

From "Beneath the Beardmore"

Three arctic adventurers encounter a strange man in the middle of the Ross Island Shelf. Unequipped with any gear and entirely alone, the three are immediately suspicious when they come across him burying something on the vast ice shelf. And well they should be; they soon learn he, is in, fact a Great Old One in a stolen "man-suit," surfaced from his ancient city below the ice.

Once unclothed of his human skin, the Great Old One speaks in verse. Below is the story he tells to the three arctic travelers.

Excerpt from "The Old One's Story"

Did I not tell you I would show you wonders?
My gift: the expansion of your hearts and minds.
See prostrate Greatness which base vileness plunders!
See boundless glory which foul Evil binds!

I make you witness our despoliation,
that you might see our conquered greatness rise
to extirpate its vile infestation

—and witness our rebirth with your own eyes.

First, then, know that *there* stands ZANADANE!
My race's home for centuries defiled
by monstrous things whose presence still profanes
her sacred precincts with their bodies vile!

Long did she flourish in her glory here
this primal home and nursery of our might
until nigh to her fifteen-hundredth year
when came eclipse! Eight hundred years of night!

Behold they still benight her, still defile
our Capital, those foul usurping throngs!
Eight centuries we've now endured exile
while Zanadane to *Shoggothoi* belongs!

We *fashioned* them, our polymorphous slaves!
Made them to toil in the abyssal deep!
Used them for salvage, miles beneath the waves
where cargo-laden vessels sank to sleep.
For know, our days of Empire and rich trade
with cities just as grand that stud these shores
saw both great commerce and fortunes made
and saw too naval conflicts and trade wars.
Much wealth was sunk—but much might be retrieved
by mighty, mindless brutes which we conceived.
Their wholly plastic metamorphic might
could pluck whole vessels from abyssal night!

That they should breed Intent, and conjure Guile
even as we bent them to our wish and whim!
That they should plot our downfall all the while
that we—complacent—wrought and wielded them!
Behold their mocking metamorphoses!
In endless flux from shape to shape they seethe,
ceaseless mutation of monstrosities!
To mock us is the very air they breathe!

Treacherous slaves! To be so new to guile,
and yet so slyly did they *mask* their wiles!
For plain we see now, in our weedy deeps,
that they grew sly while our wits lay asleep,
and while they practiced cunning, kept it cloaked,
then overthrew us with one mighty stroke.

A mile offshore the seafloor plunges steep
nigh two leagues down to zones of benthic murk
where vast-jawed things do sprawl, but never sleep
devouring lesser giants in the dark
in which deeps myriad shoggoths all cohered
into one night-black muscle two leagues wide
which, with a mighty shoreward thrust, upreared
a tidal wall which swept in to collide
with Zanadane's, and seized in foam-white jaws
full half our folk from off her walls and towers
who fed at once those shoggoths' acid maws
and augmented their imitative powers!

While we survivors, in those towering tides
were dragged offshore, our tenure thus annulled
And in those deeps our nation still abides
To haunt the citadel that once we ruled!

Conceive! In the vast reflux of such seas
Groping for weapons that we could not find!
Torn from anchorage we could not seize!
Wheeling and tumbling! Broken and bludgeoned and blind!

Oh feel with me our wretched outcast state!
We who could build a citadel like this!
To be o'erwhelmed by brutes we did create!
To be compelled to haunt the dark abyss
whence oozed those monsters who now throng our walls!
Who lord it in our mansions and our halls
whilst here we lurk like banished criminals!

But why, with strangers from a happier race
Should I our dolors, our despair rehearse?
Why thrust on you our grief and our disgrace
Even now, when our ill fortune is reversed!?
Oh my dear so comically-shaped friends
(my penance done in one of your odd frames
for that epithet will surely make amends?)
But friends, it seems a thing contrived by Fate
That you stand this moment at my city's gate!

For why was I abroad up in your world?
I and many *cohorts,* truth be told.
Stand and see, the mystery's unfurld.
Stand and hear, the history is told!
Sweet fruition of a long-sought bliss!
My allies now converge on every fortress
five hundred leagues up-coast and down of this!
And *yours* the rarest luck to stand in witness!

And when these vile *Shoggothoi* are slain
And purged and cleansed are all our citadels
Then there shall echo o'er the heaving main
the solemn sounding of our temple bells.
And when we've purged as well those citizens
Who made vile Treaty with vile Shoggoth Lords,
And transformed them to sea-floor denizens
Then—pure, renewed—begins our Afterwards!

Life is pretty fucking complicated. In the head we hold our howling hells and soaring fugues of paradise, while yet the good and evil within the reach of action is of lesser magnitude: we throw our burning cigarette butts out the window (but the forest does not burn), we throw coins to cripples (yet the maimed still crawl). If we could sin as largely as the evil in us, or make as big a beauty as we understand, we would realize life. But instead the two forces grind each other to bits in a dense and endless tangle of litigation and we end up with just barely enough moral energy to cut our fingernails.

—MICHAEL A. SHEA

Tributes

Shine On, Dark Star

Laird Barron

Michael Shea came into my life in the latter 1980s courtesy of his majestic and horrifying novella, "The Autopsy." I was a skinny kid with fourteen Alaskan huskies and a few books for company. I lived in a cabin in the Petersville Hills, spitting distance from bloody old Mount Denali, The Great One, devourer of mountain climbers of a double-dozen nationalities. Twenty-five years have rolled past in the rearview. The dogs, the cabin, the skinny kid, all gone, and now Michael too, and too damned soon. Not the stories, though. And not the memories of what it all meant to me.

"The Autopsy" detonated in my mind, although the shockwave only fully arrived in stop-motion frames a decade later. Unsurprising, perhaps, that deep psychological impact. It's a popular tale for a reason, reprinted plenty, just like his classics, "Fat Face" and *The Color out of Time.* Popular tales, excellent tales, but not half of what the man proved he could do time and again. Michael's literary remit was broad. Among other specialties, he excelled at psychological horror, science fiction, and baroque fantasy. He internalized and filtered the weird in an essential way that rivaled Clark Ashton Smith, Fritz Leiber, and Jack Vance. The proof is there in the work. "That Frog" reminds me of a contemporary fable as spun by Ambrose Bierce on a whiskey bender. "Uncle Tuggs" is a morbid ghost story with black humor so finely deployed, the first time I read it I fell out of bed laughing through a score of blood-soaked punch lines. "The Extra" remains one of the most blistering satires of dystopian North America.

Beyond the mentoring I received through dissecting his bibliography, I'm fortunate to have spent time with Michael and his wife, Linda. Since the early years of this century our paths intersected time and again. We attended the H. P. Lovecraft Film Festival in Portland, Oregon, World Fantasy Conventions in Saratoga Springs and San Jose, and once they dropped from out of the blue into my reading at the KGB Bar in New York. In 2009, I visited their place in Healdsburg, gorgeous and serene wine country. We took a long walking tour of the mountainous neighborhood and Linda inspired me to write a novel simply from her description of a particularly strange photography assignment she'd undertaken. They told me about Moose, a massive old dog their children had loved so long ago—the kids had clung to his shaggy fur like Greek heroes hiding among Polyphemus' sheep. Drinking in that vista of rock and wood and terraced grape rows, looking past to the upper valleys and deeper forests, it was evident why Northern California had so indelibly marked Michael's writing, why it had overwritten and defined so much about him as a man.

On another occasion, an occasion that will haunt me unto the end of my days, Michael and I sat in a corner during a World Fantasy Convention mass autograph session. The crowds gathered around one media sensation or another. He and I sat, largely unnoticed, behind our handwritten signs, and watched the masses teem. He told me in his quiet, melancholy fashion about the tragic death of a relative that had occurred many years prior. He'd seen the body, a body devastated by sudden and violent destruction, and explained how the experience had been a revelation, how it had opened a keyhole in his mind. He testified that death was simultaneously hideous, yet beautiful. Our flesh a thin and fragile veneer over a chasm of ultimate, unknowable depths. He understood that death follows us always, cold hand upon our shoulders. He was more at peace with its inevitability than anyone I've known.

Years back in another essay, I described Michael Shea as a dark star illuminating this strange field of the fantastic and the weird. Stars die, but their light lives on, travels on. Keep traveling, Michael. We'll see you again one day, out there in the beyond.

A Memory of Michael Shea

Cody Goodfellow

The first time I saw Michael Shea, he reminded me of the Spaceman of Ocean Beach. A colorful hippie character from my screwy hippie childhood, he had that same serenely spacey smile as we got to talking, that same bemused acceptance of the fundamental absurdity of existence. It wasn't until we'd talked and shared various kinds of smoke that I was able to drag out of him who he was, and was belatedly overwhelmed by his humility, as much as his stature as an artist.

My friend Adam and I were honored to publish Michael's collection, *Copping Squid,* and had the indescribable pleasure of his company whenever he came to Southern California. He had a poet's gift for bringing the weird and impossible to life, but also an explorer's talent for delighting in the commonplace that made every experience an adventure.

The last time he came down to LA with his wonderful wife, Linda, I took them downtown to see some readings and bands, and lost my car to a parking lot that inexplicably closed at 9 on a Sunday night, when we were done at 10. Trapped on foot in the most ped-hostile city in America, we had to wander the streets of downtown until 12:30, when we found an active bus route on the advice of a public-spirited panhandler. As indifferent police and insidious street-freaks prowled past our lonely bus stop vigil, I never stopped apologizing, but they never once complained that they were having anything less than a magical evening. The opportunity to walk down the streets of downtown without the noise and traffic, one might have thought, was a thoughtful surprise I cooked up, instead of an idiotic and potentially fatal screwup.

When the bus back to Burbank finally came, some asshole accosted us, and Mike, nearly asleep on his feet, literally threw him out into the street through the door the driver obligingly threw open. Embarrassed by this entirely justified show of force, Mike was quiet the long walk back to my house.

He fell asleep talking to me at my dining room table at 4:30, and then woke up half an hour later to go catch a plane home. We talked about Perilous Press digitizing his back catalogue of short fiction and about some new stuff he was working on, and promised to get back to him soon.

Mike was truly wonderful, in the most literal sense: full of wonder. He was always energized, inspired, and engaged with the mystery, the secret magic that suffuses all life, if we could only hear it. His was never a loud self-congratulatory voice, but almost a window through which that strange music just seemed to come rolling, with his self-effacing, gentle humor for a melody. A fearless explorer of inner space, he taught me that which has served me most of all in my own travels, to find joy on whatever alien shores we discover, in or out of our minds.

How I Met Michael Shea

Sam Hamm

I first met Michael Shea in Brooklyn, New York, in the fall of 1980. I have no idea where he lived at the time, how he looked, what he was doing. Me? I was a newly professional writer, having, through a series of freak accidents, gotten a rewrite job on a Disney nature picture called *Never Cry Wolf* that was, at the time, roughly halfway through a multi-year shoot near the Arctic Circle. It was a long commute from Brooklyn.

My usual subway stop, the Clark Street Station, opened into a shopping arcade on the ground floor of the Hotel St. George. One day, as I passed the newsstand on my way to Henry Street, I saw the new issue of the *Magazine of Fantasy & Science Fiction.* The cover, by Ron Walotsky, featured a man floating weightlessly above an equally weightless mortuary slab in a starry void. A scalpel hovered near his head. He looked like an older—or nowadays, a younger—Alex Trebek.

The cover, I soon discovered, illustrated a story called "The Autopsy," by a writer I did not know, Michael Shea. He was the fifth of six contributors listed on the cover. I took a quick glance at the first few paragraphs, and then, more or less against my will, I kept reading, and by the time I got to the end of it I was pretty much ruined for the day.

The brilliant awfulness of the setup, the oppressive tactility of the language were lodged in my head—permanently, it turned out, although I couldn't know that yet. The next day I found a Shea story I'd somehow missed, "The Angel of Death," in a back issue of *F&SF,* and from then on I sought out his byline wherever it appeared. "Polyphemus." *Nifft the Lean.* "That Frog." "Uncle Tuggs." He was plainly a writer of mercurial gifts, equally adept at tall tales, Lovecraftian horror, black humor, interplanetary adventure, and sword-and-sorcery. What did the stories have in common? They were all smart, they were all written, and I loved them. Whenever I read one, I felt like the committee of blind men discovering a new chunk of anatomy and having to revise their overall picture of the elephant.

By the mid-eighties I had moved to San Francisco. One evening my friend Peter Crosman called and asked if I would like to come over to his house, which was a few blocks from mine in Noe Valley. Peter's wife Deborah had an old friend in town—Linda—and Linda's husband was some sort of science fiction writer, and Peter knew I liked that sort of stuff. "What's his name?" I asked. "You probably don't know him," said Peter. "Michael Shea."

Moment of silence. Then: "I'll be right over."

And that is how I met Michael Shea in person. He turned out to be a big guy. Later Algis Budrys would describe him, in a review of his story collection *Polyphemus,* as "young and tough; a blue-collar roustabout . . . the kind of Irishman who would have gone out in his oyster-boat with Jack London" (Budrys had been expecting "a bookish type in a tweed jacket, perhaps a little nerdy"). None of that was wrong, but despite his burly aspect Shea gave the impression of deep gentility, of courtliness. His manner of speaking seemed oddly measured, not just because he was careful about words (he was), but because he plainly did not want to strike the wrong tone or give offense: at times it seemed he was on a two-second tape delay, reviewing his own comments in case he needed to censor them. He wanted, I thought, to be a gentleman in all things, and he was willing to put some work into it, and that made him a serious person in my book. Despite his massive gifts he was genuinely humble. He was also very funny. After a long period of skepticism he finally accepted my enthusiasm for his work, and we became friends.

I was starting to have some luck in movies about then, but I did not know any working science fiction writers. Through Michael I met Marc Laidlaw, Rudy Rucker, Pat Murphy, Richard Kadrey, Larry Tritten, the whole San Francisco SF gang. And he was interested in my racket as well; he'd started work on a screenplay called *Atomic Lifer,* which I don't believe he ever finished, although we got together with Laidlaw one Sunday morning and tried to iron out the plot kinks over pancakes with orange butter.

Alas, Michael was not much good at the rackety aspects of the racket. One evening a producer was coming through town and wanted to have dinner, and I told him he had to meet this guy Shea, friend of mine, fountain of ideas, incredible writer. Michael, who had never been cursed with an overabundance of salesmanship, was petrified at the prospect. "Come on," I said, "it's just a howdy-do meeting. He'll pitch us something, we'll pitch him something. It'll be fun!" When the evening was over, and no fun had been had, I realized that Michael put all his energy into building those sinewy Latinate sentences that overwhelm the senses and blot out our view of the ordinary world. When it came time to hawk the finished product, he had very little juice left.

I like to think—I hope—that our brief mutual forays into Darkest Showbiz might have generated just a little of the apocalyptic vitriol that fuels *The Extra.*

The last time I saw Michael in person was a couple of years ago, at Charlie Jane Anders's Writers with Drinks (guest-hosted, that particular month, by Beth Lisick). In the meantime I had written a couple of episodes for the cable anthology series *Masters of Horror;* I desperately wanted to adapt "The Autopsy," but despite my best efforts I could not talk the producers into buying it for me. ("Too static." "Too interior." Well, no, not the way I would have done it.) But Michael's career was on the upswing nonetheless; he'd reworked an old but eerily prescient *F&SF* story into a full-length novel, *The Extra,* and Tor Books had asked him to expand it still further, into a trilogy, to be published in hardcover with a decent promotional budget. Patton Oswalt, a smart guy, had already optioned the film rights. On this night Michael stood confidently at the mike, read from that fine mordant tome, and kept a crowd of boozy Mission-district hipsters absolutely spellbound; in fact, he fit right in with born raconteurs Mary Gaitskill and Jerry Stahl, who were there hawking new books of their own.

Afterwards we hung out, shot the shit, made plans to get together, went our respective ways. We traded occasional emails but never wound up in the same room together. Linda sent me galleys of *Assault on Sunrise,* book #2 in what was to be the Extra trilogy.

And then in February of last year she emailed me, asking me to call her, and when I did she told me that her husband, her great "hyperbolicker," as he called himself, was gone. Once a few people die on you, you get used to the pointlessness of it, but this one rattled me. I hated the idea that, without knowing it, I had already met Michael Shea for the last time.

And then I met Michael Shea again—in the pages of this book.

If you know anything about the market for poetry, you know that there is no market for poetry. That goes triple for narrative poetry, and quintuple, if not worse, for narrative poetry of the déclassé rhyme-and-meter variety—which means, of course, that the very existence of the volume you hold in your hands is a marvel.

I was certainly aware that Shea's novels were studded with verse—ogres and witches spit out rhyming imprecations at the drop of a hat, and bards quote at length from the Quimble Bay parchments—but until I saw the table of contents for this book, I did not appreciate just how much poetry he had shoehorned into his prose works. And I did not appreciate why, either, until I read "The Mines of Behemoth in Heroic Couplets," which I saw for the first time in the proofs of this volume. Midway through it revelation dawned, and my tiny shriveled raisin of a heart swelled with glee.

I had first read *Mines* in paperback, having somehow missed its original publication as a serial in the short-lived *Tomorrow* magazine, edited by Michael's literary champion Algis Budrys. As you know if you follow fiction magazines—there are six or eight of us left who do—the latter installments of serialized novels are usually preceded by a brief synopsis of Our Story So Far, so that the reader who skipped April (or repressed the memory of it) will not feel hopelessly over his head when diving into May. These synopses tend to be pretty dry stuff, the literary equivalent of the whispered conversation you have when your movie date returns from the restroom having missed a major plot revelation onscreen; you keep it terse and factual because the people around you will get irritated if you don't. Those who do not need the synopsis avoid the synopsis.

They avoid it, that is, unless the writer of the synopsis is Michael Shea, and he has decided to render this lowest of subliterary forms, the plot summary, in heroic couplets, as if he were Pope translating Homer.

At first you wonder why he would put himself to the trouble, and then, as you read, you hear his ghostly cackle, and soon you are cackling yourself, at the audacity of the stunt and the brilliance of the pastiche. Michael's kids grew up in a house where he would routinely thunder out great chunks of Milton or Shakespeare whenever the mood struck, and it is not hard to imagine him doing the same with Spenser, or Donne, or even the Puritan wild man Edward Taylor ("Who in this bowling alley bowled the sun?"—my favorite theological metaphor, my favorite cosmological metaphor, and a line I would love to hear delivered in Michael's characteristic rasp). Shea was a scholar, all right, but he was no dutiful academic. To him there were no dead authors, only working writers. He read the classics with an autodidact's sense of discovery, internalizing the loopy cadences, the archaic locutions, the contortions of syntax. He wanted to learn those tricks—and then, of course, he wanted to show what he had learned, what he could do, in whatever venue he could co-opt.

When *The A'rak* was published, Marc Laidlaw and I traded a series of emails expressing awe at the beauty and muscularity of individual sentences, lamenting the fact that they would go largely unread by the sort of people who do not buy paperbacks with giant spiders on the covers and largely unappreciated by the sort of people who do. We lucky few who inhabit that small sweet spot on the Venn diagram, we giant-spider-loving connoisseurs of fine prose, now have this book of poems, in which we catch Michael Shea in the act of entertaining himself. Could there be any purer expression of the great, crazy joy he took in writing?

For the benefit of the completists among us, I would like to do a little shoehorning of my own. There is at least one Shea poem that is not in the table of contents. It can only be found on the flyleaf of my Centipede Press edition of *The Autopsy and Other Tales:*

Dear Sam:

I blush to plunk this porker on your shelves—
The crooked craftings of much earlier selves.
But curse me not—oh, sir, forbear to damn!
No! Blurb me rather! Write how slick I am!

Here, Michael, is the blurb I owe you:

Michael Shea was a great writer. I loved him. I miss him.

"Grab the Morning, You'll Have the Day": An Elegy for Michael Shea

Maya Khosla

Lights out, ear plugs in, headphones tight
in silent mode, a screen's wan light spilling
on face, keyboard, hands. Your hands tapping
across darkness rich as soil, across rain falling
like fine steel, thin as spider-webbing, across
corridors of roaring pine, winds, sparrow bones
whistling like flutes, across hefts of switchback
and trail, a savanna where bison roam seas
of grass. And someone calls—half a shout
arriving, the other half snatched off. Your words
racing after, under skies blurred with streaks
of soliloquy, a flock of waxwings searching
for yesterdays dripping with sun. The drops
everywhere are vanishing the instant they hit
leaf, bark, cheek, sepal, shingle and stair.
Drops forming runlets hurry to the basement
of time where all words merge with the grand
story, the bedrock, silt and sediment of all
stories, equipped with densities of iron, porosity
of sand. Now the narrative everywhere at once—
grains in pockets, grit between teeth, slivers
of blood dripping from a dead bobcat lying
on the road, still warm, your feet thudding
across miles of earth, the limitless circle
whose rains are home on arrival, whose thousand

incantations begin with fingers tapping *"Grab*
a morning, you'll have the day; lose a morning,
you'll have nothing." The words link themselves
to black chains of rock tying a lake to itself,
words feed forests no longer in existence
to forests our great-grandchildren will witness.
We hear you from your depths of darkness,
from silences achieved with earplugs,
headphones, lights-out, door-latch fastened,
where page after page, screen after screen
hurries towards the river that carries all,
into which we, anchored, finned or feathered,
must plunge.

Memories of Michael Shea

Marc Laidlaw

In the summer of 1988, near the end of a cross-country drive that would culminate with Michael throwing his typewriter into a deep Maine lake, the Sheas, Michael and Linda, stayed overnight with us on Long Island. The summer rain was torrential but sporadic, so that we had plenty of time to sit in the yard sweltering and tending to the barbecue. Michael carried with him on this journey a large box of signature pages for a limited-edition anthology—a collection that had already been signed by a number of other authors and now required only Michael's signature in order to be bound.

Michael, as was often the case, had yet to be paid for his contribution to the book, and that was among the subjects of his endlessly soaring flights of spontaneous poetry and wordplay. When he spoke, it was hard to see what tethered him to earth. His sentences were like balloons full of noble gases, going aloft and pulling him with them. It didn't matter what the subject was, he sent them off in flights that left other writers dazzled by their deftness. If you have read his lush, fantastic prose, you might just possibly be able to imagine him speaking; yet the fact that these were not sentences laboriously composed, but extemporized, made listening to him a differently dazzling experience than reading him.

Eventually we retreated into the house, and into the night.

The rains returned.

I rose in the morning and padded past the slumbering Sheas on our sofa bed, glanced out the window, and gasped. In the middle of the patio table, in a puddle of standing water, stood the box of signature pages Michael had carried from California.

I woke him, and he went outside with a grim look, cursing under his breath. Opening the box, he discovered that only a few pages on the top and bottom had been damaged. Almost instantly he devised a ghoulish plan. He would send the publisher waterlogged pages one at a time, with a renewed demand for payment: "If you ever want to see your precious pages again . . ."

We laughed harder then than we had the night before, but his was the sardonic humor of one who had missed meals due to missing payments. The adulation of fans, the respect and admiration of his so-called peers (the word "peer" used strictly in the social sense, not that of artistic equivalence), even the awards—none of these translated into commercial success. In fairness, it rarely does. But did this stop him? No. I think sometimes it staggered him however.

Michael was a writer whose stories traveled by word of mouth, by reputation. In 1979, home from college that summer, my best friend called to tell me about a story he had read in the latest *F&SF*. From his brief description alone, I received chills. It was Michael's early classic, "The Angel of Death," which worked fantastic changes on the topical Summer of Sam that had obsessed a culture. We sensed instantly the arrival of a master. Several years later, at a gathering of writers and fans, someone mentioned in similarly breathless tones a new tale by Shea: "The Autopsy." It was the sort of gathering where I could quickly lay hands on a copy of *F&SF* and scurry to a corner to gulp it down; it is not always obvious that a classic has been delivered. In this instance, it was obvious.

Not long after that, I first met Michael and his wife, Linda. A steely, unpretentious man, he kept his intelligence hooded like a lantern until he felt he was in trustworthy company; he was as mordantly dark as Linda was golden and bright. We spoke of horror, of course. A series of barrel murders in Golden Gate Park was headline news. To these Michael added a supernatural flourish—a shapeshifting creature identifiable only by a shackle and chain it could not alter, no matter its form.

Through the years, I met my own wife and as a couple we grew closer to the Sheas. They took their small kids and bailed out of San Francisco, which played too harsh a tune on Michael's strings, and took up various residences in the wine country. Michael still drank then—when I first met him, a bottle of peppermint schnapps was his bosom buddy—but a temporarily crippling and all but fatal collision with a semi finally convinced him to put an end to that. Such eye-to-eyes with death, in addition to the spark and energy of his young children, seemed to drive him to a firmer embrace of life. He became a dedicated runner. Whenever we visited, he was always up early for his miles of running, looking faintly weather-beaten in his shredded T-shirts and ragged sneakers. I remember his laughter like sand and smoke. He worked hard, and so little of it was at writing—painting houses, spreading asphalt, carpentry. We moved far away and saw the Sheas infrequently, much to our sadness. I knew that little by little, Michael had eked his way to a degree and begun to teach. All these occupations surely fed his fiction and his poetry, but it's hard not to resent them, as they took him away from the one thing he could leave us.

The irony is that no one wrote more richly or beautifully of the physical aspects of death. No other theme brought out such voluptuous verbosity. I know that he had stared death full in the face several times in his life. This alone does not make him remarkable. But it was Michael's special grace to wrest incredible beauty from these trysts with mortality, without losing sight of their gruesome nature. It seems fitting that he will be remembered for some of the most beautifully morbid passages ever penned.

Somewhere, in a rare collectible edition, you may find Michael's signature on a page inexplicably warped and waterlogged. He never followed through on his ransom demand, but I hope all the same he was paid, and well, by whoever was lucky enough to have a new Shea story. We owe him a great deal more than that sum for the priceless visions he brought into being, from the rich landscape of his imagination, wherein he now entirely resides.

Read More Michael Shea

John O'Neill

Michael Shea taught us a valuable lesson in his poetry.

Of course, he imparted some golden wisdom in his prose, too—things like the true value of friendship, and the pleasures of adventure, and that wit is more valuable than gold and steel. (Especially gold. Steel, as it turns out, is pretty reliable when things get tough.) And most especially, when things really start to go sideways, stay close to the rogue.

But what I want to talk to you about today is the much simpler, and more elegant, lesson he imparts in his poetry.

Poetry shows up in all of Michael's epic fantasy. His works are soaked with it. Let's look at a few of my favorite examples. In his marvelous fantasy *In Yana, the Touch of Undying,* our heroes Hex and Sarf are rescued from a shipwreck by a majestic giant, Kagag Hounderpound. In thanks, they offer to do the giant a solid: rid him of two witches who pester him from shore with dark magics.

Hex and Sarf are straight-up guys, good as their word (mostly). They're on the verge of ridding the world of two witches when by chance they overhear the witches' curse and come to understand that not everything is as it appears. The witches are the only things standing between a ravenous giant and his mainland prey.

> Curse you, Kagag Hounderpound!
> We damn and ban you from this ground!
>
> Withhold your huge, unmaking hand!
> This patiently wave-hammered sand—
> This smithied gold—won't feel your touch.
> No, nothing that breathes
> Outside the seas

Will strangle in your envy's clutch,
Nor shall your claws unshape this land!

Or consider the surprising poem that Cugel glimpses as he dashes across a bridge in *A Quest for Simbilis,* inscribed by a heartbroken Mage whose son was killed by card sharks. The monster whom Cugel must best to cross the bridge has been set there to unmask card cheats—because the only way to cross is to play the creature, and the only way to win is to cheat. Cugel cheats, of course, but cleverly evades death . . . but he cannot avoid the lesson about loss that the poem teaches us.

Though now you face a cheerless waste,
You are alive to see at least,
Your blood pounds, you can hear, and taste,
You're free to dance till the sun's decease,
If dance you will.

You've thus won more than one before,
Whom cardsharps stabbed in a den of lies
And robbed of what is not restored.
From him they took heart, ears and eyes.
Thus have I wrought to publicize
That cards work ill.

Or let's consider Patti, from the diabolical masterpiece "Fat Face," wooed by no less than a shoggoth. Her suitor writes her love letters, which she doesn't really understand. But the poems buried within contain some of the only warnings to her fate that she receives . . . had she but the wit to recognize them.

Shun the gulf beneath the peaks,
The caverned ocean black as night,
Where star-spawned gods made their retreat
From the slowly freezing world of light.

There are many more splendid examples of course, but I think you get the idea.

In prose we find glorious lies, and epics of adventure and faraway lands that never were. There are life lessons, and people we fall in love with, and joy and heartrending loss.

And in poetry?

In poetry there is truth.

I was proud to know Michael for a brief time here on Earth. I was proud to get to know him and publish his work. And I'm proud to have been given the chance to say a few words to you now. You can safely ignore everything I've said up till now if you like. Because here's the heart of it, the truth I can share with you, the payload.

Read more Michael Shea.

Remembering Michael

W. H. Pugmire

In preparation to write a wee memoir of Michael Shea, I decided take a quick glance through those of his books that I own and read over some few of his stories. I couldn't, because once I began dipping into *The Autopsy and Other Tales* and *Copping Squid* I found myself so newly captivated by the work that I had to keep on reading. *The Autopsy and Other Tales* was the first Centipede Press book I had purchased, in the dealer's room at World Fantasy Convention in 2007 at Saratoga Springs.

It was at that convention, too, that I first met Michael and Linda and we all became instant friends. Michael and I had one extensive sit-down conversation where we spoke of many things, and he mentioned writing a novel that was inspired by H. P. Lovecraft's "The Hound." As he spoke of it, I became absolutely fascinated with the idea (for that is one of my favorite Lovecraft tales), and I ached to read that novel. I heard no more about the work until late last year.

I read very little modern Cthulhu Mythos fiction because I find so much of it unimaginative and poorly written. The finest collection of such fiction to emerge in recent time is Michael's *Copping Squid,* released in 2009 from Perilous Press.

One of the things that I love about the book is that its tales are honest-to-Yuggoth Mythos stories; the Mythos elements are essential to the tales, not something added on so that cool Lovecraftian words and names can be sprinkled throughout. Each story in the book is unique. One of my all-time favorites is "Nemo Me Impune Lacessit," a playful homage to Poe with a mock-somber narrative that is delightful.

Completely different in every way is "Copping Squid," an extremely modern story that contains the cosmicism that Lovecraft felt was essential to good weird fiction.

Another wonderful aspect of these stories is the very fine writing, prose that is never ostentatious and always effective.

I am delighted with this fine collection of poetry—especially with that section devoted to *Mr. Cannyharme,* the novel that Michael mentioned to me in 2007. Word has it that the novel may be close to seeing publication, and that enthralls me, because I know it will be fantastic, and I will then have a brand new work by this fabulous writer to devour.

Michael was a sweetheart, and everyone who knew him loved him. His friendship was free and easy, and it was always a cause of joy whenever we met at horror conventions or the H. P. Lovecraft Film Festival. He was genuinely interested in whatever new thing one might be working on, and he shared a love for writing that was infectious. Michael was a cool modern dude, unpretentious and able to instill his friends with deep affection. Linda tells us that he was writing all the time, and so we can hope that there are unpublished gems waiting to see print. I feel very fortunate to have called him amigo, and hope to see him again beyond the wall of sleep.

Abysses, Mountains, and Skies; or, How My Vision Was Enlarged

Jessica Amanda Salmonson

"Did I not tell you I will show you wonders?" Why yes. Yes you did. And thank you so much for doing so.

My first exposure to Michael Shea was *A Quest for Simbilis* in 1974. As a huge fan of Jack Vance's Dying Earth stories, I was bound to go into this book ready to be critical: how dare anyone try to match that level of genius? But it was just a gosh-darned great read. The one and only flaw I could see was the fact that it owed so much to Jack Vance, and Michael Shea was too grand to be writing other peoples' characters.

By the time *Nifft the Lean* came along—more doomful version of Vance's Cugel the Clever, in a high-decadent world—it seemed to me to be exactly right that it would garner the World Fantasy Award in 1982, though odd it should be in the novel category when it's a collection of tales. It became one of the very few and select books I immediately had to read again, and in years after again and again (another such is *Maldoror*), and I had to share my feelings about this work in an essay for the *New York Review of Science Fiction.*

I can't convey how much I've always loved heroic fantasy, which I personally consider a literary form that comes closer to the animal heart of our species than any other. It gets a lot of criticism for being dumb and juvenile stuff, and it just soothes my soul to see the criticisms disproven by such work done at this height of excellence, proving that the oldest form of storytelling is by no means worn out.

I'd already known the character of Nifft from an earlier appearance of "Pearls of the Vampire Queen" in Wayne Warfield's splendid *Phantasy Digest* in 1977. Nifft was unexpectedly a character who was just "with me" a lot, for years and years. I'd suggest he was my #1 favorite heroic fantasy character, but then there's also Fafhrd and the Grey Mouser as well as Cugel to consider, and I can put them in no order; they are collectively #1.

And by the time of the publication of "Fat Face" in 1987, I realized Michael Shea was additionally one of the greatest living writers of modern horror, Lovecraftian or otherwise, and when that fat bastard speaks in his last poetic grotesquerie, by gum, my gosh, that was going to be with me the rest of my life. You know how many thousands of stories I've read and forgotten? To make a lasting impression like this is the hallmark of something, don't ask me what.

Sometimes when a reader discovers an author whose work is truly arresting so that it becomes important in one's life, then meets that author at conventions, and they're geeky drunkards or handsy around twelve-year-olds or egomaniacal asshats, it makes it harder to enjoy their work. Evangeline Walton was the first author who ever said to me, "I don't like to meet authors whose works I enjoy," because not being the equal of their work drags down the enjoyment thereafter.

But meeting and corresponding with Michael made his work even more deeply important to me, as he turned out to be, basically, a long-legged rawboned figure not unlike Nifft the Lean, a man of humor and dark reflection who "got" me when I said things some people found too dark or just offending. He struck me as a heroic figure out of a Sam Peckinpah western, sexy and handsome; he could have been a movie star.

As a poet it could actually pass unnoticed he was great at that too. Unnoticed because so many of these pieces were sewn into stories, and a reader is so submerged in the world of the larger work that it's rare to stop long enough to think, "Oh, that's a good poem," and the effect is quite different removed from their larger context, judged on their own merits.

They are of themselves frequently little tales such as bards of old may have sung and told, of heroic cause, and angers and desires, doomful rants and cruelties, jeweled dreams of an appalling Otherwhere. And if betimes the reader giggles to embrace a rhyming jest, it's because we too are by turns heroic and cruel, mud on our souls. They are essentially escapist pieces, and yet too enticing to be considered minor. Well, I think so because they are so very much in keeping with my tastes, and because I write such things too, I can only wish so well.

Of these pieces, however, I have to admit "Gil Gomez and Monkey-Do" took me so much by surprise that it made me smile with its imagination and absurdity and humorous language, and as of right now it's my favorite. Of all the gloomy otherworldly choices for a favorite, it's ridiculous I like this one best, but I do.

Until my own passing, I will always know that I was so fortunate to have known this man, and to have been, in return, liked by him, since not everyone thinks I'm at all pleasant, nor should they, though I might wish they did. My antisocial nature largely vanished in the light of Michael and Linda. The joy of knowing that such a talent and a decent human being like Michael Shea lived in the same world as I was horrifically spoilt by his unexpected passing. To have known him makes me feel that I, too, have "met a Titan on the earth," and I can't help but be tragically startled that even Titans die.

My Memories of Michael

Jerad Walters

I first met Michael Shea in 2005 at the World Fantasy Convention in Madison, Wisconsin. I was just a couple of years into publishing and had only had around three books published. Always looking for new material, and already a large fan of Michael's, I sought him out and found him outside smoking with John Pelan. I remember that first meeting most vividly because the picture of him on his website at the time made him look like a bearded giant, very heavy and very round. But when I met him in person, he was a thin, fit man, not at all the physical giant I had expected.

Then and there I proposed a project to Michael. The book was to be a collection of all his major short fiction. We agreed on terms, signed contracts, and *The Autopsy and Other Tales* came into being. But for me, the collection really solidified when Michael praised it at its first appearance at the World Horror Convention in Salt Lake City in 2008. I was thrilled. It was also the first time we really had some time to sit and talk. We spent a lot of time bantering about books and films, and by the end of it, the relationship had easily turned into a friendship.

At the 2009 World Fantasy Convention in San Jose, Michael and his wife, Linda, graciously put up my wife and son and me in their home. We had a wonderful time—I recall that Laird Barron was there for a couple days as well. As we left San Jose and got on the highway to San Francisco, Michael's expletive-ridden cursing as he dealt with California highway traffic horrified my wife a bit—our son Adrian was only five at the time—but I found it hilarious. Even part of his charm.

Because whether cursing or reciting poetry, Michael's voice was full of a warmth and concern that, coupled with a raspy quality, was immediately endearing. You had the feeling that with Michael, every word mattered, whether spoken or written. He was generous and warm-hearted. He listened to what I had to say and took me seriously. For someone like me, always tongue-twisted, it was a great boost of confidence. And as much fun as it was to work with Michael on the book and other projects, it was even more fun just hanging out with him and his wife, talking about our kids and experiences and things we did.

One of the last times I saw Michael was in Portland at the H. P. Lovecraft Film Festival in 2010. We didn't have a whole lot of time to talk during this show. I greatly regret that. We kept in touch over the phone but, as it always seems, that didn't happen with nearly the frequency it should have. Our last project together was just before he passed away. He wrote an original story for an anthology that I was publishing and S. T. Joshi was editing, "Beneath the Beardmore."

Michael Shea

Jason V Brock

I will not write a lengthy testimonial to the great talent and stirring imagination of the late Michael Shea; I feel certain that terrain will be amply covered by the works contained herein, as well as the reminiscences of others in this volume. Besides, Michael's work needs no champion—we all know it was and is fantastic, singular, irreplaceable. Instead, I would like to spill a few words in tribute and reflection on how I first met him, and what happened afterward.

My wife, Sunni, and I were attending the H. P. Lovecraft Film Festival and CthulhuCon in Portland, Oregon. This was in 2010, and I was a guest. Michael, of course, was a *special* guest, along with other luminaries of weird fiction. I was on a panel with the esteemed Mr. Shea about the "Cosmic Horror Movement," featuring W. H. Pugmire and Caitlín R. Kiernan, and moderated by author Cody Goodfellow. I was unavoidably detained by another writer in the lobby and wound up being a few minutes late to the proceedings, in full swing by the time I took a seat at the end of the table. As we puzzled through the topic at hand, it was obvious that there was no clear definition about what this "movement" really was, and lively discussion ensued. As usual, Mr. Pugmire was wonderfully rhapsodic about his love for the latter-day flowering of this type of writing. Ms. Kiernan was insightful and matter-of-fact with regard to her convictions that this had actually been a longstanding tradition that the public was now catching up to; Cody was sharp as ever with his observations and questions related to the (at the time) recent trend of Lovecraft's global popularity, currently well-entrenched, and what that heralded for the future.

Michael sat quietly at the opposite end of the table from myself, and we both simply listened for a time. Finally, he made a fantastic group of statements, as I recall, about his personal take on what this tradition meant, and why it was now being seen for what it always was: not so much a relic of the past dragged into a modern context, but a dynamic representation of prescient future-thought by Lovecraft and his allies. Michael's points were aligned with Kiernan's and even took them a tad further by suggesting that Lovecraft actually understood that his conceptions were too ahead of the curve to be appreciated in his own time. I elaborated on this idea and coined an insight into Lovecraft's personal worldview that I deemed "cosmic introspection." What I meant was that Lovecraft was able to find meaning in the universe by embracing his insignificance and spreading this idea like a virus to his other writer friends. I would later write a very long piece with this title for Centipede Press's fine publication *Weird Fiction Review,* where I went into this notion in greater depth.

After the panel, Michael came up to me and said "Wow! You're really intense!" and we struck up a conversation. After a few minutes of discussing the panel and weird literature, I thanked him for his time and went on to my reading, as far as I can recollect, and thought that was that, as I knew Michael would be too busy with his duties and such for excessive chit-chat over the weekend.

But I was wrong. As I went to my next panel later in the evening, whom do I spy out in the audience but Michael Shea! After the discussion, I went down to thank him for attending, as I knew he was busy. He smiled at me, laughed, and said something that blew my mind: "Are you kidding? I came to the panel just to watch *you* in it! You're smart!" After that, we talked for about fifteen or so minutes until he was called away. That's the kind of person he was, though: generous, kind, willing to make everyone else feel like they were the most important person in the room. I was sort of in shock, but excited, and quite humbled. Throughout the weekend, we kept checking in on one another, and I could tell that we had made a connection—intellectually and personally.

After the con, we kept in touch on Facebook and with e-mail. In fact, my wife and I had planned to visit him and his wife, Linda, at their home in California (we drive from Portland, Oregon, to Los Angeles a few times a year for various appearances in the area). Sunni and I are wine enthusiasts and were looking forward to dropping in on the

Sheas, not only because they are talented, smart, fun, and interesting, but also because the area they live in is known for its wine—what's not to love about all that?

Days come and go; plans bloom and are put off. . . . As the seasons change and we get too busy with life, reality has a way of correcting us about what really matters. Therefore, it was with it was with great sadness that I learned of Michael's sudden passing in 2014. His death was a stunning jolt to the system, and it left both Sunni and me lamenting those trips where we *wanted* to make that detour, but were too pressed for time to stop over, always thinking that we'd do it *definitely* "on the next trip." Of course, now it's too late. The lesson here is: don't let those times slip away. Instead, hold those moments close; reach out to the people you resonate with; cherish them as deeply as you can, for as long as you are able . . . one can never tell when circumstances will change—for as sure as there will be a sunrise in the morning and darkness with nightfall, only change is constant.

Rest in peace Michael. You are missed.

Images

Michael Whelan: Cover for *Nifft the Lean* (DAW, 1982)

Alan Clark: "The Goddess in Glass," from *Nifft the Lean*, commissioned by Michael Pearce

Alan Clark: "The Fishing of the Demon Sea," from *Nifft the Lean*, commissioned by Michael Pearce.

Alan Clark: "Pearls of the Vampire Queen," from *Nifft the Lean,*
commissioned by Michael Pearce

John Stewart: “Polyphemus,” from *Polyphemus* (Arkham House, 1987)

John Stewart: "The Angel of Death," from *Polyphemus* (Arkham House, 1987)

John Stewart: "The Horror on the #33," from *Polyphemus* (Arkham House, 1987)

Allen Koszowski: "The Presentation," *Inhuman* (December 2005)

Allen Koszowski: "Pick and Grim," *Inhuman* (Fall 2011)

Steve Gilbert: frontispiece, *Copping Squid and Other Mythos Tales* (Perilous Press, 2009)

Afterword

Michael Shea

Horror in its first coinage is a ripple of the flesh—as in horripilation, when the tremor brings our hair erect. It is the shudder of awe and ecstasy at reality's unbearable grandeur and beauty eternal, that seizure of fear and laughter that takes us when we remember where we *really* are: spinning inside a discus of dust and fire flung out by the first heartbeat of time.

What, after all, is our landscape when we lie sleeping? When we've laid by our tools and folded ourselves into darkness? We surf the methane storms of Jupiter, stride in our nakedness across the razor-sharp, uneroded stone of the moon, indestructible wraiths fast as light, absolute zero our element, deathless diamonds our brains. We live in the *Universe* then, and deep in our spines, live *always* in the Universe.

Come sunrise, we walk around with our skull boiling with hierarchies, histories, holocausts, hymns and hyperboles . . . but our souls know always we have only our monkey-bones to scaffold our galactic visions, have only one fist-sized heart to hold the ice-white constellations, the wild-haired comets, and old Sol's nightly hemorrhage on a jade and amber sea. Horror is just our dying amidst the hair-raising wonder and heart-breaking glory that is flying apart all around us. Our knowing and feeling this—that is our soul.

I mean to say that Horror is never mere butchery. Certainly, Universal Recycling *can* be stressful. Time and gravity hammer us all back down to hydrocarbons, if nothing else gets us first, and we feel always the tug of this grand transaction's approach. But without the wild beauty of what we are losing, where *is* the Horror, really? Without the soul's hair-raising cry of heartfelt awe, what's been lost?

A Michael Shea Bibliography

A. Separate Publications

1. *A Quest for Simbilis.*
   a. New York: DAW, 1974.
   b. London: Grafton, 1985.
   Translations:
   i. *Reise in die Unterwelt.* Ratstatt/Baden: Erich Pabel Verlag, 1977.
   ii. *Simbilis.* Rome: Fanucci Editore, 1980.
   iii. *Ravasz Cugel* (Russian). Cherubion Könyvkiadó, 1994.
   iv. *La Revanch de Cugel L'Astucieux.* Paris: Editions Payot et Rivages, 1997.

2. *Nifft the Lean.*
   a. New York: DAW, 1982.
   b. London, Grafton, 1990.
   c. Eugene, OR: Darkside Press, 1994.
   Foreign editions and translations:
   i. *La Quete de Nifft le Mince.* Paris: Nouvelles Editions Opta, 1984.
   ii. Tokyo: Hayakawa Publishing, 1985.
   iii. *Die Reise Durch Die Unterwelt* and *Fischzug im Damonenmeer.* Frankfurt am Main: Verlag Ullstein, 1985 (2 vols.).
   iv. *La leggenda di Nifft.* Milan: Arnoldo Mondadore Editore, 1990.
   v. Markku Sadelehto, ed. *Pimeyden linnake* (anthology featuring "Come Then, Mortal," one of the four segments of *Nifft the Lean*). Helsinki: Kustannus Oy Jalava, 1991.

Note: Winner, World Fantasy Award.

3. *The Color out of Time.*
   a. New York: DAW, 1984.
   b. London: Grafton, 1986.

4. *In Yana, the Touch of Undying.*
   a. New York, DAW, 1985.
   b. London: Grafton, 1987.
   Translations:
   i. Japanese edition,1993.
   ii. *Yana.* Rome: Arnoldo Montadori, 1993.

5. *Polyphemus.*
   a. Sauk City, WI: Arkham House, 1987.
   b. London: Grafton, 1991
   Contents: "The Autopsy," "The Angel of Death," "Polyphemus," "Uncle Tuggs," "The Pearls of the Vampire Queen," "The Horror on the #33," "The Extra."
   Note: Finalist, World Fantasy Award.

6. *Fat Face*
   a. Eugene, OR: Axolotl Press, 1988.

7. *I, Said the Fly*
   a. Seattle: Silver Salamander Press, 1993.

8. *The Mines of Behemoth.*
   a. New York: Baen, 1997.
   b. Eugene, OR: Darkside Press, 2003.
   Note: First published in *tomorrow,* July, August, and September 1996.

9. *The Incomplete Nifft.*
   a. New York: Baen, 2000.

10. *The A'Rak.*
    a. New York: Baen, 2000.

11. *The Extra.*
  a. New York: Tor, 2010.
  Note: Book 1 of The Extra Trilogy.

12. *Assault on Sunrise.*
  a. New York: Tor, 2013.
  Note: Book 2 of The Extra Trilogy.

13. *The Autopsy and Other Tales*
  a. Lakewood, CO: Centipede Press, 2008.
  Contents: "The Angel of Death," "The Horror on the #33," "Fast Food," "Grunt XII Test Drive," "Salome," "Fat Face," "Uncle Tuggs," "Fill It with Regular," "Nemo Me Impune Lacessit," "Polyphemus," "That Frog," "The Extra," "The Growlimb," "The Autopsy," "The Rebuke," "The Delivery," "For Every Tatter in Its Mortal Dress," "The Pearls of the Vampire Queen," "I Said the Fly," "Tsathoggua," *The Color out of Time.*

14. *Copping Squid and Other Mythos Tales.*
  a. Lynnwood, WA: Perilous Press, 2010.
  Contents: "Tsathoggua," "The Dagoniad," "Copping Squid," "Nemo Me Impune Lacessit," "The Pool," "The Battery," "The Presentation," "Fat Face."

B. Stories and Novellas

1. "Pearls of the Vampire Queen."
  a. *Phantasy Digest* No. 3 (1977).

2. "The Angel of Death."
  a. *F&SF* (August 1979).
  b. In *Grotte des Tanzenden Wildes Werner Fuchs.* Munich: Knaur Science Fiction, 1982 (as "Der Engel des Todes").
  c. In *Polyphemus.* Sauk City, WI: Arkham House, 1987.
  d. In *The Autopsy and Other Tales.* Lakewood, CO: Centipede Press, 2008.
  Note: Finalist, Nebula Award.

3. "The Autopsy."

a. *F&SF* (December 1980).

b. In Ed Ferman, ed. *The Best from Fantasy and Science Fiction.* New York: Scribner's, 1982; New York: Ace, 1983.

c. In Frank D. McSherry Jr., Charles G. Waugh, and Martin H. Greenberg, ed. *A Treasury of American Horror Stories.* New York: Crown, 1985.

d. In Martin H. Greenberg, ed. *Fifty American Horrors.* New York: Crown, 1986.

e. In David Hartwell, ed. *The Dark Descent.* New York: Tor, 1987.

f. In *Polyphemus.* Sauk City, WI: Arkham House, 1987.

g. In Ed Ferman and Ann Jordan, ed. *The Best Horror from Fantasy and Science Fiction.* New York: St. Martin's Press, 1988.

h. In Karl Edward Wagner, ed. *Intensive Scare.* New York: DAW, 1989.

i. In David Hartwell, ed. *The Dark Descent 1: The Colour of Evil.* London: Graftons, 1990. New York: Tor, 1991.

j. In Ed Ferman and Ann Jordan, ed. *The Best of Modern Horror.* London: Penguin, 1990.

k. In Markku Sadelehto, ed. *Outoja Tarinoita 3.* Helsinki: Kustannus Oy Jalava, 1991 (as "Ruumiinavaus").

l. In Jack Dann and Gardner Dozois, ed. *Aliens among Us.* New York: Ace, 2000.

m. In *The Autopsy and Other Tales.* Lakewood, CO: Centipede Press, 2008.

Note: Finalist, Nebula Award; Finalist, Hugo Award.

4. "Polyphemus."

a. *F&SF* (August 1981).

b. In Donald A. Wollheim, ed. *The 1982 World's Best Science Fiction.* New York: DAW, 1982.

c. In *Polyphemus.* Sauk City, WI: Arkham House, 1987.

d. In *The Autopsy and Other Tales.* Lakewood, CO: Centipede Press, 2008.

Note: Finalist, Hugo Award.

5. "Nemo Me Impune Lacessit."

a. *Whispers* (March 1982).

b. In *The Autopsy and Other Tales.* Lakewood, CO: Centipede Press, 2008.

6. "That Frog."

a. *F&SF* (April 1982).

b. In *The Autopsy and Other Tales.* Lakewood, CO: Centipede Press, 2008.

7. "The Horror on the #33."

a. *F&SF* (August 1982).

b. In Art Saha, ed. *The Year's Best Fantasy Stories #9.* New York: DAW, 1983.

c. In Markku Sadelehto, ed. *Kuoleman Kirjat 1.* Helsinki: Werner Soderstrom Osakeyhtio, 1982 (as "33. linjan bussissa").

d. In *Polyphemus.* Sauk City, WI: Arkham House, 1987.

e. In *The Autopsy and Other Tales.* Lakewood, CO: Centipede Press, 2008.

8. "Grunt-12 Test Drive."

a. *F&SF* (February 1983).

b. In *The Autopsy and Other Tales.* Lakewood, CO: Centipede Press, 2008.

9. "Creative Coverage, Inc."

a. In Stuart Schiff, ed. *Whispers IV.* New York: Doubleday, 1983.

10. "Fill It with Regular."

a. *F&SF* (October 1986).

b. In John Pelan, ed. *Axolotl Special #1.* Seattle: Pulphouse/Axolotl Press, 1989.

c. In *The Autopsy and Other Tales.* Lakewood, CO: Centipede Press, 2008.

11. "Uncle Tuggs."

a. *F&SF* (October 1986).

b. In *Polyphemus.* Sauk City, WI: Arkham House, 1987.

c. In Ed Ferman, ed. *The Best from Fantasy and Science Fiction: A 40th Anniversary Anthology.* New York: St. Martin's Press, 1989.

d. In Markku Sadelehto, ed. *Kuoleman kierjat 3.* Helsinki: Werner Soderstrom Osakeyhitio, 1993 (as "Eno Tuggs").

e. In *The Autopsy and Other Tales.* Lakewood, CO: Centipede Press, 2008.

12. "The Extra."

a. *F&SF* (May 1987).

b. In *Polyphemus.* Sauk City, WI: Arkham House, 1987.

c. In *The Autopsy and Other Tales.* Lakewood, CO: Centipede Press, 2008.

13. "The Delivery."

a. *F&SF* (October 1987).

b. In *The Autopsy and Other Tales.* Lakewood, CO: Centipede Press, 2008.

14. "Fat Face."

a. In Ellen Datlow and Terri Windling, ed. *The Year's Best Fantasy and Horror: First Annual Collection.* New York: St. Martin's Press, 1988.

b. In Karl Edward Wagner, ed. *The Year's Best Horror Stories XVI.* New York: DAW, 1988.

c. In Ellen Datlow and Terri Windling, ed. *Demons and Dreams.* New York: Legend, 1989.

d. In Markku Sadelehto, ed. *Mustava kivi.* Helsinki: Werner Soderstrom Osakeyhtio, 1995 (as "Laskinaama").

e. In Jim Turner, ed. *Cthulhu 2000.* Sauk City, WI: Arkham House, 1995.

f. In *The Autopsy and Other Tales.* Lakewood, CO: Centipede Press, 2008.

g. In *Copping Squid and Other Mythos Tales.* Lynnwood, WA: Perilous Press, 2010.

15. "I, Said the Fly."

a. In Ellen Datlow, ed. *The Sixth Omni Book of Science Fiction.* New York: Zebra, 1989.

b. In *The Autopsy and Other Tales.* Lakewood, CO: Centipede Press, 2008.

16 "Salome."

a. *Cemetery Dance* No. 21 (Summer 1994).

b. In *The Autopsy and Other Tales.* Lakewood, CO: Centipede Press, 2008.

17. "Pick and Grim."

a. Alfred Hitchcock's Mystery Magazine 39, No. 10 (October 1994).

18. "Johnny Crack."

a. *tomorrow* (December 1994).

19. "Tollbooth."

a. *tomorrow* (August 1995).

20. "Fast Food."

a. *Century* No. 3 (Winter 1995).

b. In *The Autopsy and Other Tales.* Lakewood, CO: Centipede Press, 2008.

21. "Upscale."

a. *Scream Factory* No. 16 (1995).

22. "Piec'a Chain."

a. *tomorrow* (February 1996).

23. "For Every Tatter in Its Mortal Dress."

a. *F&SF* (February 2000).

b. In *The Autopsy and Other Tales.* Lakewood, CO: Centipede Press, 2008.

24. "The Rebuke."

a. In Elizabeth R. Wollheim and Sheila E. Gilbert, ed. *30th Anniversary DAW Fantasy.* New York: DAW, 2002.

b. In *The Autopsy and Other Tales.* Lakewood, CO: Centipede Press, 2008.

25. "The Growlimb."

a. *F&SF* (January 2004).

b. In Stephen Jones, ed. *The Mammoth Book of Best New Horror, Volume 16.* London: Robinson, 2005. New York: Carroll & Graf, 2005.

c. In *The Autopsy and Other Tales.* Lakewood, CO: Centipede Press, 2008.

Note: Winner, World Fantasy Award.

26. "The Presentation."

a. *Inhuman* (December 2005).

b. In *Copping Squid and Other Mythos Tales.* Lynnwood, WA: Perilous Press, 2010.

27. "The Pool."

a. *Weird Tales* (February–March 2007).

b. In *Copping Squid and Other Mythos Tales.* Lynnwood, WA: Perilous Press, 2010.

28. "Tsathoggua."

a. In *Copping Squid and Other Mythos Tales.* Lynnwood, WA: Perilous Press, 2009.

29. "Copping Squid."

a. In *Copping Squid and Other Mythos Tales.* Lynnwood, WA: Perilous Press, 2009.

b. In S. T. Joshi, ed. *Black Wings: New Tales of Lovecraftian Horror.* Hornsea, UK: PS Publishing, 2010. London & New York: Titan, 2012.

30. "The Dagoniad."

a. In *Copping Squid and Other Mythos Tales.* Lynnwood, WA: Perilous Press, 2009.

31. "The Battery."

a. In *Copping Squid and Other Mythos Tales.* Lynnwood, WA: Perilous Press, 2009.

32. "The Recruiter."

a. In Ellen Datlow, ed. *Lovecraft Unbound.* Milwaukie, OR: Dark Horse, 2009.

33. "Beneath the Beardmore."

a. In S. T. Joshi, ed. *A Mountain Walked: Great Tales of the Cthulhu Mythos.* Lakewood, CO: Centipede Press, 2014. Portland, OR: Dark Regions Press, 2015.

34. "Under the Shelf."

a. In S. T. Joshi, ed. *The Madness of Cthulhu, Volume 1.* London & New York: Titan, 2014.

Notes on Contributors

The Editors

Linda Cecere Shea is a visual artist whose background is in holography, illustration and faux painting. She currently owns her own architectural finishing company and provides custom murals, faux painting, and design to her clients. She was married to Michael Shea for more than thirty years, until his passing in 2014. She and their children Della and Jacob reside in northern California.

S. T. Joshi is a leading authority on H. P. Lovecraft and has compiled many anthologies of weird fiction, including *American Supernatural Tales* (Penguin, 2007), *Black Wings I–VI* (PS Publishing, 2010–16), *Searchers After Horror* (Fedogan & Bremer, 2014), and *A Mountain Walked: Great Tales of the Cthulhu Mythos* (Centipede Press, 2014), several of which included the work of Michael Shea.

The Contributors

Laird Barron is the author of five collections of short stories—*The Imago Sequence* (2007), *Occultation* (2010), and *The Beautiful Thing That Awaits Us All* (2013), *A Little Brown Book of Burials* (2015), and *Swift to Chase* (forthcoming, 2016)—along with two novels, *The Light Is the Darkness* (2011) and *The Croning* (2012). He is a three-time winner of the Shirley Jackson Award.

Jason V Brock is an award-winning writer, editor, filmmaker, and artist whose work has been widely published in a variety of media (*Weird Fiction*

Review print edition, S. T. Joshi's *Black Wings* series, *Fangoria,* and others). He is also the founder of a website and digest called *[NameL3ss]*; his books include *A Darke Phantastique, Disorders of Magnitude,* and *Simulacrum and Other Possible Realities.* His documentary films include *Charles Beaumont: The Life of Twilight Zone's Magic Man,* the Rondo Award–winning *The AckerMonster Chronicles!*, and *Image, Reflection, Shadow: Artists of the Fantastic.*

Cody Goodfellow has written five solo novels—his latest is *Repo Shark*—and three more with John Skipp. His latest short story collection is *Rapture of the Deep and Other Lovecraftian Tales* (2016). He is also a director of the H. P. Lovecraft Film Festival in Los Angeles and cofounder of Perilous Press, a micropublisher of modern cosmic horror, including, most notably, Michael Shea's *Copping Squid.* He "lives" in Burbank, California.

Sam Hamm's movie credits include *Batman, Batman Returns, Monkeybone,* and *Never Cry Wolf.* He created the TV series M.A.N.T.I.S. with Sam Raimi and wrote two episodes of the Showtime series *Masters of Horror,* for which he had hoped to adapt Michael Shea's "The Autopsy." He has also written comic books, basketball recruiting coverage, and political commentary. It was his great honor to supply the front cover for Mr. Shea's gleefully subversive novella *The Extra.*

Maya Khosla has written *Web of Water, Life in Redwood Reek, Tapping the Fire: Securing the Future with Geothermal,* and *Keel Bone* (Dorothy Brunsman Poetry Prize). She has received writing awards from Flyway Journal, Headlands Center for the Arts, Hedgebrook Foundation, Ludwig Vogelstein Foundation, and Poets & Writers, and filming awards from Patagonia, Save Our Seas Foundation, and Sacramento Audubon Society. Her new film is about the wild after wildfire in the Sierra Nevada–Cascades region.

Marc Laidlaw is the author of several novels, including *The 37th Mandala,* many short stories, and the Half-Life series of videogames. In the 1980s and '90s, he and his wife lived in the San Francisco Bay Area, where they struck up a friendship with the Shea family and spent many treasured hours in their company.

John O'Neill was the editor of *Black Gate* magazine during its ten-year run. He now maintains the Hugo-nominated website BlackGate.com. He is a Canadian living in St. Charles, Illinois.

W. H. Pugmire has been writing Lovecraftian weird fiction since his days as a Mormon missionary in Ireland in 1972. His latest Hippocampus Press collection is *Monstrous Aftermath: Stories in the Lovecraftian Tradition* (2015). He has appeared with Michael Shea in such anthologies as *The Book of Cthulhu, A Mountain Walked,* and *New Cthulhu 2* (a book dedicated to Michael's memory). He and David Barker have completed a short novel set in Lovecraft's dreamlands, and he will have a new collection from Centipede Press in 2017.

Jessica Amanda Salmonson is the author of the punk rock–era horror novel *Anthony Shriek.* A new (and first hardcover) edition is forthcoming from Centipede Press. She wrote a trilogy of high fantasy novels about women samurai. The Tomoe Gozen Saga. Her poetry collection *The Ghost Garden and Further Spirits* is forthcoming from Hippocampus Press.

Dan Temianka is the author of *The Jack Vance Lexicon: The Coined Words of Jack Vance, from Ahulph to Zipangote,* and its expanded second edition, *from Abiloid to Zygage* (Spatterlight Press). He is a retired physician and lives with his wife in Pasadena, California, where he enjoys music and woodworking and develops the legacy of his later father, the great violinist Henri Temianka.

Jerad Walters is the publisher of Centipede Press, an award-winning small press that has gained celebrity for perpetuating the fine art of book production and for the wide range of its publications in the fields of weird fiction, crime/suspense fiction, and film criticism. He published a large omnibus of Michael Shea's short fiction, *The Autopsy and Other Tales* (2008).

CPSIA information can be obtained
at www.ICGtesting.com
Printed in the USA
LVOW07s1701171017
552750LV00012B/1357/P

9 781614 981794